"Captain, I don't date marines. Is that clear?"

"Sure is." He cocked his head, holding her furious gaze. "My invitation just kinda slipped out."

Libby avoided the warmth in his voice and eyes. "I've just got some touchy spots in my life regarding the Marine Corps," Libby muttered.

"Mind if I asked why?"

Hurt rose up in Libby at the softness in Dan's voice. Then tears unexpectedly stung her eyes. She turned away so he wouldn't see them. "Captain Ramsey, I won't discuss my personal life with you or anyone else."

If she stayed one more minute, she was going to break down and tell Dan everything. Worse, she had wanted to walk into the safety of his arms and be held. Just be held . . .

Dear Reader,

Welcome to Silhouette Special Edition...welcome to romance. We've got six wonderful books for you this month—a true bouquet of spring flowers!

Just Hold On Tight! by Andrea Edwards is our THAT SPECIAL WOMAN! selection for this month. This warm, poignant story features a heroine who longs for love—and the wonderful man who convinces her to take what she needs!

And that's not all! *Dangerous Alliance,* the next installment in Lindsay McKenna's thrilling new series MEN OF COURAGE, is available this month, as well as Christine Rimmer's *Man of the Mountain,* the first story in the family-oriented series THE JONES GANG. Sherryl Woods keeps us up-to-date on the Halloran clan in *A Vow To Love,* and *Wild Is the Wind,* by Laurie Paige, brings us back to "Wild River" territory for an exciting new tale of love.

May also welcomes Noreen Brownlie to Silhouette Special Edition with her book, *That Outlaw Attitude.*

I hope that you enjoy this book and all of the stories to come.

Happy Spring!

Sincerely,

Tara Gavin
Senior Editor

Please address questions and book requests to:
Reader Service
U.S.: P.O. Box 1325, Buffalo, NY 14269
Canadian: P.O. Box 1050, Niagara Falls, Ont. L2E 7G7

LINDSAY McKENNA
DANGEROUS ALLIANCE

Silhouette®

SPECIAL▼EDITION®

Published by Silhouette Books
America's Publisher of Contemporary Romance

To Jeanmarie Swalm, a woman of immense generosity
straight from the heart. Too bad they broke the mold
when they made you. You're a wonderful humanitarian
and role model. Thanks for "being there."

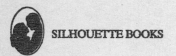 SILHOUETTE BOOKS

ISBN 0-373-09884-7

DANGEROUS ALLIANCE

Printed in U.S.A.

LINDSAY McKENNA

spent three years serving her country as a meteorologist in the U.S. Navy, so much of her knowledge comes from direct experience. In addition, she spends a great deal of time researching each book, whether it be at the Pentagon or at military bases, extensively interviewing key personnel.

Lindsay is also a pilot. She and her husband of fifteen years, both avid "rock hounds" and hikers, live in Arizona.

CALIFORNIA

Santa Barbara

Santa Barbara Islands

Los Angeles

San Bernardino Mts.

Camp Reed,
U.S.M.C.

San Diego

PACIFIC OCEAN

MEXICO

All underlined places are fictitious.

Chapter One

"Ms. Tyler, you can't go in there!"

Libby brushed by Colonel Edwards's secretary and made a beeline for the provost marshal's office, her heart pounding.

"I need just a minute of his time," she pleaded, sidestepping the older woman's hand with a limberness and calculated ease born of years of equestrian training.

Colonel Edwards looked up with disapproval from behind his oak desk. Dark horn-rimmed glasses emphasized his thick eyebrows, peppered with the same graying hair that showed at his temples.

Libby forced a slight smile that she hoped looked apologetic as she came to a halt inches from his immaculately kept desk. In the corner behind him the American flag stood next to the red Marine Corps flag, and his walls were covered with photos, certificates and a set of crossed sabers.

"Colonel, I'm Libby Tyler, one of the riding instructors at the base stables." She glanced apprehensively back at the grim-faced secretary following her through the open door. "Please... I know I don't have an appointment, but this can't wait, and I'm convinced it's in your interest to hear what I have to say."

Edwards put aside his gold pen, nodded to his secretary and then gave Libby a curious look. "Very well, Ms. Tyler. Ardella, it's all right. Just close the door, please."

The shaken secretary gave her a disgruntled glance, her face sour with disapproval at Libby's boldness. Libby managed a placating smile.

"I'm sorry for the intrusion," she offered sweetly to the departing secretary. Libby had learned much about military politics and protocol since she'd married marine captain Brad Tyler six years ago—and certainly it was not a good idea to ruffle the feathers of the secretary of the head honcho.

The secretary appeared mollified as she quietly closed the door. Libby returned her attention to Colonel Edwards, an important honcho indeed as provost marshal of Camp Reed, one of the largest Marine Corps bases in the United States. "Colonel, I'm dreadfully sorry for barging in here—"

"No, you aren't, Ms. Tyler, or you wouldn't have done it." He looked at her, one black-and-gray eyebrow raised skeptically, and Libby felt suddenly awkward, dressed as she was in English riding breeches and a short-sleeved white blouse. "Now, I'm a very busy man as I'm sure you know. And my secretary had an impeccable record of stopping anyone who wanted to get in here without an appointment—until just now." He sat back in his chair and appraised her. "You're a military dependent, correct?"

Libby moved from one foot to another, smarting under Edwards's straightforward, insightful remarks. Well, what did she expect? The provost marshal's office handled legal problems and controlled the military police, one arm of their law-enforcement jurisdiction.

"Yes, sir, I am," she agreed. Although it wasn't quite the truth, it wasn't a lie, either. When Brad was alive, she had been dependent. Now she was employed as a civilian on the sprawling base that took up a sizable chunk of valuable southern-California real estate.

"Hmm."

That meant, "You knew better than to barge in here," Libby realized. Not only that, but she had skipped the golden chain-of-command rule that the military lived and died by. "Colonel, if I didn't think this was important—and if my boss, Stuart Garwood, had been willing to listen to me—I wouldn't be standing here."

"Stuart Garwood is a fine man, Ms. Tyler." He scowled at her. "And horse business is hardly provost marshal business."

Inwardly, Libby flinched. "Yes, sir, Mr. Garwood is a wonderful boss. I've worked for him the past three years." She shifted nervously from one booted foot to the other. "But there's a problem. At least, I perceive a problem."

"And it requires provost marshal attention?"

Libby saw the doubt on Edwards's heavily lined face, reminiscent of a terrain map Brad had once showed her. "I believe it does."

"And Mr. Garwood. What does he think?"

Libby tried very hard to stand still. She knew her energy and restlessness often translated as nervousness and made people, particularly stoic military types, look at her as if she were some kind of hyperactive child. Lacing her fingers together, she said in the most serious voice she could muster, "Colonel, someone is riding five stable-owned horses at night. And not just one joyride. I've noticed it four months in a row now. I've spoken to Mr. Garwood about it each time, but he just shrugs it off. These horses are owned by the Marine Corps and are being ridden very hard for a long time. Then they're left in the paddock without being brushed down or cared for. That's not right."

Edwards's eyebrows moved up like two fuzzy caterpillars, and he growled, "Ms. Tyler, I really don't think your charges hold any water. This is a stable matter, one I think Mr. Garwood is consummately capable of handling. I'm sure if he thought it was a genuine problem, he'd have contacted our office."

"But, Colonel—"

"This is not a law-enforcement matter, Ms. Tyler. Good day."

Libby watched the officer pick up his pen. Frustration thrummed through her. "Colonel, I'm trying to be reasonable about this! Those five horses have nearly been ridden to death. For two days after each experience, they just stand or lie in the corrals, they're so exhausted." Her voice turned strident. "You must investigate!"

"Ms. Tyler, go back to Mr. Garwood. He'll deal with this the way he sees fit."

Backing away from the desk, Libby whispered, "Colonel, my boss doesn't seem to care one whit about those horses or their condition. I'd hoped to handle this through military channels, but if I can't get any satisfaction through your office, I'm going to the *Oceanside Register* to talk to a reporter!"

Edwards snapped a look across the desk at her. The silence grew heavy and strained as he drilled her with a scathing glare. Finally, with deliberation, he laid the pen on the papers.

"Very well, Ms. Tyler, since you feel so strongly about this, I want you to go down the hall. My new assistant, Captain Dan Ramsey, will take care of your complaint."

"Thank you, Colonel. You won't regret this, I promise!" Libby quickly made for the door. She knew the marines hated for the civilian press to delve into anything that went on within Camp Reed's one-hundred-twenty-five-thousand-acre territory. Edwards was throwing her a bone, intending to foist her off on some unsuspecting captain who would sweep her plea under the carpet. Well, that wasn't going to happen!

"Good day, Ms. Tyler. Anything further regarding this case is to be handled by Captain Ramsey. Understand?"

Libby smiled and opened the door. What Edwards meant was, "Don't ever come barging into my office with an idiotic complaint like this again."

"Of course, Colonel. Thank you for your time."

Ardella gave her a dark look as Libby passed, but Libby smiled and called, "Thanks," as she sailed out the door.

Once in the hall, its floor lined with highly polished green-and-white squares of tile contrasted by battleship gray walls, Libby walked slowly, reading the names on each of the office doors. The provost marshal's office was part of the Headquarters building complex that sat off Teddy Roosevelt Boulevard, the one and only main highway loop that connected everything of importance on Reed.

Libby made it to the end of the hall without finding a Ramsey listed. Two rooms, doors shut, had no names on them. She wondered if Edwards was giving her the runaround. The military was famous for it, as Libby knew all too well from personal experience. Brad had been killed in a helicopter accident, and the Marine Corps had done everything possible to hush up the matter with interested civilian reporters. They'd even tried to avoid telling Libby the whole truth until she'd squeezed it out of them, with similar methods to those she'd just used on Edwards.

A tall, darkly tanned marine, showing three dark green staff-sergeant stripes and a rocker arm beneath it on his summer tropical-weight short-sleeved shirt, appeared out of a nearby office. Libby had heard of brig chasers, marines who formed a special arm of the provost marshal's jurisdiction, charged with transferring dangerous prisoners to and from bases, but she had seen few close up. Still, she was certain this man was one. His harsh features included merciless-looking blue eyes and a mouth compressed into a hard line. Although she judged him to be in his late twenties, tension and power radiated around the man. The black nametag over his right breast pocket read Donnally, J., Corrections Div.

"Excuse me, Sergeant," Libby called, lifting her hand.

He halted and slowly turned toward her, his eyes quick and appraising. "Yes, ma'am?"

"I'm looking for Captain Dan Ramsey's office."

The sergeant nodded differentially. "Third door on the right, ma'am."

"Thank you."

She moved with respect around the sergeant and headed for one of the closed doors with no name on it. Libby hesitated momentarily, knocked on the opaque window, then entered.

Dan Ramsey was down on his hands and knees, surrounded by a dozen boxes, when he heard someone knocking on his door. Before he could say, "Come in," the door opened to reveal a woman in highly polished black boots, yellow breeches that outlined her form to perfection and a simple white blouse. He sat back on his heels and looked up at her as she stood poised in the doorway. Some things Dan had just never expected to see at HQ. One of them was a beautiful woman horseback rider. And God, was she beautiful. Not in a classically pretty way, but because of a unique combination of features that made her stand out like a wildflower in a meadow of dried grass.

"Hi . . ." Libby said hesitantly. "Are you Captain Ramsey?"

Dan grinned, liking the coverlet of freckles across her wide cheekbones and her nose. Her eyes were a glorious green that reminded him of new leaves in springtime. "Yes, ma'am, I am," he agreed. The life in her eyes struck him deeply, as if sunlight danced in them. His gaze moved to her nose, which was crooked as if it had been broken at some time, but which suited her oval face. Dan's eyes continued their inspection, coming to rest on her full, expressive mouth, parted and breathless looking, as if she weren't sure she should be in his office. He quickly got up from the tile floor, dusted off his hands and stood awkwardly.

"I'm Libby Tyler, one of the base equestrian instructors," Libby explained, offering her hand. As her fingers gripped Ramsey's, she felt their latent power. She could tell so much from a handshake. She distrusted men who gave her a wimpy, weak one—and equally disliked those who tried to grind the bones of her hand together in a macho power display. But Ramsey's warm, dry grip was strong without being overpowering, exerting just the right amount of pressure. And she liked the warmth and interest banked in his intelligent blue eyes.

Realizing he still had a hold on her hand, Dan reluctantly released her fingers. "Glad to meet you." He looked around, a wry smile on his mouth. "I'd offer you a seat, but I've got boxes piled everywhere."

"Are you moving in or out?" Libby asked, her hopes falling. It would be just her luck if Ramsey was moving *out* of the office.

"In." Dan's smile deepened. Libby's sable hair was shoulder length with just a bit of curl, dancing with reddish highlights. He felt inexplicably drawn to her, but there wasn't time to ask himself why.

"Oh, good," Libby whispered, pressing a hand to her heart in relief. "Colonel Edwards told me to come down here and talk to you. He said you'd handle my case."

Frowning, Dan looked around. His small office, painted a pale green and lighted by two windows covered with venetian blinds, was in a state of chaos. "Well...Ms. Tyler, I just got here this morning. Two hours ago, as a matter of fact." What the hell was his boss doing, sending him a case to investigate? Wasn't he supposed to move in and get briefed before he started taking on a caseload? He'd seen Edwards first thing this morning and had figured him as a no-nonsense officer like himself. But throwing him a case like this was unheard of in Dan's book.

Libby shifted from foot to foot. "I know this is unusual. And from the looks of it, Colonel Edwards didn't take my case seriously, or why would he give it to someone who's still moving in?"

Grinning, Dan nodded and put his hands on his hips. "It does seem odd, Ms. Tyler."

"Call me Libby. I can't stand marine formality. It just drives me crazy."

"All right...Libby." He liked her friendliness in this world of ceremony and protocol. She was tall—at least five-nine or -ten—and medium boned. Dan had always wondered why the advertising industry touted women who were little more than skin sagged over tiny skeletons. Libby probably weighed around a hundred and thirty or forty pounds, and on her tall frame it looked good. Damned good. She was curved and firm, a testament to her demanding physical job. Her shoulders were thrown back, her chin held proudly. He supposed it was riding that had given her such an elegant carriage.

"This is crazy. The colonel doesn't care about what I've seen. He's just dumped me on you. I'm sure he's hoping I'll just let it go."

"Whoa, slow down." Dan turned around and took two boxes off the leather chair in front of his desk. "Here, have a seat." He went around his gray metal desk and removed several more boxes from his chair, a metal contraption that was unmercifully squeaky when he sat down. Fumbling for a pen from the pocket of his shirt, he finally found one, then hunted for the Investigation Report form that had to be filled out. It took nearly five minutes of rummaging through desk drawers to find what he wanted. He noticed Libby sat fretfully, crossing her legs first one way, then the other.

"Are you always in a hurry?" he teased, laying the forms on his desk."

"Not usually." Libby forced a smile as he arranged the items he'd need to take her report. Dan Ramsey was around thirty, she guessed, with dark, walnut brown hair cut military short. And he must be a good two inches over six feet tall. Like the man she'd seen in the hall, Ramsey was powerfully built, with an aura of latent power swirling around him. He must be part of the brig-chasing team, too, she guessed. She'd noticed that brig chasers were a lot like recon marines—set apart from other marines. There was a special look to them. A bearing, perhaps. Libby couldn't put her finger on it, but Ramsey had it.

She liked his square face and intense blue eyes, which danced with obvious amusement. She just hoped he wasn't laughing at her.

When Ramsey looked up from the form, Libby added, "I have to teach a class of nine year olds in about half an hour, that's why I'm antsy."

"I see...." Patiently, Dan filled out the required information at the top of the form. Like it or not, things only got done when forms were filled out properly.

"You're Libby Tyler, riding instructor? Correct?"

"Yes." Even though Libby had sworn she'd never be interested in a marine again, she found herself continuing to absorb Dan Ramsey. The summer uniform he wore, consisting of a short-sleeved shirt and trousers, looked good on him. He was broad shouldered, his arms darkly tanned, with a fine carpeting of dark hair across his forearms. His hands were large and callused, indicating he was a field officer who really didn't want to be in an office. What attracted her to him? Was it his features? Those alert eyes that seem to look into her soul with ease? That hawklike nose? Or perhaps his mouth? Unexpectedly she wondered what it would be like to kiss him. The thought nearly unseated her. There was no way on earth she was ever going to be interested in a marine again. Not *ever.*

Squirming all the more in response to her unbidden thoughts, Libby saw him lift his head momentarily from the paperwork.

"Are you like a little schoolgirl who can't sit still for two minutes?" Dan asked, baiting her.

Libby smiled broadly. "How'd you guess? I drove my teachers crazy in school. They thought I was hyperactive, but I wasn't. I just hate sitting around. I'd rather be outside." Why on earth was she telling him this? she wondered distractedly, even as she noticed the warmth that settled in his gaze at her admission.

"That's why you're a riding instructor and not stuck behind a desk like I am."

She smiled at his insight. "You don't belong behind a desk, either," she guessed.

"Good observation," Dan commented dryly. "But orders are orders."

"Are you an attorney?"

"Yes, I am."

"Oh, good...."

"Did you think the colonel threw you a curve and sent you to some poor schmuck who didn't know anything?"

Libby had the good grace to blush. She lowered her lashes. "He wasn't very happy when I interrupted him without an appointment," she admitted. "I thought he might not take my complaint seriously." Looking up and meeting his interested gaze, Libby offered, "You're not too shabby in the observation department yourself."

"It's my job."

"No, it's a definite skill. Sometimes a talent."

Dan smiled. "We agree." He had only half an hour to spend with this woman. Suddenly he wanted a lot more. Conversation seemed highly personal between them, which struck him as unusual. For the first time in two years, Dan realized he felt lighter, happier, as if the heaviness he'd carried in his heart for so long had dissipated at Libby Tyler's unexpected and sunny entrance into his life. Well, maybe she wasn't exactly like sunshine, he amended. More like a hot thoroughbred racehorse being asked to stand quietly in a stall when all she wanted to do was run.

"Okay, let's get on with this report. Please understand it's going to take me a while to move on this investigation."

"No problem," Libby assured him. *He cares.* The discovery, and accompanying emotion, flowed through her like a warm spring wind after a very cold winter. But the undeniable concern showed in Dan's eyes, in the tilt of his head when he looked up at her. Libby swallowed convulsively. Her pulse seemed to be jagging through her, she realized with dismay. No man since Brad had ever set her heart to skittering this way before.

"So what's the problem?"

Libby leaned forward, her hands resting on her thighs. "Captain, someone's been using five horses from the stable. They're riding them at night, after the stable's shut down. No one except dependents who board horses there are allowed to ride after hours. But these are owned by the Marine Corps' Special Services branch. The horses are ridden by off duty marines who can't ride worth beans, and they're exhausted at the end of the day. They're not available for evening rides."

"What time does the stable close?" Dan asked, struggling to act official when all he wanted to do was stare across the desk at Libby like a lovesick kid. She was so alive, so vital in a way he'd never seen in a woman.

"Nineteen-hundred hours," Libby responded, offering the military terminology for 7:00 p.m.

"Five or seven days a week?"

Libby liked Dan's attention to detail, and she felt a bit more reassured that he might actually be able to solve the mystery. "Seven days a week. The marines can go out on trail rides, in groups of twenty-five, with an instructor during the day. All kinds of riding activities are going on all day long. After that, the stable is available only to those who own horses here on base. And everything is shut down by 2100."

"So what's the problem?"

"For the last four months I've noticed something really strange, Captain Ramsey. The five horses I mentioned are being illegally ridden after hours. Now, it doesn't happen all the time, but when it does, these poor animals are being ridden to death. Yesterday I came in to work early, at 0700, and there they were—heads hanging down, their feet spread apart so they wouldn't collapse and fall down from exhaustion. Not only that, but their coats were still damp, and they were covered with sand. You know how the dust and sand is at Reed. No, I guess you wouldn't, since you just got here. Anyway, for a horse's coat to gather that much dust, the animal would have to be ridden for an awfully long time and a very long way.''

Dan scowled as he recorded her story. He liked the husky timber of Libby's voice, and her concern and sincerity touched him. When he looked up and saw the fire and care burning in her emerald eyes, something walled and hidden deep in his heart seemed to break loose. He hadn't been interested in any kind of an intimate relationship with a woman since his divorce from Janna, two years ago. But the fierce determination and anxiety in Libby's eyes was toppling his defenses.

With a shake of his head, Dan forced himself to get back to the business at hand.

"What's wrong, Captain?"

"Nothing...."

"You shook your head."

He smiled wryly. "It had nothing to do with your case, Libby."

"Oh...good. Well, as I was saying, these same five horses have been used like this at least four months in a row. I've been at the stables for three years now," she added.

Dan glanced up. "Who's in charge of the stables?"

"Stuart Garwood. He's very well known and respected in eventing circles."

"Eventing?"

"Yes. You know—a cross-country jumping course, a dressage competition and stadium jumping—the three events that test a horse and rider on all levels of stamina and ability."

"Right..."

"Captain, do you know very much about horses?"

"I know you ride them."

Libby groaned and rolled her eyes.

Ramsey laughed outright and sat back in his chair, enjoying her spontaneity. Where had this sprite of a woman come from? Time was running out. He only had ten minutes left with Libby Tyler.

"I have a feeling that anything I don't know about horses you'll teach me," he told her, trying to maintain an air of gravity. He caught a whiff of her perfume, a distinct odor of cinnamon combined with a subtler spicy fragrance. Without thinking, Dan inhaled deeply and felt the stirring of dormant longings he'd thought had died years ago.

"You can't realize the seriousness of my charges unless you know about horses."

"I'm sure you'll fill me in."

Libby frowned, not at all sure he was taking her allegations seriously. There was something magical about Ramsey. He had an inner flame that Libby had never encountered. "Are you making fun of me?" she demanded.

"No."

"Then why are you laughing? I see it in your eyes, Captain."

Dan moved uncomfortably in his chair. Libby's insights seemed as sharp as his. "The truth?"

"Nothing but. I've been accused by my friends and enemies alike of being too blunt and direct, but above all else, Captain, I value a person's honesty. I want the truth, even if it hurts."

"Well," Dan said blandly, "this shouldn't hurt you at all. I was smiling to myself because I was enjoying you as a person. I've never met a woman like you in my life." He held her startled gaze. "That's a compliment, in case you were wondering. And I take your charges about these horses very seriously."

"Oh..." He liked her. Flustered, Libby looked away. He didn't wear a wedding band. Neither did she. Was he making a pass at her? Taking her case for personal reasons rather than professional ones? She suddenly stood up and began pacing around the boxes in the small office.

"Captain, I care for the horses. All horses. Too many people treat them poorly out of ignorance. These five have been ridden into the ground! Yet Mr. Garwood doesn't seem to care about it, which I find highly unusual. He's always had the horses' care high on his list of priorities. Why not these five? I've brought them to his attention, but he ignored me." Libby swung around and held Ramsey's azure gaze. "I'm not going to let this drop. If you don't help me, I'm going to go to the civilian paper in Oceanside and make waves."

"You don't have to threaten me, Libby. I'll assign someone to investigate as soon as I can get moved in. Fair enough?"

Libby stopped pacing, her gaze mercilessly probing his. "I know Mr. Garwood and Colonel Edwards think I'm some kind of flaky idiot for bringing this up. Many things in my life touch me, but kids and animals are especially important to me. If one of the children in my classes has a problem, I try to help. If one of the horses in my classes is hurt, I make sure it gets vet attention." Her voice lowered with even more feeling. "I want to find out who is riding those horses after hours. One of these days, those poor animals will end up lame, or worse. It's not fair. They need someone to fight for them."

Dan rose and nodded. "I like your concern, Libby. I promise I'll get someone from the PM's office on this as soon as humanly possible. Deal?"

Libby wondered if Ramsey was just giving her words she wanted to hear. "How long?"

"How long what?"

"How long before someone comes to investigate?"

"Within the next forty-eight hours. Is that soon enough for you?"

Relief flowed through Libby. "Yes." She moved forward suddenly, extending her hand. "Thank you, Captain. You've been very patient and understanding." She gripped his hand and shook it with feeling. "Mr. Garwood and Colonel Edwards think I've gone off on a tangent or something...."

The last thing Dan wanted to do was release Libby's artistic fingers. Her hand was long and lean, like her, the nails cut no-nonsense short. She wasn't the type of woman to use hair spray, nail polish or much makeup, he thought. No, Libby Tyler was a wildflower who thrived on fresh air, lots of sunshine and a demanding physical job.

"Perhaps they've misinterpreted your care for something else," Dan told her quietly. Her eyes widened beautifully, and he had the powerful urge to take her in his arms and kiss the hell out of her. Shocked by the intensity of the feeling, Dan stepped back, afraid he'd really do it. Libby was like a magnet, inviting spontaneity and erratic behavior. He was sure the children in her classes loved her fiercely, because she'd never lost her own ability to be childlike.

Libby walked to the door and opened it. "Thank you, Captain." She hesitated. For some reason, she wanted to stay. She liked Dan Ramsey's ability to put her at ease, as well as his sincerity. Gripping the doorknob, she walked out.

Dan stood, hands on hips, and shook his head. His first case. Although he wasn't supposed to get into normal PM investigative matters, he didn't mind taking Libby's case. The real reason he'd been transferred from the Yuma Marine Air Station to Reed was his unceasing efforts to eradicate drugs from the marine base. Colonel Edwards had heard about his success in Yuma and had pulled strings to get him here, to set up the same kind of program. So why had Edwards assigned Libby Tyler's case to him? It certainly wasn't drug related.

Then Dan laughed, something he hadn't done often in the past two years. Maybe Libby's tornadolike presence had so discombobulated Edwards that he'd foisted her off on the first person he could think of. Well, Edwards's loss was his gain.

"Sir? Did you say something?"

Dan looked up. A marine staff sergeant stood in the doorway dressed in his summer uniform. "Uh, no...I was muttering to myself." And then Dan became all-business. "I'm Captain Ramsey, the new assistant PM."

The marine stepped forward and offered his hand. "Sergeant Joe Donnally, sir. I'll be working with you. In fact, I'll be your right-hand man around here."

"Good, you're just the person I wanted to see," Dan said, turning around to pick up the report. "I've got a case I want you to investigate for me."

"A case? Already, sir?"

"I know the feeling. I've only been here two hours." Dan smiled slightly, liking the alert, predatory look in the sergeant's eyes. "Think my name precedes me or something, Sergeant?"

Donnally tentatively returned the smile and perused the carefully printed report. "Must have, sir." He frowned. "Is this a drug case?"

"No. Just a pedestrian one, Sergeant."

"But...I was told you were going to set up a drug-rehab unit here on base."

Dan waved his hand. "That's correct, Sergeant. Read the report, and if you have any questions before you begin the investigation, come and see me."

"Yes, sir. But I could send this over to Captain Adams's people to handle. He usually deals with stuff like this."

"No, don't do that. We'll take care of it."

"Sure, sir?"

"Positive." Libby would think he was passing the buck if he did that to her. And for some reason, Dan cared what she thought of him. "I'm sure it's going to be a simple matter to clear up, Sergeant. No, we'll handle it here through our office."

Joe shrugged. "Fine with me, sir."

Dan sat back down. "Stay a minute, Sergeant. If you're my assistant, I'd like to know a little about your background. Have a seat."

Joe did as he was ordered, sitting at attention in the seat facing the desk. "Colonel Edwards chose me to work with you, sir, precisely because of my background. I was born and raised in National City, close to the Mexican border."

"A lot of drug activity around your hometown?"

"Yes, sir. I ran with a Hispanic gang growing up, and I know the southern-California territory."

"Did you sell drugs?" Dan knew the man could lie to him if he chose to, but he wanted to gauge his reaction.

"No, sir," Joe returned steadily.

"Why?"

With a shrug, Joe said, "I lost my sister, Maria, to drugs. I saw what it did to her and what her death ended up doing to all of us. No, sir, I never used drugs. I hated them. And I hate the people who sell them to the kids."

"I'm sorry about your sister, Sergeant," Dan said, meaning it. Donnally's story hit too close to home. He'd lost Janna to cocaine addiction. Since then, all his anger toward the drug culture had been turned into a personal war that included cleaning up the Yuma air station, and now Reed.

"Sir, if I can be bold, there are a couple of other good men who really hate drugs that could be assigned to your office."

"Excellent. Give me a list of names, Sergeant. We'll be building this rehab clinic and an undercover interdiction unit from the ground up. I can use all the good men I can get."

Joe nodded, liking his new officer immensely. Word had come down that Ramsey was a tough officer. Well, Joe didn't mind that type, as long as they were fair-minded. Hope rose in him. Ramsey seemed a hell of a lot better than his predecessor, Captain Jacobs. Suddenly, excitement thrummed through him.

"Sir, when will you let us in on your plans and ideas for the base?"

Dan hid a smile, liking the sergeant's intensity and enthusiasm. "Just as soon as we can get a pool of people who hate drugs as much as you and I do."

Joe jumped up and came to attention. "Permission to leave and get started on this, sir?"

"First things first, Sergeant." Dan motioned to the report in his hand. "Let's get Ms. Tyler's investigation out of the way, shall we?"

"Yes, sir. This'll be a piece of cake."

"I hope so. Dismissed, Sergeant."

Dan pushed his fingers together in a steeple as he thought about Donnally. He liked the staff sergeant, who seemed to couple intelligence with enthusiasm—the combination Dan was searching for in the team he'd put together for Reed. Brig chasers were big, mean marines who reminded him of the old corps before all the changes. As a group, they had one hell of a reputation, and no one messed with them. Not even the highly vaunted recon marines. No, brig chasers were the perfect instruments to use against the drug world.

Glancing at the phone on his desk, Dan wondered how long it would be until it would be ringing off the hook with drug-related problems. Once he'd put his drug unit together in Yuma, the phone had become a living being, stalking him twenty-four hours a day.

Reed was a lot bigger than Yuma, boasting 48,000 military personnel and 4,200 civilian employees to the Arizona air station's 12,000 military personnel. He exhaled heavily, wondering if the drug problems at this base could be corralled and eradicated. No matter what happened, Dan knew he had to give it his best shot. If people such as Donnally were available to him, his job would be a lot easier. Still, from what Rose, his new secretary, had told him, his office and personnel were in dire need of being shaped up. Captain Jacobs had left the unit in shambles, the morale low. It would only make his job tougher if he had to whip his men and women back into line.

As Dan continued to ponder, his thoughts revolved back to Libby Tyler. If she was this upset about those five horses, why wasn't her boss, Stuart Garwood? Or was she one of those people who did, indeed, go off on a tangent and make mountains out of mole hills? Dan grimaced, wishing mightily that he was the one going out to the stables to investigate Libby's allegations rather than Donnally. Somehow, Dan had to figure out a way to see her. Somehow.

Chapter Two

"Chaos." Dan muttered under his breath so no one passing his office door could hear him. "Utter chaos." He'd been at Reed exactly three days, and everything was a mess. The officer whom he'd replaced, Captain Arthur Jacobs, had somehow managed to transform his fifty-person contingent into a surly group who were bordering on disrespect—except for Donnally, who was turning out to be a godsend.

His desk was scattered with papers. The In basket was full and teetering with files begging for his attention. It was only a matter of time until the pile toppled.

"Captain?"

Dan looked up. Rose Tannison, his GS-12, government civil service secretary, stood in the doorway. She was a civilian who worked for the military. Her bulk filled it amply. "Yes, Rose?"

"We've got a problem." She removed her bifocal glasses from the end of her nose. "Mind if I come in and shut the door while we talk?"

Groaning inwardly, Dan guessed it to be another personnel problem. Right now, he wanted to strangle Jacobs, a short-timer whose bitter attitude toward the Marine Corps had rubbed off on the enlisted people who worked under him. "Sure." Dan glanced at his watch: 1145. For once, if this didn't take long, he was going to be able to grab some lunch.

Rose smiled and sat down after closing the door. She fluffed her full pink cotton skirt. "Have you met Howard Parker, the police chief from Oceanside, yet?"

"No." Oceanside bordered Reed's territory and was a military town with all the inherent problems that accompanied such a dubious title. And Dan knew working closely with civilian law enforcement would be vital for his plan to be successful.

"Well," Rose said, placing her glasses back up on her bulblike nose and peering over them at him, "you'd better pull out a big box of Band-Aids. He's on his way here."

"What does that mean?" Dan rested both his elbows on the desk.

"May I be frank?"

"Yes." Rose had worked in Reed HQ for eighteen years, and Dan was finding her indispensable for the straight scoop on what was going on around the base.

"Trouble with a capital *T*. His wife was formerly married to a marine sergeant. Unfortunately, the sergeant died and she married Parker on the rebound, six months later. The chief has never forgotten his wife's first love was a marine. He's always been the jealous type."

Mouth quirking, Dan leveled a stare across the desk at Rose. Her black hair was pushed up into a haphazard knot

on top of her head, and she wore long, dangling red earrings that matched her red-and-pink cotton blouse. "And
so," Dan said, "he doesn't like marines very much at all
and is a pain in the rear in any working relationship with
marines. Right?"

Rose beamed. "Go to the head of the class, Captain
Ramsey." She grinned impishly. "They said you were a
tough officer. But I think you're *smart* and tough."

Grinning, Dan leaned back. "Being tough isn't going to
smooth out this problem, Rose. Do you think a little diplomacy will work with Parker?"

"Captain Jacobs hated the police chief, and vice versa.
But then, Jacobs couldn't get along with his own shadow.
I think if you appear willing to work with Parker and let
him think he's running the show, there'll be room to maneuver."

"I don't know what I'd do without you, Rose. Okay, so
handle Parker with kid gloves and pull his strings without
him knowing it. Can do." He frowned. "I just wish my own
people weren't so damned sluggish and morale wasn't so
low."

"Joe Donnally's squared away," Rose assured him. "He
and Captain Jacobs got along like a dog and cat. He'll level
with you the way I do. But he needs your permission to
speak frankly, while I don't. Ask him for his opinion and
use his suggestions. He's been at Reed for two years. As a
brig chaser and a people manager, he's the best. I think if
you shower your people with a little attention and pats on
the back for a job well done, they'll snap back into line real
quick."

Laughing softly, Dan nodded. He picked up a pen and
tapped it against the desk. "At least there's some light at
the end of the tunnel."

"You got handed a can of worms when you came here, Captain." She grinned lopsidedly. "But then, I feel you're just the kind of man to handle a can of worms. My money's on you."

Glancing out the venetian blinds, Dan saw a police car pull into the parking lot. A heavyset man in a dark blue uniform stepped out. He had a bulldoglike face, jowls and all. "Keep telling me that, Rose. I think Parker's arrived."

"Uh-oh." Rose got nimbly to her feet. "I'm outta here. Want me to send him in and get coffee?"

He nodded. "Yes, thanks."

"Good luck."

Dan smiled and watched her leave as silently as she'd come. Rose must weigh at least two hundred and fifty pounds, he thought, but for all her bulk, she was surprisingly agile and quiet. As he pulled the blind aside a bit more to take a good look at Parker, Dan's mind shifted unexpectedly to Libby Tyler. Her file was still sitting in his Out basket. He just hadn't had time to contact her yet with the results of Donnally's investigation. That was one woman he wanted to see, but the pressures and demands of his job were drowning him. She probably thought he'd buried her investigation in the circular file. He'd have to get the report over to her soon.

With a sigh, he released the blind and went over to his desk to tidy up the piles of work. Might as well make a good first impression on the police chief. At least his summer uniform was perfectly pressed, the ribbons on the left side of his chest in order and straight.

Rose knocked on the door and opened it. "Captain Ramsey," she sang out, "Chief Parker's here to pay his respects."

Dan rose and smiled. "Thanks, Rose. Chief, come on in."

Parker glared as the door shut behind him and Dan offered his hand. Grudgingly, he shook it.

"Captain."

"Sit down, Chief. Rose will bring us coffee."

"I'm not staying that long, Ramsey." He took off his cap and tucked it under his left arm. "I'm making this call because it's necessary, not because I want to do it."

Resting his hands on his hips, Dan coolly held the chief's belligerent stare. "Okay, Chief. What can I do for you, then?"

Parker stared at him. "I hope you're nothing like Jacobs."

"I didn't know the man."

"We didn't get along."

"So what will it take for us to mend some of those bridges, Chief? We don't have a choice in this matter."

Parker looked around the office and then back at the marine. "You got any background in law enforcement?"

"I'm a lawyer."

Parker's eyebrows rose and fell. "What else?"

"Drug enforcement is my jurisdiction, Chief, which is why I've been assigned to Reed. I'm interested in stopping any trafficking going on inside the base or around it. I'll need your support and, sometimes, your help."

"Captain Jacobs didn't give a damn about anything except how much time he had left before he got out."

"I'm looking at a thirty-year career, Chief, and I can promise you I'm in for the long haul, particularly in regards to drug enforcement." Dan saw Parker's face turn a dull red. "Have a seat, Chief," he coaxed. "I'm interested in your assessment of drug traffic through your city. And I want to know how we can help you. Of course, I'm primarily interested in marines either selling or using drugs, but I'll work just as hard to see to it we help you nail civilian drug pushers, too."

"Humph, sounds like a lot of bull to me, Ramsey."

Dan sat down. "Try me, then. I don't mind being put on the hot seat. I'm used to being there," he offered, letting a grin leak through his professional demeanor. Gradually, Parker was losing the chip on his shoulder. Dan was confident of his diplomacy skills. What excited him most was getting the best out of each person he met. Parker was no exception, so Dan took up the challenge of changing the chief's perception about working with the marines of Reed.

Rose poked her head around his door after Parker had left. "Not bad, Captain. He stayed a whole hour. What'd ya do? Hog-tie him?"

"Almost," Dan said dryly. He pulled his sack lunch out of a drawer in his desk. "I'm starving to death."

"Sorry, Captain, but you've got another visitor."

Frowning, he unwrapped the beef sandwich he'd fixed for himself earlier that morning at his apartment. "Who now?"

"Don't get that unhappy look on your face. This one will make you smile. Libby Tyler's here."

Libby. Dan set the sandwich aside. "God, I promised her I'd get back to her before this." He started rummaging frantically through the teetering stack of files on his desk. "Send her in, Rose."

"Sure thing, boss."

Locating the file, Dan pulled it out. Just as he opened it, Libby entered his office and suddenly his pressured, demanding day melted away. Her sable hair was caught in a loose ponytail tied with a yellow ribbon, and she looked like a freshly scrubbed college girl. Escaped tendrils curled at her temples, and the thick bangs across her brow emphasized her large green eyes. She wore a long-sleeved, pale yellow cotton blouse that complemented her canary yellow riding breeches. More than anything, Dan liked the flush to her freckled cheeks and her sensual mouth.

He stood quickly, nearly tipping over his chair as he rose. Grimacing, he caught it and dropped the file on the desk. "Hi, come on in."

Libby hesitated in the doorway. Yes, Dan Ramsey was still just as pulverizingly handsome as she'd remembered. For three days now, she'd been trying valiantly to push him out of her mind—and heart. "I was in the neighborhood and thought I'd drop by, Captain."

"Sure, no problem," he said, bending down to retrieve the file. "Sit down. I'm glad you dropped by." He liked the way she walked, with a fluid kind of grace. Despite her height, she reminded him of a quietly flowing river. Did horseback riding impart that ballerinalike quality? It must. "I've got to apologize," he said, motioning to his overflowing investigation files. "I think everyone on base heard I was here. The cases coming in have been more like an avalanche than a dribble."

She nodded and sat down. "Then you must be very good at what you do." Her pulse bounded when he smiled ruefully and sat, opening the file in front of him. Libby found herself wanting to stare deeply into his amused azure eyes. The crow's-feet around Dan's eyes were deep, as were the lines around his mouth. This man knew how to laugh, how to find the positive in life, she thought, violently fighting the desire to like him even more.

Seeing the opened sandwich and paper bag at his right elbow, she felt bad at having interrupted his late lunch. "What did you find out about the horses?" she asked eagerly.

Dan rapidly read Joe's typed report. "Mr. Garwood feels it's a group of teenage dependents doing it, Libby."

Libby stood up. "Boys! He told me the same thing four months ago! I didn't buy it then, and I don't buy it now."

Dan held up his hand. "He promised my sergeant that he'd post one of his men at the stable for the next seven nights and catch them." Looking up, he saw Libby's disgust and agitation. "Isn't that enough?"

"Oh, I don't know. My gut feeling tells me it isn't a bunch of rowdy dependents looking for a good time."

Sitting back, Dan absorbed her fiery beauty. She had the most beautiful green eyes he'd ever seen—like emeralds held up to sunlight. Right now, they were narrowed, reflecting her agitation. "Listen, I haven't even had lunch yet. How about I take you over to the Officers' Club and we'll grab a bite to eat and discuss this issue further?" Dan suggested, as surprised as she apparently was that he'd asked her out. After grieving for the loss of his marriage, he'd carefully avoided any kind of relationship—until now. He noted the way her lovely eyes had gone wide at his invitation, a pink flush delicately tinting her freckled cheekbones.

Was it Libby who had aroused this sudden change in him? Or was it the fact that he was finally starting to come out of his long tunnel of grief? Dan digested the possibilities, acutely attuned to her reaction.

She motioned to his desk. "What's that on your desk, Captain?"

"Er...oh, that." He grinned sheepishly. "Just an old beef sandwich. Something I threw together this morning. I'm not much of a cook," he offered. He'd forgotten that it had been sitting at his elbow all along. *Not a very smart move, Ramsey. Not smart at all.* He hoped Libby would buy his explanation.

"I doubt very seriously we would have anything to discuss about this investigation that would take up a whole lunch hour," Libby said, her words clipped.

She was angry. Why? "I just thought that if there was any background information you didn't fill me in on that might help this case, we could do it over lunch." Dan was damned if he was going to let go of the opportunity and back down. He wanted to know Libby a hell of a lot better.

Squirming, she shoved her hands into the pockets of her breeches. "Captain, I don't date marines over issues of business or for pleasure," she rattled in a low, off-key voice. "And I don't like you trying to take advantage of the situation to maneuver me into going to lunch with you."

Dan felt heat rushing to his face. Was he blushing? Maybe he ought to be, under the circumstances. "I just thought that—"

"Captain, I don't date marines. Is that clear?"

"Sure is." He cocked his head, holding her furious gaze. "My invitation just kinda slipped out."

"I don't know whether to be insulted or complimented," she admitted.

"It was a compliment, believe me."

Libby avoided the warmth in his voice and eyes. "Never mind, Captain. I've got a short fuse about the topic of marines, that's all."

"I didn't mean to imply that if you didn't go to lunch with me, the investigation would be dropped. It won't be, I promise."

"I know, I know. I've just got some touchy spots in my life regarding the Marine Corps," Libby muttered. The frightening thing was, a part of her *did* want to go to lunch with Dan. She couldn't figure out why he wasn't married.

Perhaps he was divorced? Libby told herself she shouldn't care one way or another.

"Mind if I ask why?"

Hurt rose in Libby at the softness in Dan's voice. Then tears unexpectedly stung her eyes. She turned away so he wouldn't see them. "Captain Ramsey, I won't discuss my personal life with you or anyone else. I just want whoever is riding those horses caught!" If she stayed one more minute, she was going to break down and tell Dan everything. Worse, she wanted to walk into the safety of his arms and be held. Just be held . . . In desperation, Libby walked out the door.

Dan looked down at his uneaten sandwich. He began to wrap it up again, his appetite gone. The tears in Libby's eyes had torn at him. "Sometimes, Ramsey, you can be a first-class jerk. Do you know that?"

"What?"

Dan looked up. Rose was at the door again.

"Nothing. What's wrong now, Rose?"

She grinned. "You're catching on fast, Captain. When I show up, you know trouble ain't far behind."

Dan sighed. "Come in and shut the door." What he wanted to do was follow Libby to the parking lot and make an apology—somehow patch up the trust he'd broken between them. It was too late now. What a hell of a welcome to Reed.

Rose sat down with a file on her large lap. "You've got a new brig chaser under your command, Captain."

"Let's dispense with formality, Rose. Call me Dan when we're alone, okay?"

"Fine. Anyway, this new kid is only eighteen and really green. He's a potential problem, as I see it. His name is PFC David Shaw."

Dan put the sandwich in the drawer and closed it. "Go on."

Rose frowned. "This morning he was to escort a murderer by the name of Coughman from the brig up to Treasure Island on the other side of the San Francisco Bay. He's driving the prisoner up right now. Just in case you don't know it, TI is a major prison for military men who've committed serious crimes."

Dan smiled to himself. "I've sent a few of them there, Rose. What else?"

"Well, when Shaw came up to me to get the paperwork this morning on this prisoner, he started acting real funny with the set of orders I prepared for him. I showed him what to read and where to sign his name. Shaw got real uneasy and started asking me a lot of questions, so I told him to read the orders. I mean, they were right in front of him, for heaven's sake. He kinda did, but then he went over to Joe Donnally and started asking the same questions of him that I refused to answer."

"Maybe the kid's just nervous, Rose. You know—double-checking before making the drive up the coast with a prisoner. Being responsible for a prisoner isn't easy, and if it's his first time, some of his actions might be understandable."

She shrugged her shoulders. "Maybe you're right, Dan." She tapped the file. "There's something funny going on with the kid. He's real tall and skinny and built like a rail." She grinned. "If only that would have happened to me. Anyway, he's not the brig-guard type of guy, if you know what I mean."

Dan nodded. Brig chasers were usually big, strapping marines, even tougher and meaner than the criminals they had to guard and move from one brig or correctional place to another. "Keep an eye on him, Rose, but give him a chance. He was probably just intimidated by Coughman's reputation."

With a laugh, Rose got up. "You're probably right. But if you're going to square this office away, things like this need to be reported to you, Dan."

"No argument from me, Rose. Thanks for bringing it to my attention."

She hesitated at the door, giving him a coy look over her bifocals. "I saw Libby Tyler hurrying out of here. Looked like she was going to cry. . . ."

Dan refused to take the bait. "She was a little upset," he answered shortly.

Rose nodded. "I see."

"I'm sure you do, Rose."

She smiled. "Pretty lady, isn't she?"

"Sure is."

"She's a widow, did you know that?"

Dan frowned and looked over at his secretary. "No, I didn't."

"Yeah, her husband was a marine helicopter pilot, a real fine officer here at Reed. Three years ago he was with his squad in a helicopter for a night patrol, and they crashed in the hills. Word is that the copilot was flying at the time and wearing those new night goggles. He flew the chopper into some power lines. All twelve men on board died instantly, including Captain Tyler."

"Damn . . ."

"Libby really forced the hand of the crash investigators to find out why her husband had been killed. They hid the facts from her at first, but when she threatened a civilian lawsuit, they leveled with her. It was a problem with the night goggles."

What a jerk he'd been. No wonder his lunch suggestion had proven painful to Libby. Chances were, Dan surmised, she didn't want a damn thing to do with marines ever again. "They've had a lot of problems with those goggles," he agreed quietly. He owed Libby a genuine apology.

"She's a real special lady," Rose went on. "Libby's program to teach the dependent children how to ride has been a roaring success around here. She's gotten them off the streets and out of the malls and interested in horses instead. She doesn't have any children of her own, but the kids just love her. Word on the grapevine was that Libby wanted a child really badly." The secretary shrugged. "Guess it wasn't meant to be, but Libby's really been a positive force here on Reed in the three years since his death."

If it were possible to feel worse, Dan did. "I guess I'd better drop over to the stables and see her," he muttered.

Rose's smile was benevolent. "I knew you wouldn't let her down, Dan."

He gave her a pointed look. "Is Libby your daughter?"

She laughed. "No, but I'd be proud to have her as one."

"Just wondering. The way you're doting over her, I thought for sure she was a close relative."

"In my book, Libby Tyler is a good-hearted person. We need more of them on this poor, suffering earth of ours. I just happen to think there's something nice between the two of you. I saw the way she looked at you."

Dan felt his skin heat up. This time he knew he was blushing. "Rose," he said in a growly tone, "don't you have something to do? Shouldn't you be getting ready for our meeting with the MP's this afternoon?"

Giggling, Rose nodded. "Yes, sir, Captain. Just pen some time in your appointment book to visit Libby in the next day or two. I'm sure it'll do both of you good."

Chapter Three

"Hey, Libby," Jenny Stevens called from her horse in the middle of the riding ring, "do you know that marine standing over by the gate?"

Libby kept her gaze on the ten children walking their horses along the arena's pipe-rail fence. Jenny was a navy corpswave nurse. On her days off, she helped Libby with her classes, acting as her assistant. Libby twisted around on Shiloh, her Trahkner gelding, a special breed of horses brought from Europe specifically for eventing because of their size and strength. She looked toward the gate. Her heart thudded hard in her breast. Dan Ramsey.

"Him," she muttered.

Jenny leaned over and gave her an inquiring look. "Him? Why, Libby, you said you'd never date a marine again. He's gorgeous. Who is he?"

"Trouble," she said between gritted teeth, "and he's not my boyfriend, Jenny." Two days had gone by since she'd last seen Dan Ramsey, and she'd never expected to see him again. Worse, she'd had a torrid dream about him this morning—which had left her in a decidedly bad mood. Now here he was, leaning negligently against the gate, looking cool and relaxed in his summer uniform. If only he weren't so heart-stoppingly handsome, she'd have a much easier time remaining immune to him, Libby thought wryly.

Jenny smiled, her eyes on the children under her tutelage, each child sitting straight and tall in an English saddle, small hands clutching the reins near the neck of their horse. The group came in once a week to learn how to ride English-style. "Trouble? I'd like to see trouble like that. I've been here at Camp Reed for a year and haven't met even one decent guy. Well, a couple, but they just didn't do much for me. Now, that captain looks *very* decent."

Libby gave her friend a dirty look. She was going to ignore Dan Ramsey for a while. Maybe he'd get the message and leave. She was willing to bet he wasn't here for business reasons. "He's as sneaky as they come."

"Oh? Did he ask you out to dinner or something?"

Squirming in her English saddle, Libby felt Shiloh start to move restively between her legs. She reached out and stroked his long, powerful neck to reassure him. She knew he was picking up on her reaction to Dan. Ramsey, she reminded herself. *Keep him at a distance, Libby Tyler. If you start calling him by his first name, it'll be too late.*

"He had the nerve to ask me out to lunch when I was over at the PM's office the other day trying to get someone to investigate about those five horses.

Jenny nodded. "Can't shoot the guy for trying," she teased. Becoming more sober, she added, "I've heard about Captain Ramsey. They say he's a real gung ho marine who's going to clean up the drug situation around here. I treated a brig chaser at the hospital last night who mixed it up over at the brig with a prisoner, and he mentioned Ramsey's name. I guess the good captain was brought in specifically to start a rehab program."

"I didn't know that."

"You wouldn't—you don't listen to base gossip. Oops, there goes Scotty. He's slipping out of the saddle. I better go over and help him."

Libby nodded and watched her assistant trot over to a small, red-haired boy who was having trouble staying balanced in the saddle. The animal wanted to stop, not walk, so Scotty was kicking it as hard as he could, slipping slowly but surely off the saddle all the while. Smiling, Libby watched Jenny, who was an experienced rider with some dressage training herself, take care of the situation. Her neck felt hot and she rubbed it, sure that Ramsey was staring at her. Too bad, let him wait.

As Libby gave Shiloh the leg signal to trot over to another child in trouble, she admitted she was afraid of Ramsey. Afraid of how easily he'd reached into her slowly healing heart and awakened her feelings. As she neared Molly, who sat on a white gelding, Libby released a flustered sigh. Ever since she'd met Ramsey he'd been popping uninvited into her thoughts at odd moments.

"Molly, honey, lift your hands," she coaxed, coming alongside her. A pure-blooded Trahkner, Shiloh towered above the white mare. The gelding was big-boned, a dark blood bay color with black mane and tail. He was seventeen hands high, a giant for a horse of almost any breed. Poor Sunny was small in comparison at fifteen hands high, and Libby had to lean down to gently reposition Molly's tiny fingers on the thick, unwieldy reins.

"There, that's it," she said encouragingly, smiling down into the girl's serious face. Molly's father was General Endicott, the base commander. Too often Libby had seen small children's natural spontaneity severely suppressed by the rigid military atmosphere they were raised in.

Molly's face relaxed once Libby had reached over and patted her shoulder. "Like this, Miss Tyler?"

"Exactly like that, Molly," Libby praised, directing Shiloh to shorten his long stride to keep her at Molly's side. Libby was still reluctant to turn around, wildly aware of Ramsey's interest in her activities. It was impossible not to look up when she gave Shiloh pressure against his barrel to make him turn and head back to the center of the arena. The afternoon sun's long rays made thin, uneven shadows across the sandy space. The few trees nearby offered snippets of shade here and there from the burning heat.

This time, Dan smiled at her. Libby's mouth went dry and her heart started an erratic pounding. She forced a slight smile of her own and quickly pretended to shift her focus back to the children. The arena was a good five hundred feet in diameter, an oval filled with soft sand and dirt, perfect for teaching riding as well as jumping. Jenny had walked her horse back down the straggling line of children, correcting posture and hand or feet positions with plenty of lavish praise. Libby loved to see how quickly the children responded to a little positive reinforcement.

Jenny trotted back to the center and joined her.

"Why don't you go talk to Captain Ramsey? We've only got five minutes left in the class hour. I can watch them."

"Thanks, Jenny, but no."

"You don't like him?"

"It's not that."

"Oh, so you do like him. Good taste."

Giving Jenny a flat stare, Libby said, "You're reading something into nothing. I know why he's here, and I don't want to encourage him, Jenny. He can wait until we're done with the class."

Chewing on her lower lip, Jenny cast her an understanding look. "I know you're afraid to get involved after your husband's death. It must be so hard to reach out and try to love or trust again."

Her stomach knotted and Libby whispered, "I'm not afraid of dating, Jenny. I just won't date a military man, that's all."

Jenny reached out and touched Libby's shoulder. "Maybe, with time, that fear will leave you. How about I take the kids back to the barn and make sure they unsaddle and put their tack away properly? You can go talk to Captain Ramsey in the meantime."

Giving her friend a resigned look, Libby said, "Okay, but I'm sure I'll be joining you in a few minutes. This won't take long."

Tossing her head, her black hair brushing her shoulders, Jenny laughed. "Okay. See you back at the OK Corral." She waved to the children to halt their horses at the gate.

With a sigh, Libby steeled herself to meet Dan. *Ramsey. Damn.* How did he get under her skin so quickly? Reluctantly, she turned Shiloh toward where he stood. Although she found herself wishing her ten-year-old gelding would actually drag his hooves in crossing the arena, it didn't happen. Libby remained seated as she pulled Shiloh to a stop next to the fence.

"Captain," she said coolly.

"Libby."

She squirmed inwardly, yet maintained a grim look on her face. "Why are you here?"

Dan looked up at the late-afternoon sky. It was a cloudless blue, the sunshine pouring across the yellowed hills of Reed. "The truth?"

"Nothing but." Her heart snagged when he cocked his head and looked up at her with that boyish smile.

"I have spring fever, and I couldn't stand one more minute in that cramped cubicle of an office of mine."

"Oh . . ." She relaxed slightly in the saddle, relieved. He wasn't pursuing her after all.

Dan hitched one highly polished shoe up on the lowest rail of the fence. "Actually, the rest of the truth is that I came to tell you I'm sorry for upsetting you the other day." Wryly, he added, "I haven't slept well since it happened." He pointed to the area beneath his eyes. "I can't handle three days in a row of guilt-ridden sleep."

Libby stared at him, not knowing whether to laugh or take him seriously. "I don't see any dark circles." She liked his eyes, the intensity in them—the promise of a man who held many secrets, some of them sad.

"No?"

"No."

"Hmm, Rose noticed them." When he saw her frown, he said, "That's my secretary. She's quite a gal. I don't know what I'd do without her."

"Your apology's accepted, Captain. Now if you'll excuse me—"

"Wait." Dan leaned out, his hand nearly brushing the rein she held.

Libby halted.

"Hell, this isn't working out the way I wanted," he grumbled, then glanced up at Libby. "It's about the other day when you told me you didn't date marines. After you left, Rose filled me in on what happened to you, Libby. She said you lost your husband in a helicopter accident here on base." Dan watched her flushed cheeks grow pale. The defiance in her eyes turned dark with undisguised anguish. "I'm sorry. I guess I don't blame you for not wanting to get involved with another marine, and I understand your reactions to my lunch invitation the other day. I didn't know." He held her vulnerable gaze. "I have a tendency toward foot-in-mouth disease. Have you noticed?"

"Oh, I have a good dose of the same disease," she muttered under her breath. Then, indignantly, she added, "What makes you think I'm the least bit interested in any marine, including you?" The nerve of this man! But when he gave her that rakish smile, all her anger melted.

With a shrug, Dan said, "I don't, not really." Did Libby realize how beautiful she was atop her bay gelding? Her shoulders were thrown back with such pride, her chin had a slight tilt of confidence and her back was ramrod straight. No denying it, right or wrong, practical or crazy, the way she sat the horse made him go hot with longing. Her thighs, outlined by the taut fabric of the yellow breeches, were long and firm. Judging from her reaction to him stepping into her life again, it was a damn good thing she couldn't read his mind. Libby would probably trample him to death with that huge horse of hers if she knew what he was thinking.

"I just felt I should come over and apologize in person," Dan said humbly, meaning it.

His humility shamed her. Libby relented a little and allowed the reins to fall on Shiloh's neck. "I'm sorry, too. I shouldn't have overreacted. I do that a lot. You can't help it that you're a marine."

"It's not a disease, you know."

She grinned and enjoyed looking at him as a man, regardless of the uniform he wore. Jenny was right. Dan Ramsey was wonderfully good-looking in a strong kind of way. He wasn't pretty-boy handsome. In fact, his face was almost leathery from so much time spent out in the elements.

"Touché. I had that coming," she said.

"Can we start over?" He saw blood rush to her cheeks, her lashes dropping to stop him from seeing what emotions lay in her emerald eyes.

"Over? You're making me jumpy again."

"I can see that."

Libby picked nervously at a nonexistent thread on the thigh of her breeches. Shiloh, too, was restive, mirroring her feelings.

"What I meant was that I'm new on base, and I think I ought to know more about the terrain of this particular area." Dan watched her chin rise as her huge green eyes settled on him, filled with an intriguing mixture of distrust and interest. "I've given this a lot of thought," he lied, "and I think I ought to inspect the surrounding areas by horseback. Of course, I'll need an expert guide. Someone like you, for instance."

"Why?"

Dan turned and pointed in a northwesterly direction from the stable. "The brig sits right over there. If a prisoner ever escapes, and they have before, there's a ninety-five-percent chance he'll come this way, toward the San Luis Rey gate right down the road. It's the fastest way to get off base and into civilian territory. And there's less chance he'll be picked up once he gets off base."

Impressed, Libby nodded. "You're right on all counts. Last year a brig prisoner got loose, and the hills around the stable were crawling with brig chasers and helicopters."

"Did they find him?"

"Sure did." Libby shrugged. "It was kind of exciting, to tell you the truth. Not much happens around here. Every once in a while a marine will fall off one of the trail horses and have to walk back to the stables, but that's about it."

"Do you ride out in these hills much?" Dan asked curiously. Last night he'd pulled out a map of Reed and plotted the escape routes attempted by brig prisoners over the past ten years. All had been recaptured in the area surrounding the San Luis Rey gate, which was only a mile away from the stables. Escapes didn't happen often, but it was a valid part of Dan's education to know the prisoners' likely routes to potential freedom.

At the same time he'd been racking his brain for a way to meet Libby again—on her turf, so she'd be more comfortable. Armed with Rose's explanation, Dan knew he somehow had to get past her distrust of him as a marine. Maybe, with time, she'd get to see the man, not the uniform he wore. He'd slept poorly after forming his plan, asking himself why it meant so much to him to pursue Libby. He didn't have an answer.

The sun was setting behind the hills, throwing deep shadows along the area's rounded, loaflike hills. Libby loved this time of day. "I often ride in those hills, Captain," she admitted. She smiled and patted her horse's neck. "This is where I train Shiloh. He's an eventing horse, and I've got to keep him and myself in peak condition for the southern-California circuit."

Dan wanted to say something about Libby's peak condition but gave it a rest. She was a no-nonsense woman of the nineties who, he was sure, rightfully disdained chauvinism and double standards.

"You teach riding *and* show your horse?"

"Yes, but I also train eventing horses over at the Crescent Stables in Fallbrook."

"You're a busy lady, then."

Grimly, Libby said, "It pays to stay busy." That way, she didn't have time to remember—didn't have to be reminded of the tragic end to her happy two-year marriage.

"What are the chances of you taking me out sometime soon to show me these hills up close?"

"Sure, anything in the name of patriotism and *Semper Fi.*"

He grinned. "Now, you don't really mean that."

"I'm being flip," Libby conceded. Every time he smiled, the creases at the corners of his mouth deepened, and so did the deviltry in his eyes. She could find nothing to disklike about Dan. Ramsey, Libby sternly reminded herself. *Captain* Ramsey. "One of my trademarks, I guess."

"I like it." *I like you.* Dan studied her mouth, sensing more than seeing the unhappiness Libby held on to. How much of her grief had she worked through? Something in him wanted to reach out to her, to help her, and perhaps in doing so, heal himself. Vestiges of pain remained in her eyes. Well, Dan knew what it was like to carry that kind of sadness around.

"So, when's a good day?"

Libby shrugged. "It's best to ride in the morning or late afternoon. The midday is murder, and I don't like to subject human or animal to it."

"How about Friday at 0900? I'll meet you here."

"Not this Friday. I have to get ready for a horse show we're having here on Saturday and Sunday." She motioned toward the arena. "It's a two-day show for the children, and I'll be helping them and giving encouragement from the sidelines."

"Okay...then how about the following Monday—at 0900?"

Libby hesitated, then capitulated under Dan's warm gaze. "Okay. Do you know how to ride, Captain?"

Dan grinned. "I'm a beginner, but I have a feeling you'll teach me."

"Better wear jeans. Do you have a pair of cowboy boots?"

"No, but I can get some."

"Good, wear them. I'll put you in a Western saddle. That way, you won't fall off."

With a laugh, Dan threw her a salute. "You're really hell on a man's ego, you know?"

She laughed. "Really?"

"Well, maybe some men, but not me. I'll see you Monday morning, Libby."

As he turned away, Libby admired the breadth of his shoulders and the inherent strength of his back beneath the snug-fitting shirt. He was in excellent shape, she could see. As Dan settled the garrison cap back on his head, Libby knew without a doubt he was proud to be a marine. There was strength in his movements, blended with confidence and pride. Suddenly, Libby wanted to know a great deal more about him. Where had he come from? How had life treated him? He seemed so positive and upbeat.

Mulling over her observations, Libby guided Shiloh out of the gate and toward the tack room below the arena. A number of trail riders were going and coming, the vociferous noise of marines on the horses echoing around the small niche in a canyon where the stable stood.

Most of the children from her class had already left, and Jenny was just unsaddling her mare when Libby arrived at the tack room.

"Long two minutes," Jenny teased.

Dismounting, Libby grimaced. "I was wrong."

"Oh?"

Unbuckling Shiloh's girth beneath the saddle flap, Libby said, "I thought he was chasing me, but he's not. He wants me to show him around the area on horseback Monday morning."

Jenny slid the English saddle off her horse and held it in her arms. "And?"

"Don't give me that look."

"What look?"

"Oh, you know which one," Libby muttered, hauling the saddle off Shiloh. "This is strictly business, Jenny. Captain Ramsey wants to become acquainted with this area because it's the direction brig prisoners always head to escape onto civilian territory."

"Sure."

"You," Libby said, following her into the darkened tack room, "are misinterpreting Dan's—I mean, Captain Ramsey's actions."

"Sure I am." Jenny giggled and hung the saddle on a long cottonwood rack, checking to be sure the iron stirrups were snugly fitted up near the back of the saddle before she wiped it down with a clean cloth.

"You're such a wiseacre, Stevens."

"My momma and daddy didn't raise a dummy, Ms. Tyler. Despite *Captain* Ramsey's seemingly innocent request, I think he's pursuing you."

"Pooh." Taking a damp cloth, Libby quickly wiped down her own leather straps and saddle. "He's new here. He's got to get the lay of the land. I give him credit, at least he's doing his homework. What other PM has ever come down to check out the terrain?"

Grabbing her purse from the tack trunk, Jenny said, "Precisely my point, Lib. Think about it. Listen, I gotta run. I have to be on duty over at the hospital in an hour. See you tomorrow afternoon." At the door she cheerily called back, "And have fun getting to know the terrain!"

Disgruntled, Libby didn't respond, merely waving goodbye to her friend instead. Quiet settled around her. The odor of leather and soap permeated the air. She inhaled the reassuring smells as she continued to clean off her saddle and then the double bridle. About fifty Western saddles lined the left wall and equally as many English saddles covered the right. The wonderful aromas made this one of her favorite rooms. Her most favorite was the hay barn, with the fragrant clover-and-alfalfa hay stacked beneath the corrugated-aluminum roof. It was too bad the perfume industry couldn't capture the essence, Libby thought. She, for one, would wear it religiously.

Without reason, Dan came to mind. He wasn't a horse person. Probably not even a country boy. A city slicker, no doubt, she judged. He didn't even own a pair of cowboy boots. With a smile, Libby shook her head. Jenny was wrong. The captain was merely being thorough about his new assignment. She liked that trait in a man. Thoroughness could save lives. The copilot who had killed Brad and his men hadn't paid attention to such small details on the terrain map as the location of the power lines, and it had killed all of them. She sighed. Finished with her task, she walked outside and prepared to rub her gelding down.

As she snapped Shiloh into the cross ties—two chains hooked to either side of massive barn timbers—Libby fought her curiosity about Dan.

"Ramsey. You've got to call him Captain Ramsey," she whispered to herself, picking up the rubber brush. Libby wondered what he would do for the rest of the day. Go back to an office he really didn't want to be in? Go home? She felt for him, understanding all too well his love of fresh air and the outdoors.

"Dan, you'd better put your seat belt and crash helmet on," Rose warned, sticking her head around his door.

Having just come in, Dan raised his brows. "I don't like your tone, Rose. What's coming down?"

"There's a Lieutenant Wood on the phone from Treasure Island, and he's furious in capital letters. He's a navy brig officer up there," she added.

He nodded. "Okay, I'll take the call in here, Rose. Did he say what it's about?"

She looked down her glasses at him. "PFC David Shaw. The same kid I talked to you about the other day."

"Okay." Rose shut the door and he picked up the phone. "Captain Ramsey speaking."

"This is Lieutenant Wood calling from the correction facility at TI, Captain. Just how in the hell are you training your brig chasers nowadays?"

Dan settled his elbows on his desk and kept a tight rein on his anger. "Lieutenant, would you like to explain? I'm in the dark about this." He didn't like navy people chewing him out in general. And specifically, he didn't like snotty officers snapping at him, regardless of rank or service.

"PFC Shaw transported Coughman from your brig to ours," Wood snarled. "And he brought the prisoner in without leg irons. Now, Captain, that's pure slop. What if Coughman had decided to run for it? All he'd have had to do was knock Shaw out and take off. Regulations specifically cite the prisoner must be bound in wrist *and* leg irons. Don't your people read the orders we give them? Just what the hell's going on down there?"

Taking a deep breath, Dan recalled Rose's warning about Shaw. "Look, Lieutenant Wood, I apologize for Shaw's performance," he said in an unruffled but authoritative tone. "I've been here less than a week, but I can promise you it won't happen again."

"It'd better not, Captain. I don't put my brig people at risk like that. Shaw's stupidity put the civilian population at risk, too. Coughman's a convicted murderer. Didn't Shaw know who he was transporting?"

"I agree with you in principle, Lieutenant Wood, and as I said, it won't happen again. You've got my word."

"I hope so."

"Thanks for calling," Dan said, keeping his voice calm as anger lapped at the edges of his control. The other officer's receiver clicked down and the line went dead. Grimly, Dan pushed the intercom button that would connect him with his secretary.

"Rose?"

"Yes, sir?"

"Is PFC Shaw on duty down at the brig?"

"Umm . . . wait a sec, let me check the daily brig roster. Yes, sir, he is."

"Get him up here on the double," he ordered tightly. "And bring in the files on Coughman and Shaw, please."

"Yes, sir!"

He'd just stood to unwind from the tension that had settled in his shoulders when his phone rang again.

"What is it, Rose?"

"Bad day, Captain. Sergeant Donnally just reported in from San Onofre. He was asked to go over there because two illegal Mexicans were found hiding behind one of the Quonset huts. Apparently they spoke only Spanish and Joe is fluent. They needed an interpreter."

"Yes?"

"He got into a fight with a couple of marines who were beating up the illegals when he arrived. Joe's on the way over to make a report to you just as soon as he drops off the Mexicans to Border Patrol authorities. He's putting the two enlisted guys who started the fight on report."

"Very well. Radio Donnally and tell him I want to see him as soon as he arrives."

"Sure thing, sir."

Great. Just great. Dan faced the window and placed his hands on his hips. One of his brig chasers had just screwed up big time, which gave him and Reed a black eye. Not a good way to start his job. And Donnally had been in a fist-fight with fellow marines. That wouldn't be viewed as positive by Colonel Edwards, either. He couldn't have his brig chasers taking things into their own hands. But he'd wait to hear Donnally's side of the incident before making a judgment. He looked out toward Teddy Roosevelt Road, running parallel to the huge two-story gray Headquarters building. When things went wrong, they really went wrong. Rubbing his jaw, Dan thought of Libby. And just as quickly, all his tension and anger dissolved. She had that kind of magical effect on him.

He heard a slight knock at his door. "Enter!" he snapped, turning around.

PFC David Shaw's hand shook as he opened the door that led to his skipper's office. Sweat had popped out along his broad brow and upper lip. Ramsey's face was thunder-cloud dark and his eyes were narrowed on him with predatory intensity. Gulping, his Adam's apple bobbing, Shaw entered the office, shut the door and snapped to rigid attention.

"PFC Shaw reporting as ordered, sir!"

Dan glared up at the string bean of a marine. His sandy hair was still short from boot-camp days. He was at least six-foot-three and couldn't weigh more than a hundred and fifty pounds soaking wet. As usual, Rose had been right: Shaw wasn't brig-chaser material. At least, not outwardly. Shaw's face was oval, his gray eyes set wide apart, and teenage acne scars were still plainly visible on his flushed skin. It was a sensitive face, broadcasting anxiety from his straight-ahead eyes. Too sensitive for brig chasing, Dan thought as he rounded his desk and thrust his face in front of Shaw's.

"Just what the hell did you think you were doing with Coughman, Shaw?" he rasped, his nose nearly touching the private's.

"Uhh . . . sir, I shoulda put Coughman in leg irons. I didn't. No excuse, sir!" he choked out, standing rigidly, his arms stiff against his sides.

Breathing hard, Dan glared into the private's frightened eyes, which were locked dead ahead. "What didn't you do, Shaw?" he shouted. Repetition was an ironclad teaching tool in the Marine Corps. Marines learned by rote.

"Sir! I didn't put prisoner Coughman in leg irons, sir!"

"Did you read the orders, Shaw?"

"Y-yes, sir!"

"It doesn't show, mister!"

"No, sir! It—" he gulped "—won't happen again, Captain. I promise! Sir!"

Dan eased inches away, not satisfied that Shaw had learned his lesson. A heavy film of sweat covered the private's face. "When you got out of boot camp, Shaw, what was your MOS, your Military Operational Specialty?"

"Motor pool, sir!"

"Then," Dan thundered, "what the hell are you doing over here in Corrections and MP work?" It didn't make sense.

"Sir," Shaw snapped, as if back in boot camp facing a DI, "I was in motor pool, but Sergeant Major Black said I couldn't cut it, so he sent me over here. Sir!"

Inwardly, Dan grimaced. Reading between the lines, he realized Black had recognized a screw-up when he saw one, and when Shaw had walked into his motor pool, he'd wisely gotten rid of him by dumping him on Correction's doorstep at the first opportunity. "How long have you been a brig chaser, Shaw?"

"Sir! Two months, sir!"

"And you had all the primary MP training offered?"

"Sir! Yes, sir!"

"Shaw, dammit, this isn't boot camp! Knock off the 'Sir, yes, sir!' Got it?"

Shaw's eyes bulged and he made contact for the first time with Ramsey's. "Yes, sir..."

Rose knocked at the door.

Reluctantly, Dan stepped away, giving Shaw one more lethal glare. The private was at stiff attention, his back bowed as if it would break. "Don't move a muscle," he rasped.

Jerking open the door, Dan took the files and thanked Rose. He shut the door loudly. Shaw jerked as if he'd been shot.

Let him sweat it out, Dan thought as he rounded his desk to sit down and study the two files. Quickly perusing Coughman's, he saw Shaw's illegible scrawl, indicating he'd read and understood the orders before transporting the prisoner.

Shaw barely breathed as the captain read through his file. Sweat beaded, then ran down his temples. Did he dare wipe it away? One look at the captain's dark, angry face and Shaw remained at attention, not moving a muscle. Couldn't he do anything right?

After five minutes, Ramsey looked up at the sweating private. "What made you join the corps?"

Stunned by the unexpected question, Shaw stared at Ramsey momentarily, then jerked his eyes away. "Wha— sir?"

Patiently, Dan repeated, "Why'd you join the corps, Shaw?"

"Uh...well, sir, I wanted training. My friend's family said education was a key to success, so I oughtta get some kind of technical training I could use on the outside once my enlistment was up, you know?''

Dan's gaze fell on Shaw's grades. They were just this side of failing in all categories. ''Motor pool would have been your best bet, Shaw. Brig chasers are a breed apart, and they're highly intelligent men and women. Also, unless you're planning on being a prison guard when you get out, this job isn't going to help you toward your goal one iota.''

Shaw remained frozen. ''Yes, sir, I know, sir.''

''Do you know why I called you in here?''

''Yes, sir,'' Shaw mumbled.

''You screwed up on taking Coughman to TI. I suppose Lieutenant Wood set you straight on correct regulations regarding transport of a prisoner?''

Ashamed, Shaw nodded and swallowed hard. ''Uh, yes, sir, he did. He, uh, was really mad about it, sir.''

''Don't you think he had a right to be?'' Dan shouted.

''Yes, sir, I do!'' Shaw's head snapped up, his eyes wide with sincerity. ''I'm really sorry, Captain. I promise, it won't happen again! I just didn't read that set of orders close enough. Coughman was my first real chase, sir. Before, I always paired up with another, experienced brig chaser. I—I guess I got overexcited or something.''

Dan leaned forward, his voice grating. ''Shaw, marines don't get excited when trouble happens. You got that? You stay calm, cool and collected.''

''Yes, sir...''

''I don't like being brought to task by another officer over one of my men, Shaw. Especially a navy officer. That's embarrassing.''

''Yes, sir...''

Exhaling hard, Dan glared at the young private. Shaw was sweating so hard that large, dark splotches showed beneath each of his arms. A part of Dan took pity on the kid, but another part didn't. Shaw could be killed if he didn't make this lesson stick. Regulations were in place to make transporting a prisoner as safe as possible for the brig chaser and the civilian population alike. A little fear was good for him. It might keep him alive. "All right, Shaw, I'm giving you one more chance."

"You are?" he gasped.

Dan made his face hard and merciless. "You screw up so much as an inch out of line, Shaw, and I'm going to make sure you get transferred out of my division and into someplace where the sun doesn't shine until your enlistment's up. You got that?"

"Yes, sir! Loud and clear, sir! I won't let you down, sir!"

"I hope," Dan whispered gruffly, "for your sake, Shaw, you don't. I don't ever want to see your face in here again on charges like this. Now get out of here and study up on the regulations for transporting prisoners. You are to know them by memory. Once you've memorized them, you are to repeat them verbatim to Sergeant Donnally. Understand?"

"Yes, sir!"

"Dismissed!"

Shaw did an about-face and left his office, and Dan leaned back in his chair. A knock sounded on his door. He glanced down at his watch. It was 1700. Already angry, he snarled, "Enter!"

Sergeant Joe Donnally entered.

"What the hell happened to you?" Dan asked, sitting upright in the chair. Donnally's face was a mess of bruises and he had a long cut leaking blood down the right side of his jaw.

Sheepishly, Joe handed over his report and pressed a green handkerchief to his face. "I mixed it up with a couple of marines over at San Onofre, Captain. A couple of

PFC's discovered some illegal aliens hiding behind a supply Quonset hut and were beating the hell out of them when I arrived. I ordered them to stop." Donnally shrugged his broad, powerful shoulders, stiffness apparent in them. "When they didn't, I waded into the fray, sir. Wetbacks might be entering this country illegally, but they don't deserve to be beaten to death. It's all here in my report."

Disbelief edged Dan's voice. "Why didn't you stop at the hospital first and get that face taken care of?"

"I figured you'd want to know what happened over there first, Captain."

"Sergeant, your report can wait until later. Get your butt over to the hospital emergency room, pronto."

"But, sir—"

"Dammit, Donnally, don't argue with me! My people come first. You should have had the good sense to get treatment. You could have radioed me from the truck and detoured to the hospital. I'd have approved your request." He gave the report a disgusted look. "This damned report can wait."

Contrite, the sergeant nodded and came to attention. "Yes, sir."

"You can fill me in on the details tomorrow morning at 0800, Sergeant."

"Very well, sir." Joe reached for the doorknob.

"Who won?"

"Sir?"

Dan motioned to Donnally's swollen and bruised face. "It was two against one. Who won?"

It hurt like hell to grin, but Joe did anyway. "Captain, you know brig chasers don't take crap from anyone." And then he added respectfully, "Sir."

Suppressing a smile, Dan kept his face carefully neutral. "I'm glad to hear you were the victor, Sergeant. Now dis-

appear and get that mug of yours taken care of. Understand?"

"Yes, sir." Joe quietly shut the door behind him. He
pressed his damp handkerchief against his jaw, suddenly
realizing the front of his uniform was splattered not only
with his blood but with the blood of the other two men.
Ramsey was proving to be a damn good officer and man—
a far cry from Captain Jacobs, who'd hated Hispanics. If
this incident had happened under Jacobs's command, the
sonofabitch would have considered it open season on illegal aliens. And he certainly wouldn't have cared if Joe had
lived or died, much less gotten over to the hospital to take
care of his facial injury. At least Ramsey put his men first
and the incident they were involved in second.

Rose gave him a wide-eyed look as he walked through the
busy fifteen-person office and stopped at her desk.

"Rose, I gotta go over to the hospital. Had a slight scuf-
fle."

"No kidding. What shape was the truck in that hit you?"

The corner of his mouth that wasn't split open and
bleeding lifted. "The other two dudes are in a lot sorrier
shape than I am, believe me. I'm checking out for the day.
Will you sign me out?" He held up his scraped and bloody
hand. If he signed out on that pristine sheet on her desk,
he'd make a mess of it, and Rose valued neatness. He didn't
want to risk her ire. One fight a day was plenty.

Rose shook her head. "Yeah, I'll sign you out. You
oughtta make that a couple of days off, Joe. Your face
looks like hamburger."

"Thanks, Rose. I can always count on you for an honest opinion," he said dryly, smiling through his pain.

She winked at him. "Take care of yourself. Is the captain upset?"

"I don't think so. He only wanted to know who won."
Rose's face grew pinched. "That's terrible!"
"No," Joe corrected as he left, "that's marine."

Chapter Four

By Saturday afternoon, totally disgusted and bored with the moving-in process, Dan sat down amid the boxes cluttering the living room of his new apartment in Oceanside. His thoughts—and if he was honest, his emotions—revolved back to Libby Tyler. She'd said she had a horse show this weekend at the base stables. Grimacing, he looked around at the half-unpacked cartons and strewn packing material. To hell with it. In one smooth motion he was on his feet. He was going to see Libby.

Not wanting to make the mistake of showing up in uniform, Dan decided the faded jeans and short-sleeved chambray shirt he was wearing would be more appropriate under the circumstances. Minutes later, as he pulled his Corvette onto the dirt road leading to the base stables, he saw cars, trucks and horse trailers lining both sides of the road. Hundreds of people dotted the rolling hills that surrounded the stables and the three riding arenas. Once he'd found a place to park, the urgency he felt to find Libby made him walk a little faster than perhaps he would have under ordinary circumstances.

Children of all ages either had horses in hand or were riding them around. The small hills that formed a backdrop for the largest of the three fenced arenas were colorfully decorated with parents watching their children compete in the riding events. Some children wore tall, shining black boots with canary yellow breeches, a white shirt or blouse, a black jacket and a black safety helmet. Others wore decidedly Western outfits and rode in Western-style saddles.

As Dan came to the fence, he saw a man out in the middle of the arena, apparently judging at least thirty children participating in an English riding competition. Where was Libby? From time to time the loudspeaker droned over the laughter and noise from the crowd. His eyes narrowing, Dan looked around for the one person he cared about finding among the thousand that must be attending the horse show.

After a good fifteen-minute perusal of the main arena, he threaded his way among the horses, children and parents who waited outside the gate for the next class to be called. Disappointed at being unable to locate Libby, his hands in his pockets, he sidestepped a fractious bay horse and its young rider in the bright afternoon sunlight. Then he heard Libby's voice. Halting, Dan turned in that direction.

Libby Tyler was dressed in a long-sleeved white blouse, form-fitting yellow breeches and calf-high black boots. Her dark brown hair, although drawn into a chignon at the nape of her neck, shone with red highlights from the sun. His breath jamming in his chest, Dan could only stare at her as she reached up to touch one of her charges, who appeared terribly nervous on board a gray horse. There wasn't anything but grace to Libby's movement as she reassuringly patted the eight-year-old girl's shoulder and smiled up at her. A tingle spread down Dan's own shoulder and he was momentarily stymied; it was as if Libby had touched him in the exact same spot. His overactive imagination, he decided glumly. Frowning, he remained out of her view, absorbing the sight of her flowing movements, her blinding smile—her laugh, and the easy way she worked with her students.

A bit of panic ate at Dan. What would Libby do if she spotted him? Give him a dark look of warning? Would the wariness creep back into her eyes? Did she not like him personally, or was it because her husband had died as a marine? Dan fervently hoped it was the latter. Taking his hands out of his pockets, he walked slowly to the pipe fence near the gate that would be opening in a moment to release the class that had just been judged.

There wasn't an ounce of extra fat on Libby's tall, lithe frame, Dan decided from his vantage point where he could see but not be seen. Every movement she made was more reminiscent of a ballerina than a rider, he thought. A slight smile curved his mouth. But what did he know about equestrians? Nothing. Ballet he did know something about because he'd attended performances over the years when possible. There was something about the sensuous grace that drew him to dance—at least in appreciation.

For the next hour, Dan remained undetected, and he wanted it that way. And in every event, it was Libby's students who kept taking top honors—whether in formal English classes, hunt classes or in a halter class, where the horses were judged on conformation. But what struck Dan most was that whether a child won a ribbon or not, Libby hugged each one as they dismounted outside the arena after the competition, offering a compliment, emphasizing what had been done right, not wrong. As each child's face lit up like sunlight beneath her touch and her genuine praise, Dan found himself wishing she would be that relaxed and natural around him.

As the evening events began, Dan went over to a food vendor serving hotdogs and soda pop. With one of each in hand, Dan found a seat in the stands near the fence. The sunlight was sliding behind the hills and the arena lights had come on. His show program in hand, Dan saw that the adult classes were beginning. The first one was for level-two dressage. Dan had no idea what that was, but as he sat munching the hotdog, he noticed Libby mounted on her magnificent horse near the entry gate. Now she, too, wore the standard black hard hat, and looked impeccable in her black jacket, fawn-colored leather gloves and black leather boots.

Dan savored the spectacle of Libby entering the arena. Behind the fence, three judges watched her with hawklike intensity. If Libby was bothered by the judges' undivided attention, she didn't show it. Her back ramrod straight without being stiff, she seemed to flow into each movement of her shining blood bay horse. It was obvious to Dan that the animal, his neck arched proudly, was completely under the control of her hands, body and legs. At a certain point in the arena, the horse broke into a trot. Dan was mystified about how, since he hadn't seen Libby kicking the horse with her heels. Indeed, as the animal went from a trot into what he heard over the loudspeaker was an extended trot, and then a canter, he saw no outward signals from Libby at all. Was the horse psychic or something?

For the next fifteen minutes, Dan felt like he was in heaven—or as close as he was ever likely to come to it. Seeing Libby flow in a singleness of movement with her horse was like watching a breathtaking dream unfolding before his eyes. The unspoken signals that were silently telegraphed between her and the horse simply amazed him. If the horse had to stop, it stopped on a dime, standing statue still, its coat shining, ears moving back and forth, attentive to carry out Libby's next unseen order. When she had completed the dressage demands and left the arena, applause erupted from the stands. Dan clapped appreciatively, too. Sliding down off the bench, he made his way toward the gate to intercept Libby, who was now dismounting.

Libby gave Shiloh a well-deserved pat on his sleek neck after she'd dismounted. "You were great!" she told the horse.

"I think *you* were."

Her head snapping to the left, Libby gasped. There stood Captain Dan Ramsey, a sheepish smile on his face. Her heart gave a huge thump in her breast and an odd tingling spread wildly through her. How handsome he looked in his comfortable jeans, shirt and old, worn tennis shoes. Gone was the military look—except for his proud bearing and his very short hair. Libby felt heat spread up her neck and into her face and groaned to herself. She was blushing! She touched her cheek.

"Cat got your tongue?" Dan teased as he moved forward to where she stared openmouthed at him.

Swallowing convulsively, Libby tried to gather her scattered thoughts as Dan approached, that bright smile of welcome still on his face. Did he somehow know how devastating his smile was to her? The warmth in his blue eyes was unmistakable, and Libby felt even more heat flowing into her cheeks. The man was impossible! Disgruntled at the profound effect Dan Ramsey had on her, she frowned.

"What are you doing here, Captain?"

Inwardly, Dan's heart sank. She'd retreated into formal military protocol with him. He reached out and moved his fingers down her horse's sleek neck, still damp from exertion. "The truth?"

Libby smiled a little nervously, watching as his fingers slid appreciatively across Shiloh's neck. The crazy thought of what it would be like to have him touch her in the same way flitted through her mind. Castigating herself, she tried to hide her surprise at his appearance. "Nothing but, Captain," she responded. Oh, why did she sound so hard and brittle? But she knew why, she realized, struggling to tame her internal panic.

"I got bored unpacking boxes back at my apartment. I sat in the middle of the living room—which looks more like a Class A disaster area than anything else—and said to heck with it, I'd rather come down here and see what a horse show was like." Dan didn't mention that he'd actually come to see her, and he noted a bit of thawing in the wary look she was giving him. Patting the horse, he added, "It's the first one I've ever seen."

His somewhat shy demeanor caught Libby off guard, and she relaxed—slightly. "I guess since you're in the provost marshal's office, you need to know and understand all of Camp Reed's activities," she offered lamely. A part of her was strangely disappointed. Why, she didn't know. She should be relieved that Dan wasn't here because of her.

Allowing his hand to drop to his side, Dan smiled and looked up at her horse. "This guy was impressive out there. What I can't figure out—" he leveled his gaze at Libby "—was how you got him to do all that stuff without moving a muscle. Are you telepathic or something?"

Laughing, Libby shook her head and relaxed. Dan seemed to have a way of getting her to do that. "No. Dressage is about riding as one with the horse. You're supposed to transmit signals to walk, trot, extend trot, canter and gallop or halt without showing any outward sign to the judges. It's not telepathy—it's hundreds of hours of hard work and training."

"Well, it certainly worked," Dan said, smiling and losing himself in her dancing eyes that now shone with happiness. "I'm an ardent fan of ballet, and I always marvel how the dancers make each move so fluid and graceful. If I tried the same thing, I'd be a klutz." He laughed. So did Libby, and Dan found himself watching the way her full mouth lifted effortlessly into a delightful curve. "You made something that's very difficult look very easy," he said, getting more serious.

"Your powers of observation aren't to be taken lightly," she teased, still smiling. "As a matter of fact, I'm glad you're not a dressage judge—you'd be almost too good at watching for nuances if you have an eye for ballet." The fact that he liked ballet surprised Libby completely. The words *marine* and *ballet* just didn't go together—at least, not naturally. Or did they? She realized just how much she was projecting her preconceptions of what a marine was onto Dan Ramsey—and he was surprising her again by stepping out of that stereotypical mold.

"I was watching you pretty closely," Dan admitted, "and I didn't see you move a muscle."

Flushing, Libby avoided his suddenly sharpened gaze. There was a hunger in his eyes, and she was old enough and experienced enough to realize why. A melting sensation flowed through her, as if to tell her that she wasn't immune to Dan Ramsey's charm—or to him as a man. Feeling uncomfortable, Libby knotted the thick leather reins in her gloved hands. "I'll find out just how much I moved, shifted weight or squeezed my legs to give Shiloh signals when the judges award the ribbons."

"You'll take first place, I'm sure."

Libby shook her head. "Captain, there are some very fine equestrians in this class." She turned, glad to shift the limelight to the horsewoman in the arena. "My friend Jenny Stevens is an excellent dressage rider. Take a look."

Dan moved to within a foot of Libby as they stood at the fence to watch Jenny on her black mare. He tried to pretend interest in the other woman, but all of his senses were focused on the tall woman who stood beside him. Realizing Libby still didn't trust him any farther than she could throw him, he kept his banter directed toward the topic of Jenny.

"She looks just as relaxed as you were," he noted.

"Yes. In dressage you want to look balanced but not stiff. There's a formality to it, but without what I call robotlike movements. Jenny's very good. She makes everything look effortless." Libby placed her hand on the pipe rail, wildly aware of Dan's nearness. He seemed so laid-back in comparison to how she felt inwardly. Maybe he was sincerely interested in horsemanship. After all, he liked ballet, and equestrian activities were similar in some ways.

"You looked like you were melted into your horse," Dan commented, his gaze on Jenny. "It reminded me of seeing international ballet stars moving together in a seamless and utterly natural dance." His eyes crinkling, he slid her a glance. "But I know what it takes in terms of work behind the scenes in ballet to make it seem that way. I'm sure at this level of riding, you're putting in a lot of hours every day to maintain it."

"Yes, I'm out here five days a week, for at least an hour, working with Shiloh on dressage movement."

Dan smiled to himself. So, Libby Tyler was out here five days a week. That was a useful piece of information. When he realized she was gazing at him with undisguised curiosity, he said, "You look a little shocked that I like ballet."

"Well..." she mumbled, "I mean, most marines wouldn't be seen at the ballet."

He grinned a little. "Is that a diplomatic way of saying most marines are insensitive to the finer, more subtle things in life? Like art? Dance?" He was baiting her deliberately.

Caught. Libby avoided his merry look. "Ouch. I guess I had that coming, didn't I?"

How badly Dan wanted to reach out and stroke Libby's flaming cheek. When she blushed, she looked all the more vulnerable. The urge to draw her into his arms became excruciating. "I guess most marines don't follow the ballet circuit," he said to soothe her consternation.

"You're very kind, Dan—I mean, Captain Ramsey."

"I think we all get trapped in stereotypes. Don't you?" That she'd used his first name—even by mistake—made Dan feel as if he'd finally breached Libby's considerable defenses against him.

Closing her eyes for a moment, Libby wished she could slide down into a hole and disappear. "I try very hard when I'm teaching my classes not to mold the children into male or female stereotypes. With you—" she lifted her chin and held his dancing blue gaze "—I find myself stereotyping every inch of the way."

At that moment, Dan felt her tentatively opening up to him for the first time, and he longed to establish this kind of rapport with her. "I think we all do," he said lightly, not wanting her to be so hard on herself. "Marines do have an image, I can't disagree. But we have soft underbellies just like anyone else."

With a grimace, Libby turned away and focused on Jenny in the arena. "Yes," she answered, her voice slightly choked, "I know about that...." It hurt to say any more.

Memories of the past, of her happiness with Brad, reminded her about the human side of marines. Libby was surprised at her response to Dan's ruminations. A sadness lingered in her heart. She missed being married, but she would never think of remarrying just to quell the loneliness. No, what she and Brad had shared had been special, and—until Dan Ramsey had crashed into her life—she'd never thought to discover those traits in another man.

Stealing a glance at his rugged profile, Libby felt the edges of her sadness, the last remnants of her grief, being soothed by his quiet presence. It was on the tip of her tongue to ask him personal questions about his life. He wore no wedding band, but then she knew many marines never wore them because of working with rifles and other weapons that could potentially snag on the ring, causing injuries. Was he married? Biting her lip, Libby forced herself not to ask.

Dan looked over at Libby. Her lower lip was tucked between her teeth, a slight frown marring her smooth brow. If his intuition served him correctly, she was upset. Because of him? Probably. With an inner sigh, he decided he wasn't going to give up and disappear out of Libby's life.

"How long does this horse show last?"

"Until 2100." Libby flushed. "I mean, nine o'clock tonight."

"Old habits die hard, don't they?" he asked gently. Dan saw her cheeks turn bright red and anguish rise in her eyes. Once the wife of a marine, a woman was inevitably tied to that way of life, whether her husband was alive or dead, in the corps or out of it. He gave her a tender smile filled with understanding.

"Y-yes, they do," Libby said, her voice hoarse with emotion. For a moment, she felt like moving into Dan's arms and just being held. The feeling was so unexpected that Libby felt ridiculous. What was happening to her? The expression on Dan's face was one of complete understanding. She looked at him querulously. Just how much did he know about her past?

"I imagine you'll be pretty hungry after all of this," Dan said, gesturing to the arena. "I'd like to take you out for a bite to eat afterward." He held his breath unconsciously, wanting her to say yes. Watching her face, Dan knew it was hopeless. The openness Libby had displayed vanished quickly.

"I—no, I can't, Captain. Thank you, but I just can't. I'm very tired." Libby hated herself for lying, but she was desperate.

"No problem," Dan said smoothly as he tried to hide his disappointment. "Are we still on for our ride to check out the area around the brig?"

Libby nodded. "Yes... of course."

"Fine. So I'll see you at 0900 on Monday?"

"Yes..." Panic ate at Libby. She had promised earlier to do it, but the prospect of spending hours with him was suddenly terrifying to her. Yet she knew she couldn't back out of it. Clearing her throat, she said, "I'll see you Monday, Captain."

Giving her a mock salute with his two fingers, Dan smiled and turned away. He realized that Libby was highly uncomfortable, and he had no wish to make her feel even more ill at ease. As he threaded his way through the crowds and horses, he hoped that her reaction toward him wasn't personal. Well, he'd find out next week when they went riding. More than anything, Dan was eager to be with her again—even if it meant riding a horse.

Libby's heart started an erratic beat as she saw Dan drive up to the stable in his red sports car Monday morning. Part of her had been hoping he wouldn't show up. Another part—the silly, dreamer part—was hoping he would be here precisely at nine. She saw that he was dressed in casual clothes and laughed to herself. No marine would be caught riding a horse in uniform! The thought made her smile a bit mischievously as she stood waiting for him on the wooden deck near the office.

Her boss, Stuart Garwood, came out and joined her. "Who is he?"

Libby smiled up at Stuart. He was a tall, distinguished-looking man who always wore English riding breeches, shining black leather boots and a white polo shirt. His black hair, thick and carefully combed into place, was sprinkled along the temples with gray, complementing his darkly suntanned face and adding to his sophisticated looks.

"Captain Ramsey. From the provost marshal's office, Stuart."

"Oh, yes." He frowned and placed his large hands on the wooden rail in front of them.

"Remember? I told you he wanted to ride around the brig area and look for possible prisoner escape routes? Captain Ramsey is new to the base."

Stuart nodded gravely and smiled down at Libby. "Do you really think he'll be able to ride a horse for a couple of hours?"

Laughing, Libby shook her head. "No, I think he's going to be very sore by the time we get done with this jaunt."

Stuart nodded and walked down the wooden steps to meet the officer. He held his hand out to the approaching marine.

"Captain Ramsey?"

Dan sized up the large, spare man in riding clothes and extended his hand. "Yes?"

"Stuart Garwood. I'm the Special Services stable manager. I want to welcome you to the base. We spoke on the phone earlier about setting up one of my wranglers to watch the paddocks at night, remember?"

Dan nodded and gripped Garwood's hand, which was strong and firm. It was obvious Garwood did a lot of riding himself. "I certainly do. It's good to meet you in person, and I appreciate your help on this investigation, Mr. Garwood."

"Call me Stuart." He turned and motioned to Libby. "I understand our premier instructor is going to take you on a ride around the brig area?"

"That's correct." Dan glanced up and nodded to Libby, who looked even more beautiful than usual, if that was possible. Her fresh white blouse accented her flushed cheeks and laughing eyes, while the canary breeches and black boots reminded Dan once again how lithe Libby was. He had to place a check on his desire simply to stare up at her.

"Well, I'm sure Libby has chosen a suitable mount for you. I've got some new horses coming in, so if you'll excuse me, I have to go down and see to them."

"Of course." Dan stood, hands on hips, watching Garwood walk quickly and with natural aplomb toward the huge area where most of the trail-riding horses stood. The morning was cool without being chilly, the sky a bright blue and the sunlight warming. He shifted his gaze to Libby, who remained on the porch.

"Howdy, Ma'am," he drawled as he walked up to the steps. "I think this here city slicker is ready for his first ride."

Giggling at his drawl, Libby moved down the steps and joined him. "You're precocious if nothing else, Captain."

"Hey, can't we be on a first-name basis?"

Libby fell into step with him as she took a narrow, well-worn path to the right. "I guess you're right—Dan."

He smiled faintly. "Miracles *do* happen."

"Your wit has improved since I last saw you."

"I've had all weekend to get my lines down," Dan said lightly. The path led up to a huge red barn. He saw Libby's horse, Shiloh, standing patiently in ties in the center of the passageway.

"Somehow," Libby murmured as she opened the sliding door to one of the box stalls on the left, "I don't think you're a man with many lines. Just straightforward talk."

Dan stepped aside as she brought out a small black horse that was already saddled and bridled. "You're right," he said.

"Come on, you can mount Fred out here in the paddock area," she called as she led the horse out of the barn and into the sunlight. Libby tried to pretend that Dan didn't look boyishly handsome in his blue jeans and short-sleeved white shirt. The aura of strength around him permeated her, lifting her and making her feel joyous in a way she'd never experienced before. Stymied by all the rampant feelings within her, Libby pulled the horse to a halt.

"You mount from the left," she said. "Watch how I do it, and then you try it."

Dan had ridden bareback as a kid growing up on the Navajo Reservation at Fort Wingate. He knew a bit more than he was letting on, wanting to enjoy every stolen moment with Libby. He stood back appreciatively as Libby placed her left foot in the stirrup and swung easily up onto Fred's back. "Beautiful," he said.

Flushing, Libby dismounted. "I'm not going to ask if you meant the horse or me."

He grinned slightly and took the reins she offered him. "There's no competition—you're the beautiful one."

Libby moved to his left, near the head of the horse. "Are you always this aggressive, Captain?"

Dan saw the merriment in her eyes and knew she was teasing him, or at least trying to deflect his compliment. He placed his foot in the stirrup and held her gaze. "Since when is a genuine and sincere compliment aggressive, Ms. Tyler?" He pushed himself up, swung his leg over the horse and settled into the Western-style saddle.

Avoiding his gaze, Libby quirked her mouth. She busied herself checking to make sure that the stirrups were the correct length for Dan's long legs. Dodging his question, she stood back, satisfied that everything was properly adjusted. "You moved into that saddle with a lot more ease than I'd have given you credit for."

"Is that a polite way of asking me if I've ever been in a saddle before?"

"You know it is."

His smile deepened. He wasn't going to lie to Libby. "I was born at Fort Wingate, New Mexico—on the Navajo Reservation. My family was more or less adopted by the Navajo while I was growing up, and they had a few ponies around to herd the sheep with, so I did a little bareback riding from time to time."

Libby gave him a flat look. "There is a lot more to you than I suspected."

"Is that good or bad?"

She almost smiled, but didn't. Dan looked supremely at ease in the saddle, slightly slouched, his hand resting on the pommel, reins between his fingers. "I don't know yet."

"At least the jury's still deliberating. I'm grateful for that."

This time, Libby laughed. "You're a first-class scoundrel, Captain Ramsey. Stay where you are and I'll go get my horse."

The sun was warm and felt good on his back as he smiled down at Libby. She seemed surprised he might know just a tad about horseback riding, which pleased him. Again, he'd broken that stereotypical mold she had him in, and from the look on her face, she was delighted with the discovery. Humming softly, he watched as Libby brought Shiloh into the paddock. It was sheer poetry watching her walk and mount. Today her hair was in a careless ponytail, tied with a red-yarn bow to tame that thick mass. Sunlight glinted off the strands, eliciting a reddish cast.

As Libby halted her horse beside him, she pointed to one of the paddocks. "I know you're working on the case, but I want to take you over and point out the five horses that are being ridden so hard every month, Dan." She gave him a stern look, as if waiting for him to say no.

"Stuart has been putting one of his wranglers out every night to watch the place, Libby. So far, no one has taken the horses. I've also asked Sergeant Donnally to interview Garwood and some of the wranglers who work here."

"I owe you an apology," Libby said as they walked their horses down the wide trail to the paddock. "I know Colonel Edwards thinks I'm going off half-cocked about this. It's true, horses and teaching riding are my life, but I'm not crazy. I've seen those horses with my own eyes, and they've been exhausted.

"You're not crazy. You care," Dan said, surveying the hundred or so horses lounging lazily in the paddock, soaking up the morning sun.

Pulling Shiloh to a halt near the pipe fence, Libby met and held Dan's gaze. *He* cared. It was so obvious. And heartwarming.

"I hope," she said in a small voice, "that Colonel Edwards knows how good a heart you have toward all things, not just people or Marine Corps matters."

The catch in Libby's voice touched Dan deeply. For the first time, he saw her drop those defensive walls she'd lived behind since the death of her husband. There were tears in her eyes, and it affected him on a level he'd never known before. "Well," he murmured, "justice is for all things, not just someone in a marine uniform."

"I like the way you see the world. I really do...." Libby caught herself. Just being around Dan was giving her foot-in-mouth disease! Pointing to the paddock, she said, "Do you see those bay-and-black horses over there in the corner?"

Dan followed her direction. A group of five dark-colored horses stood together in companionable fashion. "Yes."

"Those are the ones."

"Okay. Sergeant Donnally is still working on the investigation, so I haven't seen a full report yet, Libby. I told him to interview the head wrangler and take a look at the horses. Joe's a city slicker, but I'm sure he'll ask some good questions about the animals involved."

Swallowing, Libby turned and looked him squarely in the eyes. "I just don't know what to make of you."

"Do you have to make anything of me?"

Libby shook her head and ran her fingers over the smooth, wide reins across the pommel of her English saddle. "No, I guess I don't. But—" she lifted her head and met his warm gaze "—I'm surprised, that's all."

"About what?"

"You. How you're handling this investigation. I mean—" she shrugged helplessly "—you could have given me lip service on the whole thing like Colonel Edwards...." Her voice ebbed into silence. "You care."

Those last two words fell softly across his heart, and he sat there enjoying the singing of the birds in the trees, the sunlight, the slight, fragrant breeze and Libby at his side.

The ache to reach out and touch her shoulder, to show her how much he did care, nearly overwhelmed him. Dan forced himself to keep his hands where they were. Although he could only see Libby's profile, he could tell she was wrestling with some unknown emotion, her lower lip again caught between her teeth.

"What do you say we get going?" he urged quietly. "I've got a feeling this ride is going to take awhile."

Chapter Five

Libby's heart wouldn't settle as they rode at a leisurely pace down one of the dirt roads that crisscrossed the base. The hills were alive with singing birds at this time of morning, and she felt like singing herself. Occasionally, Dan's leg would touch hers, and each time a tingle moved through her. The brown hills were dry except for the greenery provided by the prickly pear cacti and the thousands of sagebrush that reached upward toward the sun.

She felt Dan's gaze on her, too, from time to time as they rode in companionable silence. Never had she been more aware of a man's presence—or of his interest in her as a woman. Libby tried to concentrate on riding, on enjoying the sway of Shiloh beneath her and the beauty of the desert morning, but her attention kept moving back to Dan. She had so many questions about him.

"You said you were born at a fort?" she asked finally, unable to stand her burning curiosity.

"Yes. Fort Wingate. It's an old U.S. Cavalry fort that was used by the army when settlers were coming west."

"Did you like living there?"

"You mean, on the reservation?"

"Yes."

He smiled in remembrance. "I wouldn't trade my life for anyone's. The Navajo people were my friends and teachers. Their way of life rubbed off on me. I've got great respect for them as a people. How about you—where are you from?"

"Me?" Libby hadn't expected him to ask in return. Fair was fair, she supposed. "I was born in Vail, Colorado. My parents own a clothing store at the ski resort."

Dan nodded. "So you traded in a set of skis for a horse?"

Libby smiled. "You might say that. Dad bought me a Shetland pony when I was seven years old, and I've been in love with horses ever since."

"I can't ski at all. The only time I tried it," Dan said with a good-natured grin, "was when I took my first ride on a ski lift, fell off at the other end and cracked my tailbone."

"Ouch."

"Yeah, it was my first and last try at skiing, believe me."

With a laugh, Libby said, "I hate skiing! My poor parents think I'm nuts, but they love me despite my eccentricities."

Dan felt a ribbon of heat bolt through him as Libby tipped her head back, showing the fine expanse of her throat, and let that husky, rich laughter escape from her lips. Swallowing hard, wishing the moment would never end, he tore his gaze from her profile.

"So you grew up with horses, too?" Libby prodded.

"Kinda. My friends were Navajo kids who lived around the fort, and we used to go riding. I'm not the horsey type, to tell you the truth."

Libby tilted her head and gave him a merry look. "What type are you then?" she teased.

"What do you think?"

"Oh, no! I'm not falling into that trap!"

"My zodiac sign is Scorpio."

"That sounds like a line."

He grinned. "It's as much as you're getting out of me about myself. I'd much rather hear about you and your life."

"I'm sure it's boring compared to yours."

"Let's find out."

Libby moved uncomfortably in the saddle. Up ahead, the road wound down into a mile-long dip, then rose up between two hills. Beyond that was the brig region. "Let's trot a bit," she suggested. "The horses are warmed up enough, and Shiloh needs to stretch these long legs of his. What do you say? Are you game?"

Dan nodded and let her get away with changing the topic. He was a private person himself, so he understood her hesitation about sharing deeply personal information. At least, not quickly. "Sure, I'll give it a try."

Pressing her calves lightly against Shiloh's shining, dark brown barrel, Libby urged the gelding forward into a fast, steady trot. The wind moved quickly past her and she turned in the saddle to see if Dan was keeping up. He was bouncing around in the saddle as Fred worked frantically to keep pace with the much-longer-legged horse. Libby didn't have the heart to make Dan suffer needlessly, so she pulled Shiloh down to a slow trot. Dan gave her a slight nod of thanks and concentrated on staying in the saddle, his hands gripping the horn.

"We can drop to a walk," Libby called.

"No," Dan said, "keep going. I'll get the hang of this one way or another. Old memories, you know? They'll come back."

Heartened, Libby thought how much she liked his attitude. A can-do attitude—and a very marine one at that. Still, she appreciated his cheerful attempt. He was giving it his best shot—which was all Libby asked of anyone.

At the end of the mile-long trot, Dan's rear was more than a little sore—it was bruised. Fred's rough gait kept throwing him high in the air. If he hadn't gripped the saddle horn and clenched the animal with his long legs, he'd have been tossed off long ago. Furthermore, every time Dan came down, he hit the rear of the saddle, and the bruises began to accumulate. The only thing that made the ordeal bearable was watching Libby and her magnificent bay horse flow together like hot butter in a skillet. Their effortless grace helped take his mind off his own discomfort.

As they rode between the hills, the brig came into view. The rectangular gray building was two stories high, surrounded by a heavy cyclone fence topped with double-edged concertina wire to prevent escape. The revolving brig siren sat on a pole a hundred feet high and was triggered at noon every day to ensure that it would work in case a prisoner escaped.

Dan halted his horse beside Libby's at the end of the dirt road. The brig was less than half a mile away. He noticed that Libby's ponytail had worked loose as she rode and half her hair now hung in dark, glorious sheets across her shoulders. Damp tendrils clung and curled at her temples, giving her the look more of a young girl than a mature woman. When she turned toward Dan and smiled, his heart melted again at the joy and life in her green eyes.

Slowly dismounting from Fred, Dan groaned. He tenderly rubbed his hip and gave Libby a sheepish smile. "Riding a horse is dangerous," he joked.

Sliding easily from Shiloh's tall back, Libby brought the reins over the horse's head. "Pretty bad?"

"Let's put it this way," Dan said mildly, "a hot bath tonight is going to feel awfully good."

"I feel terrible. We could have stopped trotting a long time ago and walked up to this point."

"No way. It was fun."

Libby peered up at him and saw that he was telling the truth. His mouth was stretched into a good-natured line as he reached into the saddlebag and pulled out a map. "Most men wouldn't even climb into a saddle, much less trot a mile. I'm impressed," Libby offered.

"You should be," Dan said as he gingerly got down on his hands and knees and spread the blue topographical map on the ground. "Come down here and help me."

Libby tied both horses to a nearby bush and joined him. Dan had picked up four hefty stones and firmly anchored the corners of the map. He was already kneeling over it when she joined him. Just being those mere inches away from him was enough to make her heart pound a little harder than normal. She watched as he got his bearings by looking up at the surrounding area, then turned his attention back to the map.

"Do you ride this area often?" He twisted to look up at her as she leaned over, arms resting on her thighs.

"All the time."

He pointed to the map. "This is a depression, like a ravine?"

Libby got caught up in his reconnoitering. Pressing her index finger to the indicated spot, she said, "Yes, it's a ravine about twenty feet wide and a good half-mile long."

"Could a man hide in there?"

"Easily."

"What's the terrain like?"

"A lot of cacti and underbrush. Large boulders, too."

Dan nodded and wrote notes on a pad he pulled from his back pocket. "Boulders big enough for an escaped brig prisoner to hide behind?"

Libby looked in that direction and thought for a moment. "Yes..."

"You don't seem sure."

"I am. It just takes me a moment to think about the location." She gestured around the stark landscape. "There are lots of boulders out there, wouldn't you agree?"

Dan smiled and nodded. "Point well taken." He forced his attention back to the map—the last place he wanted to focus it. For the next half hour, Libby gave him good information on the terrain and he made notes. The sun was becoming hot and he realized by looking at his watch that it was nearly 1100. Slowly getting to his feet, he turned and offered his hand to Libby to help her stand.

Libby stared at Dan's strong and capable hand. For a moment she hesitated, because to touch him would be like touching fire. Then, lifting her hand, she placed it in his. The firmness of his fingers wrapping around hers sent a jolt of need through her. Need? As she rose easily to her feet, she felt stymied. The years without Brad had shut down many desires within her, Libby realized. But somehow Dan Ramsey seemed to awaken those sleeping needs, and it was disconcerting as well as confusing.

"Thanks," she whispered, reclaiming her hand from his supportive touch. As she went to retrieve the horses, she realized how much she'd missed that kind of taken-for-granted support. Emotional support. Physical support.

She'd buried her life in horses, teaching riding and participating in equestrian events.

As she mounted Shiloh, she found herself smiling. Dan wasn't exactly graceful about mounting Fred, but he got the job done. When he arranged himself in the bulky Western saddle, picked up the reins and lifted his head in her direction, her smile increased.

"I'll give you credit, Captain Ramsey—you aren't a quitter. With as many bruises as you say you have, most marines would be walking the horse back to the stable, not riding him."

Chuckling, Dan pulled Fred alongside Shiloh. "Touché. But the way my logic works is that Fred can walk a lot faster than I can, which means I can get back sooner—which means less time to suffer."

"You're incorrigible!" Laughing, Libby directed Shiloh to turn and they began their walk back toward the stables. She saw Dan looking around, a frown working deeply into his brow as they rode. After ten minutes, she broke the silence between them.

"What are you worried about, Dan?"

He roused himself and glanced over at Libby. The fact she'd used his first name again was heartening. "I was mentally going over the map, the terrain around the brig."

"What do you think?"

His mouth quirked. "I think that a prisoner has a good chance of escaping if he heads toward the nearest gate, which means he'll go right through the stables area to get to it."

"There have been brig escapes before, but the brig chasers have always caught them."

"That's not the point." He moved uncomfortably in the saddle. "You ride in this area frequently."

"Every day."

"Then you're setting yourself up as a target if a brig prisoner escapes."

She laughed lightly. "What a worrywart you are! Dan, I've been riding these hills for the last six years. I think we've had exactly two escape attempts, and no one got hurt."

"Still," he persisted darkly, "it's a risk you're running, Libby."

"The hills around here are steep, and that's what I need to keep Shiloh in peak performance for my three-day eventing competitions."

"Why won't the hills to the north do the job?"

"They're lower and not as physically demanding." She leaned over and ran her fingers down Shiloh's neck, which was glistening in the sunlight. "We both need the challenge, Dan. I'd have to ride him twice as long to get the physical exercise for both of us that I can get right here."

Frowning, Dan said nothing. He was worried for Libby's safety, but she obviously wasn't.

"May I ask you a personal question?" she asked.

He raised his head and held her gaze. "You can ask me anything," he said, meaning it.

Libby fretted inwardly over the sincerity of his statement. She got up enough courage to point to his hand. "I know a lot of marines don't wear wedding rings because of the equipment they have to use. I was just wondering . . . well, if you have a family here with you."

Pleased that Libby was interested enough to ask, he said, "I'm divorced. My ex-wife lives in North Carolina."

Rather than satisfying her curiosity, the answer made her want to know more about Dan. "Divorces seem to be a way of life nowadays," she commented.

"They happen."

"Did you have any children?"

Dan shook his head. "No, but I was hoping some-day..."

Libby heard pain in Dan's voice and saw him frowning again. "I'm sorry. I've really overstepped my bounds. I shouldn't have been so nosy...."

Dan roused himself and managed a tight smile. "It's okay. The divorce was two years ago, but I guess the wounds take longer to heal than I'd like."

"You don't seem the kind of man to take marriage lightly," Libby said.

"You're right. When I married Janna, it was forever. And, to be honest, she felt and thought the same way. That was seven years ago." Pain moved uncomfortably around his heart and Dan took a deep breath and released it. Libby's look of compassion made him continue. "I met Janna in law school. After we graduated, we got married. I wanted to make a career out of the Marine Corps, and she was a red-hot criminal lawyer. I was making my mark in the area of the provost marshal's office, and she was building a name with a law firm in Raleigh."

"Sounds like you had a lot in common." Libby couldn't stop herself from wanting him to continue revealing his personal side. "And usually, that's a good sign the marriage will last."

With a slight grimace, Dan nodded. "We had everything going for us, Libby. There was only one fly in the ointment—Janna is a drug addict."

"Oh, dear..."

Dan held her sad gaze. "I didn't know it for a long time. I guess I should have been more alert. Something. She hid it well."

"Often there's a family history of alcoholism or addictions?"

"There was," Dan concurred grimly, "but in my idealism, I dismissed that red flag. Janna's father is an alcoholic. Was. When he died, it tore her apart, and that was when I first realized she was using cocaine. She'd actually been using it for ten years before that, but I had no idea...."

"Did she want to get help?" Libby asked softly. Dan struck her as a man who, once he'd identified a problem, would go after it and fix it.

"No." Heaving a sigh, he looked around at the bright, sunlit day. The brilliant blue sky made everything seem so alive, but he felt none of that as he dragged up his unhappy past. "Janna was bullheaded and swore she didn't have an addiction problem. But over the next three years, our marriage eroded into a hell that just got worse with every passing day. I loved her, but I couldn't help her if she wouldn't help herself. Finally, we agreed to a divorce. I refused to be Janna's enabler, so the only choice left to me was to leave. I didn't want to...."

Libby reached out and briefly touched his arm. "You did everything you could, Dan."

Her touch was soothing to his unleashed feelings and the guilt he still carried over leaving his marriage. "To this day, especially at night when I can't sleep, I go over things again and again. I ask myself whether, if I'd done 'this' instead of 'that,' we'd still be together."

Libby hurt for Dan. Suffering was clearly etched in his features and his eyes were shadowed. "One of my students, the daughter of a colonel, has a similar problem. Patty is only ten years old, but her father's a heavy drinker. I see what it's doing to her, and I try to single her out for special attention when I can during class. It hurts, Dan. I know a little bit of what you must feel. Patty comes to riding class so unhappy. Sometimes I'll find her in the tack room crying. But when I go to hold her, she pulls away. It's as if she has walled herself off to protect herself, and she can't accept anyone's help.''

"Exactly.'' Dan smiled a bit and said, "Patty's lucky to have you around. Don't ever stop trying to hold her when she cries. That little girl could easily grow up to be like Janna. Children of alcoholics carry a lot of baggage into their adult lives.''

"But Janna's problem was more than that,'' Libby said, "if she's got an ongoing drug habit.''

"Yes.'' Grimly, Dan threw back his shoulders as if to toss off some invisible weight he carried. "I did everything I could, Libby. I went to Alanon meetings. I went into counseling with Janna, hoping that would help. But the bottom line was, she didn't want to help herself. So, I could either stay in the deteriorating situation and become a crutch to her habit, or I could leave.''

"You seem to think you could have done differently.''

Libby's insight startled him—but then, Dan was quickly discovering that she was a woman of great depth when it came to the human condition. "I have doubts. Maybe if I'd stayed, she would have changed. It got pretty heated at the end. I said a lot of things I shouldn't have. I contributed to the marriage dying, too.''

"I can't imagine what it was like,'' she said softly, holding his anguished gaze. "But I do know from working with Patty this past year that she has temper tantrums and will lash out and hurt the very people who are trying to help her.''

"Janna was the same way,'' Dan agreed sadly. "Sometimes it seemed the more I tried to help her, the more she resented me. I couldn't do anything right. At least, that's how I felt. It got so I'd get up in the morning and wonder what kind of mood she was in. Then, depending on her mood, I'd adjust the way I'd behave to avoid a fight.''

"Like walking on eggshells?"

"Exactly," Dan muttered. "And I cracked my share of them, believe me."

"You're too hard on yourself."

He twisted to look in her direction. "Remember? I'm the guy who thought marriage was forever? My mom and dad have been married almost forty years. They're happy. Sure, I saw them fight sometimes, but they never fought personally, they argued about the topic at hand—and there was never any screaming or yelling. I was like a fish out of water when I realized Janna's problem. I came out of a pretty great family situation where I got love and support. With Janna, I didn't know what would happen from one hour to the next—how she was feeling, if she'd explode, cry or accuse."

Aching for him, Libby saw the amount of injury Dan had suffered. "Is she getting help now?"

"No," he rasped. "I have a good friend at the law firm where she works and he keeps me posted on how she's doing. Her work is starting to suffer now...."

"I guess," Libby said, her voice wobbly, "love isn't enough sometimes." And she thought of Brad, her husband, and his love of flying—even though it frightened her to death. How many times had she begged him to quit flying helicopters and get into some safer career? But Brad wouldn't listen, and he'd died—just as her dreams had warned many times before the actual accident occurred.

Wrestling with a barrage of feelings, Dan shrugged helplessly. "I always thought love could fix everything. I thought that if I loved Janna enough, she'd get well." His voice became flat. "I was wrong."

"You did the best you could, Dan," she said again, holding his bleak stare. "At least you tried."

"For three hellish years we tried," he agreed grimly. Rousing himself, he looked around and then back at Libby. "Maybe you missed your calling," he teased somberly.

"What do you mean?"

"I'm spilling out my heart and soul to you. Sure you aren't a therapist in disguise?"

Her lips pulled into a tentative smile. "I like people, Dan. I think we've all been through our own battles and wars and learned a little from them. At least, I hope I have."

Rubbing his chest, Dan said, "I don't know about you, but I feel better having talked about it. Thanks."

At that moment, Libby wanted to halt the horse and throw her arms around Dan and just hold him—because that's what he needed more than anything in the world. How many times had her students needed a hug? A reassuring kiss on the brow? Adults were no different, Libby knew. Afraid to risk the intimacy because she felt so powerfully drawn to Dan, she withdrew, and they rode toward the stables in silence.

They followed a winding trail that crossed a small, rocky creek, then curved up to the barn. It was noon by the time they dismounted. Dan moved stiffly, and Libby realized he must be in a lot of physical pain. Taking the reins from him, she said, "Why don't you call in to the office and take the rest of the day off to go home and soak?"

Gingerly rubbing his hip, Dan smiled a bit. "Just getting off the horse will help. No, I've got a lot going on at the office." He took the map out of the saddlebag. Turning, he stood before Libby. How wild and untamed she looked with her hair loose and falling across her proud shoulders. The parted softness of her lips drove him to wonder what it would be like to lean down, capture them and kiss her breathless. Dan saw her green eyes widen, and in that moment, he knew that she'd seen what he was thinking, what he wanted to share with her.

"I've got to get going," he rasped, and forced himself to take a step back. Holding up the rolled map, he said, "Thanks for your help on this."

"You're welcome...." Libby had to catch herself. She'd seen the burning desire in Dan's eyes, felt his penetrating stare and absorbed the hunger that emanated from him. He had been about to kiss her; she knew it in every level of her being. And worse, she'd desired it just as much as he had! Consternated, she raised her hand in farewell. As she led the horses into the barn, she wondered what was happening to her. Dan's tragic story of his marriage had touched her far more deeply than she'd realized.

As she slipped the bridle off Fred and hung it on a wooden peg, she frowned. Every time Dan looked at her, she seemed to melt a little more inside. Her heart was responding regardless of what her head was shouting at her. What was she going to do?

"Captain Ramsey?" Rose's voice echoed down the passageway as Dan approached.

"Trouble," Dan muttered. He knew his secretary well enough to know that sweet tone was a bad sign. Rose raised her hand and pointed toward his office. With a nod, Dan opened the door and allowed her to enter first.

"What's up?" he growled. "I can tell by the way you look it's not good news."

Rose halted near his desk and watched him make his way around it and carefully sit in the wooden chair. "Looks like you're a little saddle sore. How'd it go?"

"Worthwhile," he grunted, sitting up and placing his elbows on the desk. "Now, tell me what's going down, Rose."

Shutting the door quietly, Rose turned and frowned. "It's about Private Shaw."

"What'd he do now?" Dan demanded, scowling.

"Now, don't go jumping to conclusions, Dan. The kid, I think, is illiterate."

"Oh?"

"You know the blunder he made taking that brig prisoner up to Treasure Island? Saying he forgot to put the guy's feet in chains?"

"Yes?"

"I think he couldn't read the instructions from the brig that came with the prisoner. I don't think he forgot anything." Rose sat down and handed some papers across the desk. "These are insurance forms, Dan. Every year, every marine signs them. When I asked Shaw to come in, sit down and read the new clauses before he signed the papers, he got real nervous. I couldn't figure it out. The kid broke out in a heavy sweat, fumbled through the papers and didn't really read anything. He pretended to read them."

"How do you know?"

"Because I tested him. I made up a lie on clause two, which has to do with dependents and the share of the money they'll get if he dies. I pointed directly to that clause and asked him to write in the names of his beneficiaries. He refused to write anything and kept telling me to do it. Finally, when I thought he was going to jump out of his skin or run screaming from my office, I wrote in their names. When I told him to sign the form on the back, he couldn't find where to sign it." She pointed to the form. "You can see where it says Sign Here. I mean, it's plain as day."

Dan studied the form and rubbed his jaw slowly with his hand. The words were printed in big red letters that even a child could see. "You're right," he murmured. He looked over the top of the paper at Rose's worried face. The signature on the paper was an illegible scrawl. "Is this Shaw's signature?"

"It is. I swear, Dan, that kid stood hunched over my desk for ten minutes, the pen gripped so tightly between his fingers I thought it would snap. It was painstaking for him even to write his name."

"Okay." Dan sighed, handing the papers back to her. "I'll take it from here."

"May I make a suggestion?"

Dan knew Rose was more in tune with the inner workings of his new job than he was. "Sure, go ahead."

"Ask Sergeant Donnally to work with Shaw. You probably don't realize it, but Shaw idolizes Joe Donnally. If there's anyone who could reach the kid, it's Joe. Maybe he could find out for sure."

"That's an excellent recommendation. Thanks, Rose."

She got slowly to her feet, smoothing her dark purple skirt. "Joe happens to be in the office. He just got back from taking a prisoner up to Fort Ord."

Dan smiled. "Okay, send him in, Rose."

"You bet, Boss."

"And Rose?"

She paused at the door. "Yes?"

"Thanks."

Waving her hand in his direction, she chuckled. "I'll give you credit, Captain Ramsey—you're smart enough to trust us old dogs who have been around this place for a while."

"I'm smart enough to listen to the *right* people, Rose," he responded dryly, hiding a smile.

Chortling, Rose opened the door. "I'll send Sergeant Donnally right down."

Dan heaved a sigh and began to look through all the phone messages Rose had taken that morning. There were a dozen to be returned. Fuming, because he'd rather be thinking about Libby, about their ride together and their conversation, than paying attention to office problems, Dan put them aside. He'd been so close to kissing her there in the paddock. So close.

"Captain, you wanted to see me?"

Dan lifted his head. Joe Donnally stood just inside the door. "Yes, come in, Sergeant."

"Yes, sir." Joe shut the door and came to attention in front of his superior's desk.

"At ease, Donnally. Sit down," Dan murmured, pointing to the chair on his left. He saw surprise on the sergeant's face, which the other man quickly hid. Dan wondered once again what kind of officer Jacobs had been to make these men and women respond so warily. Donnally sat on the edge of the chair, hands on his thighs, attentive.

"How well do you know Private Shaw?"

"Sir?"

Dan scowled. "Do you get along with Shaw?"

"Yes, sir."

Realizing the sergeant's wariness could slow down communication, Dan decided to spill everything, then ask for Donnally's response. "We've got a problem, Sergeant, and I believe you can help." Again, Dan saw surprise on Donnally's set features. The enlisted people around the office weren't accustomed to being referred to as "we." Jacobs had set up a them-and-us dynamic that Dan found sad, because he saw enlisted people and officers as a team, not as singular entities working at cross purposes.

"What can I do to help?" Donnally asked, clasping his hands.

Smiling to himself, Dan knew that this last simple exchange had just worked a minor miracle with the sergeant. Good. "Rose has just told me that she thinks Shaw is illiterate."

Donnally raised his dark brows. "Sir?"

"Evidently he can't read, nor can he write very well." Dan got up. "Look, Joe—" he purposely used the marine's first name, which he knew was unusual for an officer to do, but he wanted Donnally's help "—I can't do this alone. Shaw is an outstanding marine. I've looked over his record. The corps has used good money to educate and train him, and I don't want him kicked out because of this." Dan came around and leaned against the front of the desk. "I understand that Shaw idolizes you."

Donnally blushed. "Well, sir..."

"Shaw tries to emulate you, and that's positive. What I want you to do is find out for sure, one way or another, if Shaw is illiterate. If he is, I want you to make sure he starts taking whatever classes he needs to correct it. If he refuses, that's another thing, but I feel since he looks up to you, he'll do it if you're there for him."

Clearing his throat, Donnally nodded. "He does follow me around like a puppy, but the kid's young, sir."

"Sergeant, I know you're a man of integrity and honor. I can't think of a better role model for Shaw." Dan jabbed his finger at the sergeant. "But I want you to support and nurture his progress to get literate. Rose and I aren't going to say anything about his problem. Keep it quiet. The kid is embarrassed enough as it is."

"That poses another problem, sir."

"Oh?"

Joe shrugged. "That means we can't trust Shaw to do any more brig chasing, which leaves us shorthanded—again."

"I'll call Personnel and see what can be done to offset Shaw's nonavailable status."

"You will?"

Dan smiled a little. "Why wouldn't I, Sergeant?"

"Well…sir, Captain Jacobs didn't give a damn if we had enough brig chasers on a run or not."

"I do," Dan said grimly, moving back to his chair. "As a matter of fact, I've got a marine in mind who's considered one of the best trackers in the business. After riding out to the brig area and studying the topography, I'm convinced we need a tracker."

Donnally nodded. "I don't mean to speak out of turn, sir, but I've been saying that since I got here. If a prisoner ever escapes, we're going to need dogs and someone who's good at picking up tracks."

"I'm glad you agree, Sergeant. The marine I have in mind worked with me back at Camp Lejune for two years, and I saw her in action. She's a legend in the brig-chaser world. Have you ever heard of Corporal Yellow Horse?"

Joe's eyebrows inched upward. "Yes, sir. But…I always thought the corporal was a he, not a she."

Jotting down the name, Dan looked across his desk. "I know we don't have many women in brig chasing, but she's the best when it comes to tracking. She's a full-blooded Navajo, and she's never lost a prisoner during transport. Over a period of two years, I saw her track down five escapees when even the dogs had lost them. No, we need someone like her here, just in case. Sergeant, I'm going to pull some strings, and unless hell freezes over, I'm going to get Corporal Annie Yellow Horse assigned to us. She'll go in your section because you're senior sergeant here at the

PM's office. Rose will let you know if I can manage to get her here and how soon. Right now, you work on Shaw and start guiding him in a big-brother kind of way. If he doesn't want to play ball, tell him he'll be getting a discharge within a week. I'm not putting any of my people's lives at risk for someone who can't read a damn set of instructions regarding the transport of a prisoner.''

"Yes, sir!"

Chapter Six

"Captain Ramsey?" Joe Donnally knocked on Dan's partially open office door.

Dan lifted his head from the mountain of paperwork before him. "Come in, Sergeant."

Joe eased his frame inside the door, a file in hand. "Sir, I've just completed my initial assessment on the investigation involving Ms. Tyler's allegations." He handed the file to Ramsey.

"Good. Come in and sit down. Shut the door, will you?" Dan took the file and opened it, as Joe took a seat. Frowning, he rapidly read Donnally's report. Another week had passed since he'd seen Libby, and reviewing the case brought her sharply into his focus. But then, Dan ruminated, as he turned the page of the neatly typed report, when didn't he think of Libby? Actually, when her face appeared before his closed eyes at night, there was no thinking involved; it was more a warm, good feeling that flowed through him. That and a gnawing ache that centered around his heart.

Dan eased back in his chair, the report in his lap, and slowly rubbed his chin. The silence deepened for a number of minutes before he looked up at the marine sergeant.

"You want to keep this case open?"

Donnally nodded. "I do, sir. I know I haven't reached any concrete conclusions yet, but according to the testimony of the wranglers, these five horses *have* been ridden hard once a month for at least the past four months."

"So Libby—I mean Ms. Tyler—wasn't imagining things?"

"No, sir. The head wrangler, an ex-marine named Pete Harkins, said he'd begun to notice and be concerned about it, too." Joe pointed to the file. "I've taken depositions from all the wranglers who work down there, and they verify the story."

"I see...."

Joe leaned forward. "Another thing, Captain—all the horses are dark colored. Did you notice that?"

Dan shook his head and leafed through the file, noting the age, color and type of horse that had been used. "No."

"I think that's a key, sir."

"How?"

Joe smiled a little. "Where I come from, if you don't want to be seen at night, you drive a dark-colored car. None of the horses have any white markings on them that would stand out at night."

Swallowing a smile, Dan nodded. Joe Donnally had been raised on the border between Tijuana, Mexico, and San Diego, California, he knew. Half-Hispanic, he'd grown up as a scrapper and gang member until he turned his life around at age seventeen. Joe was a junkyard dog who knew what it was like to grow up poor, using his wits to survive.

He had joined a gang that had made trips back and forth across the border transporting illegal aliens—so he knew nighttime tactics better than most. Dan lifted his gaze to the marine sergeant.

"Nighttime activities?"

"Yes, sir."

"What kind?"

With a shrug, Joe said, "I don't know, Captain."

"Conjecture, will you?"

Sighing, Joe lifted his hands. "I haven't ruled out that a bunch of local teenagers get together once a month to go on a hell-bent-for-leather ride."

"Sort of like joyriding in a stolen car?"

"Something like that, sir, only they're doing it with horses."

"Or?"

"I don't know. Nothing else really makes sense. You know how dependents are—their fathers are in the military and usually lean hard on their kids not to get into trouble. You might have some kids who want to raise hell but have picked on horses instead of tearing around in a car and possibly getting caught by the police outside the gates."

"A 'safe' kind of joyriding?"

"Yes, sir."

Dan continued to read. Joe Donnally was a thorough investigator, and that pleased him immensely. "I see you've contacted the principal of the high school in Oceanside."

"I did. I wanted to see if they had a club activity that involved horses, and I wanted a list of teenagers from the base who have been in trouble at school but not to any high degree."

Smiling slightly, Dan murmured, "Kids who walk the fine line between getting into real trouble and behaving—

rebels who do things that won't have the principal calling their folks?''

"Exactly, Captain. I've got the list and I checked it against the kids who either have horses boarded at the Special Services stables or who go riding a lot on the trail rides. There are seven boys who fit the ID.''

"Ms. Tyler said that the horses were ridden every new moon, when it's the darkest. I see you're suggesting a stakeout at the stables at that time, by yourself.''

"Yes, sir. Mr. Garwood had a wrangler stay for seven nights at the stable and he didn't report anything unusual. This time, I don't want Mr. Garwood to know what we're up to.''

"Why? He's the manager.''

Joe frowned. "Just a gut feeling, Captain. He was helpful about putting that wrangler on night duty, but he seemed irritated about it at the same time. I can't be any more specific, sir.''

Dan shrugged. "Garwood seemed okay to me.''

"Maybe, Captain, but I'd like to try a stakeout without him knowing it.''

Dan raised one brow and held the sergeant's dark blue stare. "Then,'' he drawled, "you make damn sure that no one knows you're there. I don't want a hassle with Garwood if he discovers your presence, understand?''

With a slight grin, Joe nodded. "Yes, sir.''

"When will you do it?''

"I've submitted a plan on the last page of the report, Captain. I'll go down there in two weeks, on the first night of the new moon.''

"You can't do it every night for seven days, Donnally. You have duties here at the PM, too.''

Clearing his throat, he said, "Well, sir, I thought since you were able to get Corporal Yellow Horse assigned and she'll be coming in next week, you might let me work nights and sleep days during that time."

"Hmm. Let me see, Donnally. No promises. Yellow Horse will need a breaking-in period around here to get a feel for how we do things."

"I know that, sir. But if she's half as good as the stories that circulate about her, then she'll adjust pronto."

"It's food for thought, Sergeant." Dan tapped the file. "You've done a good job. I'll let you know."

With a nod, Joe got to his feet. "Thanks, Captain."

"Dismissed."

Dan watched the sergeant leave as quietly as he'd come. He was pleased with Donnally's thoroughness, and that made him draw a deep breath. With only two weeks on the job, Dan was finding that the people under his command were basically good workers who had been dealt a raw hand by Jacobs. Even Shaw, whom Donnally had approached, was turning around. The young marine was taking night classes to learn to read. And Joe had wisely taken Shaw under his wing and given him less-important assignments where someone else was in charge to read transit orders on brig prisoners. Yes, things were starting to shape up around here.

His mind automatically gyrated back to Libby. He was restless and didn't want to work. As a matter of fact, for the week since he'd seen her, he'd been more like a growly old mountain lion around the office than his normal easygoing self. Glancing at his watch, he saw it was noon. The files on his desk pleaded silently for his attention. Colonel Edwards had told him he expected great things from him regarding drug enforcement on board the base, so he'd best keep his nose to the grindstone.

When 1700—quitting time—came, Dan promised himself he'd go to the stables in hopes that Libby would be there, either teaching a class or training her gelding. Besides, he rationalized, he wanted to tell her the results of the investigation thus far—a valid reason to see her.

Libby pulled Shiloh to a halt after jumping five wooden fences set up in the large arena. The gelding snorted and tossed his head as if to congratulate himself on his flawless performance. Patting him, Libby happened to look toward the main stables. Her heart gave a leap and then began to pound as she saw Dan Ramsey, still in uniform, emerge from his sports car. On the steps of the office stood Stuart Garwood, who instantly scowled. Why?

Libby was torn. For seven days she'd neither heard from nor seen Dan. And every day she'd missed him—his banter and his insights. She wanted to know much more about him, about his life—more than she deserved to know, she told herself. How tall and confident he appeared as he approached Garwood. Had Dan come to see her boss? Instantly disappointed, Libby tried to chastise herself for the inappropriate feeling. She'd made it perfectly clear to Dan that she wasn't interested in dating a marine. And she still found it tough to talk about Brad and his death, even after three years.

Her heart pulsed strongly when she saw Stuart point toward the arena where she sat astride her horse. Dan turned and began walking toward her. Had he come to see her, after all? Happy and frightened simultaneously, Libby dismounted and waited for him. Allowing herself the privilege of watching him walk with that proud, sure stride, Libby swallowed convulsively. There was such integrity in his face, in the way he held himself. As he drew closer, she saw his mouth curve into a welcoming smile meant only for her. Libby felt a flush move with startling quickness up her throat to stain her cheeks. Blushing hotly, she avoided his warm, dancing gaze and smile by pretending to brush off her boots.

"Hi," Dan called in greeting as he stopped at the fence that separated them.

"Hello."

"Looks like you took the big boy for a round on the fences," Dan observed. He tried not to stare like a starving animal, but he couldn't help it. Libby was dressed in her normal English riding attire, but today, for some reason, she looked even prettier. Her hair was tucked into a chignon and she was wearing a steel helmet covered with black velvet. A few dark brown tendrils stuck out from beneath the cap and curled along her temples, giving her an ingenuous look.

"Yes," Libby said a little nervously, patting Shiloh, "I train him over jumps at least twice a week."

Dan rested his elbows on the pipe and absorbed Libby's hesitancy. "So, how are you?" he asked, still gazing at her intently.

"Fine."

He cocked his head, his smile broadening. "I'm glad to see you again."

It was a risk to admit it, but Dan no longer cared. Libby had to know how he felt—one way or another. Still, the shock that registered on her face made him tense inwardly. "As a matter of fact," he went on smoothly, "I'm here for business *and* pleasure."

"The business I can handle," Libby said, trying to sound firm and uncompromising. Oh, why did Dan have to look at her in that heartwarming way that made her feel so special?

"Okay, I'll start there," Dan conceded, and proceeded to tell her about Donnally's investigation thus far into her complaints about the five horses. The wariness in Libby's eyes disappeared as he detailed the investigation. And the hope he saw flare in them when he told her about Donnally's intended stakeout made him feel good.

"I'm trying to swing it so Donnally can be here all seven nights, but I've got to wait until our latest brig member gets transferred onto the base."

"I didn't think you cared that much," Libby whispered, suddenly emotional. "You keep surprising me, Dan."

"Good surprises, I hope," he said, his voice rough with feeling. Libby's eyes shone with unshed tears, and he realized how easily touched she was by simple gestures from others. But then, Libby had a heart that held the hope of the world in it.

Self-consciously wiping her eyes with her gloved fingers, Libby gave him a soft, hesitant smile. "You've been a good surprise from the beginning, Dan." She saw his face lose its military hardness and grow more open. "I mean—"

"No, say it," Dan urged. "Don't keep hiding from me, Libby."

Her lips parted as she stared up into the intensity of his burning blue gaze, which spoke to her of his real feelings. Tearing her eyes from his, she knotted the reins nervously between her fingers. "I'm sorry, Dan, I don't mean to, but . . . it's the past—my past . . ."

"Talk to me," he rasped, and placed his hand on her shoulder momentarily. Libby looked ashamed and guilty. "Please . . ."

His husky voice caressed her and gave her the courage to overcome her fear. Looking up, Libby moved closer, inches from the pipe fence. "Dan," she began in a low voice, "you have to understand why I can't get involved with you. It's not you. It's me."

Dan knew it had to do with the death of her husband, Brad. Libby's face was filled with real suffering, and Dan saw the anguish shadowing her eyes. Maybe, if she would confide in him, it would remove one more obstacle between them.

"Let's talk this out, Libby," he pleaded. "Rose told me about your husband, but I'd like to hear it from you."

Glancing up, Libby said, "Last week you told me about your marriage to Janna, and my heart bled for you. I know you're the type of man who wouldn't give up easily on something. Brad, my husband, was a lot like you in that way." She took a deep, unsteady breath and plunged on. "I married Brad just after he came out of pilots' school in Pensacola, Florida. He loved flying, and more than anything, his life was helicopters. Sometimes I think he thought he was part bird and not a flesh-and-blood man. He lived to fly, Dan."

Libby sniffed and quickly wiped away the tears. Her voice was wobbling. "From the time I married him, I had horrible nightmares of him crashing and burning up in a helicopter. I tried to persuade him to change his job, but he wouldn't do it. Over the years, it caused tension between us. Then he was assigned here, and we moved. My nightmares came a lot more often out here, and I didn't know what to do. Brad and I loved each other, but we fought a lot.

"One night they were on maneuvers. There was a crash. When Brad's commanding officer showed up that evening at the apartment, I knew . . . I just knew . . ." Libby closed her eyes and bowed her head, the grief overwhelming her. She felt Dan's hand move gently across her tense shoulders to give her solace. Gulping back a sob, she lifted her head. Dan's face was blurred, but she could see the grim set of his mouth and the understanding in his eyes. "It was awful. Brad was letting his new copilot fly the helicopter, using those night goggles. They flew into electrical wires near the beach and crashed.''

Dan tightened his grip on Libby's shoulder as she stood there with her head bowed, wrestling with so many emotions. ''They had a lot of problems with those goggles about that time,'' he said hoarsely.

Nodding, Libby lifted her head, glad that Dan's hand rested on her shoulder. ''Yes, they did. Brad had come home any number of times complaining about them, how they made flying extra dangerous. He hated wearing them, hated flying with them.'' She made a small, choking sound. ''The worst of it was that I was three months pregnant with our first child.''

Dan's eyes narrowed. ''You were pregnant?'' Rose hadn't told him that.

''Yes...'' Libby's voice cracked.

''Rose never mentioned that part to me, Libby. I didn't know...''

''No one knew. I never told anyone. I lost the baby from the shock of Brad's death. I remember the commanding officer telling me that Brad was dead, and the next thing I knew, I'd fainted. The days after that were a blur of grief. A week after Brad was buried back East at his family's farm, I began to bleed. I should have paid attention to it, but I was in a daze. I refused to take any sleeping pills because of the baby, and finally, I slept for the first time in a week. When I woke up the next morning, I was in horrible pain.

''I called my next-door neighbor and asked for help. She called an ambulance, but it was already too late. I'd lost the baby....''

Dan's fingers tightened on Libby's shoulder. Her face was taut with pain. ''My God,'' he rasped unsteadily. ''I'm sorry, Libby. So sorry....'' And he was.

If she didn't step away from Dan, she was going to move into his arms, whether that pipe fence separated them or not. The fear was stronger than her other needs, so Libby pulled slowly out of his grasp. Fighting tears, fighting her ache to be held, she said brokenly, "That's why I'll never date another marine. Their jobs are too dangerous. They can get killed. Three years have gone by, and for the most part, I'm over Brad's death, my baby's death...." Struggling, Libby moved closer to her horse. "That's why there can't be anything between us, Dan. I know you like me, but it's no good. My nerves just can't handle it. I want to marry again, but it has to be a civilian, somebody safe."

Shaken, Dan absorbed Libby's trembling words and understood as never before why she had tried so hard to shun him. "Marines mean death."

"Loss," Libby agreed hoarsely. "Terrible losses in so many ways."

Dan drew in an unsteady breath and released it, looking beyond Libby to the brown hills dotted with sagebrush and cacti. "I understand better now," he told her quietly. Leveling a look into her misery-laden eyes, he tried unsuccessfully to smile, if just a little bit. "You've lost so much, Libby. Of all people, you didn't deserve that. I see how much you love kids...."

"Children mean the world to me, Dan. I—I wanted at least four of them—and I thought it would happen. Brad and I were both so happy when we found out I was pregnant."

Nodding sadly, Dan raised one polished shoe to rest on the lowest rung of the fence. He leaned his elbow on a higher rail. "Janna was pregnant a couple of times, too," he admitted in a low voice. "But she always miscarried." With a grimace, he said, "I think it was for the best. Knowing what I know now, if those babies had survived, they'd have been drug dependent. I tell myself it was better that Janna lost the babies, but I don't know. Losing them devastated her like nothing else ever did. She kept saying she wanted a career, but each time she found herself pregnant, she'd be happier than I'd ever seen her."

"Life isn't easy, is it?"

"No," Dan whispered, "it isn't. I do know one thing, Libby."

She lifted her head and met his tender gaze. "What?"

"That regardless of the pain I've gone through, life is still worth living, still worth reaching out to grab hold of."

Studying him in the silence, Libby not only heard, but felt his words. "Then you've got more courage than I do," she quavered.

Holding her shaken look, Dan said, "You're stronger than you think, Libby."

"Not anymore. The deaths of Brad and my baby broke me in a way I can't even begin to describe."

"What do you do when you fall off Shiloh?"

She gave him a quizzical look. "I get back on."

"That's right, you do. And I'll bet there have been a few times when you've taken some pretty serious falls."

"Yes." Frustrated at the sudden switch in topic, Libby said, "What are you driving at?"

"Make a comparison, Libby. Life is like Shiloh. There are good days when everything goes according to plan. Then there are other days when it's rough, even dangerous. But despite it all, you're still riding, aren't you?"

"I don't see your point, Dan."

Patiently, his voice remaining low, he said, "You had a lot of happy years with Brad before he died. Are you going to let one incident, one injury or fall, if you will, keep you from climbing back on board that saddle of life and trying to live again? Maybe even fall in love? Even if it was with a marine?''

Gasping, Libby clenched the reins in her one hand. She heard the challenge in Dan's voice. "How dare you!''

"Me? What about you, Libby? We all get dealt bad cards in life. I grant that some people get worse hands than others, but don't let it scare you into not living anymore." Dan looked around the arena. "Don't let it scare you so much that you never love again—or let someone love you."

With a gasp, she took a step forward. "You have no business saying that!''

Grimly, Dan held her blazing gaze. "I think I do. We've both suffered losses, Libby. The difference between us is that I'm willing to try and get on with my life, and you aren't.''

Libby's mouth dropped open. Just as quickly, she snapped it shut. "Where do you get off saying that to me?''

"I happen to like you, Libby. And I don't think it's fair that you judge me because I wear a marine uniform. I want to know you better—''

"Forget it, Dan!'' Badly shaken, she turned on her heel and started to lead Shiloh toward the gate at the far end of the arena.

Dan slid easily between the rails. He caught up with Libby and reached out to grip her elbow. In one smooth motion he halted her and turned her around to face him. Her expression was one of outrage and fear—fear of living again. "Don't do this to us," he rasped, keeping his grip on her gentle.

"Us?" she croaked, yanking away from him. Stumbling back a few steps, tears flooding into her eyes, Libby cried, "There is no 'us'! Leave me alone! Just leave!''

His mouth set, Dan stood firm, taking all her rage. He understood she was still angry at the Marine Corps for taking her husband's life from her, for jolting her to the miscarriage that took her baby from her. Slowly placing his hands on his hips, he held her glare.

"It's not that easy," he growled.

"Like hell it isn't!" Libby cried.

"I happen to think you like me," he rasped.

Startled, Libby took another step backward. "You're wrong!"

"I don't think so." Dan walked slowly up to Libby. It hurt him to see the tears staining her suddenly pale cheeks. The last thing he wanted to do was hurt her. "This is a two-way street, Libby. I know you like me. We're not kids. We've been around, and we understand chemistry between a man and a woman."

"You're crazy!" Libby spun away, nearly running for the gate.

Dan caught up with her again, matching her stride for stride. "I'm crazy, all right," he said darkly. "I'm crazy about you, Libby!"

"No!" The cry was like a howl of pain from a wounded animal. Libby leaped away from him, startling the horse, who skittered sideways. Stunned, Libby stopped and spun in Dan's direction. "Get out of my life, Captain Ramsey! I never wanted to see you in it, anyway. You're the one who has been pursuing me, stalking me. I don't like you! I hate that uniform you're wearing!"

She was bluffing and Dan knew it. A terrible, gut-deep feeling moved through him, and he held up his hands and took a step back. "Okay," he murmured, "I'll leave for now, Libby."

"Now? You'll leave for good, Captain! I don't ever want to see you again. Do you understand that?" Libby gulped, tears burning in her eyes. Her heart ached and she didn't know why she was saying all these horrible things to Dan.

Frightened as never before, she repeated, "I don't want to see you again—not ever!"

Dan stood in the arena, watching Libby walk hurriedly away, her horse in tow. Breathing hard, he allowed his hands to slip off his hips. He hadn't meant to get in a fight with her. But dammit, she was running away from life. Hurting for her because she'd lost a husband and a baby within a week of each other, Dan slowly walked from the arena. Somehow, he couldn't leave Libby like this. Vowing to apologize, he decided to call her that evening.

When Libby arrived home to her apartment in Oceanside two hours later, she was shocked to find a dozen yellow roses in a vase sitting on the porch. Uncertainly, she picked up the card and opened it.

Dear Libby,
I hope you can forgive a thick-headed marine for overstepping his bounds. Your friend, Dan.

Her hands trembling, Libby slipped the card into her pocket. The roses were too lovely to throw out. Still upset, she picked up the vase and unlocked the door. Dan's words haunted her. Worse, his analogy about falling off a horse and getting back on ate at her. Setting the vase on the kitchen table, she went on into the bedroom to change into slacks and a blouse.

She muddled through dinner, too upset to eat much. Sitting in the living room, not really paying attention to the television's drone, Libby tried to work out her weekly riding-class schedule. Finally, making a frustrated sound, she put the schedule aside. A photo of Brad, proud in his dress blue Marine Corps uniform, sat atop the television. Tears stung her eyes, and the memory of Dan's words haunted her.

Near ten o'clock, Libby took a bath and got ready for bed. She wasn't sleepy—far from it. Instead, Dan's voice echoed in her head. Placing a cup of fragrant lemon tea on the bedside table, Libby shrugged out of her pink silk housecoat. The phone rang. Frowning, she hesitated. No one ever called her this late. Suddenly panicked, wondering if something had happened to one of her parents, she scooped up the receiver.

"Hello?"

"Libby? It's Dan. I hope I didn't call too late."

Her heart pounding, Libby sat down. "Oh, God, I thought one of my parents was sick or something. I never get calls this late."

"I'm sorry. Let me call you tomorrow then, from work."

"...Uh, no. What is it?" Libby hated herself for not slamming down the phone. The fear in her ballooned, and she wondered what had made her say that. Maybe it was the low tenor of Dan's voice, the heartfelt apology of the roses and note. She wasn't sure.

"I just called to say I'm sorry for this afternoon, Libby. I had no right to say those things. I guess some buttons got pushed for both of us, and we took it out on each other. I didn't mean to. I really didn't. I got upset when you told me about the baby you lost. It brought back a lot of memories and feelings I thought I'd worked through, but I guess I hadn't...."

Gripping the phone, Libby closed her eyes, an ache centering in her chest. "I guess I knew that, but I couldn't help myself, Dan."

"Will you forgive me?"

"Yes. And I'm sorry for yelling at you. I never yell at anyone. Ever."

Dan chuckled a bit. "It didn't upset me that much, Libby. It really didn't. I think I know where that anger was coming from."

"Did Janna yell at you a lot?"

"Yes. After a while—" he sighed "—you get used to someone slamming you broadside with personal attacks."

"You had every right to turn on me," Libby whispered. "But you didn't."

"No." The silence deepened. "Libby?"

"Yes?"

"I learned a long time ago to be brutally honest with myself and the people I care about. You said a lot of things out there today, and I've got to know if you meant them or not. If you did, I won't ever bother you again. But I wasn't sure..."

Pain sheared through Libby. She'd hurt Dan badly. She really hadn't meant to. "Oh, Dan..."

"I know you're scared, Libby. So am I."

"You are?"

He laughed a little. "Yeah, scared to death. When I met you, my world just kind of fell apart around my feet. The day you walked into my office, you turned my world upside down."

"Oh, dear..."

"In a good kind of way," he assured her. "We've been sharing our underbellies with each other, Libby. We've gone through hell with the partners in our lives. And I'd like to know if I have a chance with you. I don't know where it will lead, but I'd like the opportunity to find out."

His words flowed over her, and she closed her eyes. "I don't know. I just don't know...."

"Libby, there's no hurry to make a final decision. I know you're hurting, and I know time will heal those things. Just tell me whether you want me in or out of your life. Whatever you decide, I'll abide by it."

The volume of fear threatened to overwhelm her. Libby sat frozen, her fingers gripping the phone so tightly that her knuckles whitened. "I keep remembering what you said about falling off the horse and climbing back on, Dan. I see the parallel, but I'm so scared I don't know if I have the guts to try again."

"That's all I need to know, Libby," he soothed. "I'll try to be less of a pain in the neck and more your friend, if you want."

With a helpless little laugh, Libby said, "Yes, I could use a friend, but I've never had a man who was one."

"Well, maybe that's a good place to start, then. Don't you think?"

Friends. Dan had been that to her already in many ways, Libby realized. The corner of her mouth quirked, and she tried to smile. "Yes, I'd like you for a friend."

"Good. No pressure on you, Libby. You call the shots, okay? I'm not a mind reader. I don't know where you're at unless you talk to me."

"I understand." She drew in a deep breath and released it. "You're a good person, Dan."

"Even if I'm a marine?"

Libby felt herself respond to his laughter. Dan had a deep, strong laugh that moved over her like moonlight across the glassy surface of a pond. It was a good, cleansing feeling. Freeing. "Yes, even if you're a marine."

"Get to sleep, Libby. You sound worn out."

"I am."

"Sometime next week I'll drop by the stables and see you—if that's okay with you?"

"Yes, I'd like that, Dan. Good night...."

Chapter Seven

Dan tried—unsuccessfully—to grapple with his anticipation of seeing Libby again. A week had passed since their heated argument. He'd wanted to give her time to feel her way through what had been said. Besides, he rationalized, as he eased out of his sports car, friends gave each other the space they needed.

As he shut the car door, Dan saw Stuart Garwood talking with one of the wranglers. Garwood was seated on a big, rawboned black gelding. The horse was wet, shining in the late-afternoon sunlight, its flanks heaving in and out. It was obvious that Garwood had ridden the animal hard.

Garwood's attention turned to him as he approached.

"Still investigating, Captain Ramsey?"

Dan smiled a little. "No, I'm here to take my first official English riding lesson from Ms. Tyler."

"Ah, a convert."

"Maybe," Dan hedged with a broadening grin. "We'll see if I can stay in the saddle."

Garwood laughed. "Learning to ride correctly in an English saddle, Captain, is an art."

"I've got the athletic part down, but I don't know about the art. See you later, Mr. Garwood."

"Of course, Captain. Enjoy your ride."

He was going to. Dan silently congratulated himself on the idea of taking a weekly riding lesson from Libby as a slow, less-pressured way of allowing her to get used to his presence in her life.

She was waiting for him, with Fred, the horse he'd ridden before, tied to the rail fence. Dan saw her expression light up with genuine warmth and felt as if he were walking on air. With a smile of his own, he entered the arena and approached her and the two waiting horses.

"Hi, stranger."

"Hi." Libby fiddled with the thick leather reins.

"Nervous?"

"Yes."

"So am I," Dan confided. He halted far enough away so that Libby didn't feel threatened by his presence. "And I'm here as a friend," he said, his voice lowering with feeling.

"I—I know. Thanks. I think it was a good idea coming for riding lessons."

Grinning ruefully, Dan patted the rear of his jeans. "In my heart I know that, but I have doubts about this body of mine taking the brutal beating it's going to get."

Libby laughed and stepped forward. She reached out and touched Dan's arm. "It's going to be okay. Really, it will."

"I don't know," he murmured, delighted with her brief, spontaneous touch. "I just saw Garwood coming in on a horse, and he looked like he belonged on him."

Frowning, Libby moved over to Fred. "Him. Did you see that poor horse? He rode him to death."

"The horse was sweaty," Dan agreed, moving to Libby's side as she gestured for him to stand beside her.

"No one should bring a horse in lathered up like that," she whispered indignantly under her breath as she checked the white horse's girth one last time. "Then, he'll just dismount and tell the wrangler to throw the horse in the paddock. That isn't right, Dan. Stuart should take responsibility to cool the poor animal down himself. Lately, he's been sloppy in his care of the horses he rides. I just don't understand it."

Without thinking, Dan placed his hand on Libby's shoulder as she fussed over the English saddle. "I like the way you care for things. Animals usually don't have a champion." He smiled down into her eyes and lost himself in their warmth. Dan felt her response to his momentary touch on her shoulder. When he realized he'd done it, he quickly removed his hand. Still, Libby's eyes were lustrous, and he felt a powerful ribbon of hope flow through him.

"Well, come on." She sighed. "I've got to forget what Stuart is doing and teach you how to ride safely. I'm sorry I spouted off."

"Don't be. Isn't that what friends are for? To confide in?"

She pulled the stirrup down and snapped the leather to make sure it was properly adjusted. "Yes."

Dan patted the docile gelding. "I'm not real comfortable getting into this English saddle."

Libby's eyes rounded and she stopped what she was doing. "Why?"

"I told you I'd done a little bareback riding with my Navajo friends growing up. All that ended when I was twelve. I was riding with them after school one evening, when a rattlesnake scared the pony I was on. It reared up and I fell off.'' Sheepishly, Dan said, "I ended up with a broken arm and a lot of hurt pride. After that I switched to a bicycle to cover up for my less-than-glorious abilities as a rider.'' He patted Fred. "So now you know the whole truth about me and my karma with horses—and I have to admit, this light saddle looks a little too much like riding bareback.''

"I'm glad you told me that," Libby said with a smile, pleased that he'd shared his fears with her. "I'll put Fred on a longe line. That will give you the sense of security you'll need. I'll be at the other end of the thirty-foot length of nylon line, on the ground.''

With a sigh, Dan nodded. "I wish I was the one on the ground."

Giggling, Libby led him around to the left side of Fred. "You're wonderfully human in a surprising kind of way, Dan Ramsey.''

"Some of that Marine Corps glitter got flaked off, did it?''

Libby felt some of the dread falling away. "Brad always wanted me to think that he was impervious, that he was strong and could do anything. I knew better, but he had this facade in place. I think that's partly what got him in trouble with the helicopter crash—he thought everyone could do things as well as he could. But we all have strengths and weaknesses. And there are times when no matter how good we are at something, we can still make a mistake.''

Dan nodded at Libby's words. She'd said them so softly, and yet with such feeling, that he smoothed his hand across her shoulders. "With me, you get the opposite—a man who wears a marine uniform during the day but is sinfully human the rest of the time.''

Another cloak of fear began to dissolve around Libby. Dan was different from Brad. The realization was as surprising as it was tempting. She brought down the second stirrup and snapped the leather against the saddle. Dan stood patiently, his hand resting on the rump of the gelding as he waited for the instruction to begin. How many men could speak about their weaknesses? Not too many. Brad certainly hadn't been one. He'd personified the Marine Corps' professed image. The comparison she was making surprised her, too. Perhaps she was over the loss of Brad. It had been three years of hell, of cycling up and down with loneliness and stormy periods of grief and depression. Libby's hands stilled on the pommel of the English saddle.

She could already see that Dan Ramsey was different from Brad in telling ways. And what she did know of Dan, she liked. She had to admit that she was powerfully drawn to him as a man—faults and all. Time, they had to have time. Her, especially, because that jagged-edged fear kept rearing its ugly head. With a sigh, she forced a smile.

"Okay, let's get on with your first riding lesson."

Dan smiled. "Just think," he teased as he came forward to mount, "next week I'll be here to haunt you, too."

"Not quite..." Libby hesitated. "I have a new trail to check out at this time next week, Dan. You'll have to come an hour later."

Gathering up the reins, Dan said, "As long as I get the lesson, I don't care what time it is."

Libby stepped back and watched his mounting ability through a critical eye. As confident as Dan was with two feet on the ground, it didn't transfer to four feet. With a slight smile, she approached him once he'd made it into the saddle, and began to point out what he'd done right and wrong in mounting the quiet horse.

* * *

The sun was hot, burning down on Libby as she rode Black Jack, one of the better stable horses. She was exploring a new trail possibility, between the swell of two cacti-dotted hills. Glancing at the watch on her darkly tanned wrist, she saw that she had two hours before she had to be back at the stable area for Dan's riding lesson. Giving the black, leggy gelding a pat on his sleek neck, Libby urged the horse into a familiar walk as he picked his way up through the gap between the hills.

The air was desert dry, the breeze welcome as horse and rider delicately weaved in and out among the rocks. Stuart Garwood had sent her out on special assignment to reconnoiter the area as a possible A trail—one that posed more challenges for qualified riders. The brig was about a mile away, and earlier she'd seen a recon-marine team scurrying over the hills. They used this area sometimes to practice their skills.

A sharp crack sounded, like a gunshot. Black Jack leaped to one side. Surprised, Libby clenched the horse with her strong legs and instantly pulled on the reins to keep him from jumping unexpectedly again. A second shot sounded, and a rock exploded as if hit by a bullet, less than ten feet from the nervous horse.

"Whoa!" Too late! The black gelding snorted apprehensively and reared skyward, his front legs pawing the air. Libby felt herself come unseated. She didn't know the horse well enough to anticipate how it might react to stressful circumstances. Few would rear, but Black Jack had. Suddenly, she was tumbling backward, heading for the rocky ground. Her last thought was to keep hold of the reins.

Pain brought Libby slowly back to consciousness. The sun stabbed into her slitted eyes. She groaned and slowly raised her left hand. The ache in her head told her she'd struck a rock when the horse had thrown her. Because a fall could be fatal, Libby took long, patient moments to allow her spinning head to settle down before she began methodically moving each extremity to check for broken bones.

Black Jack stood tensely above her, his head lifted, ears pricked forward, watching something in the distance. The reins were still gripped in her gloved hand, and Libby was glad the automatic had kicked in. If the horse hadn't been held, he'd have hightailed it for the stable, and she would have had to walk the more than three miles back.

Groaning, she sat up. Dizziness assailed her, and she placed her head between her knees until it abated to a degree. Conscious of a warm sensation spreading down her right temple, she lifted her gloved fingers and met blood. Her eyes widening slightly, Libby realized it was her blood. The heat of the sun and the relentless, dry breeze seemed to accentuate her predicament. So far, no broken bones, she reassured herself—just a lot of bruises and cuts on her elbows and forearms.

"Lucky," Libby muttered softly to herself. "I was lucky...." Dazed, she sat there for at least ten minutes, trying to understand what had spooked Black Jack. Had it really been a gunshot? Even now, the gelding was tense, like a statue above her, his nostrils flared. Slowly moving her head to the left, Libby tried to figure out what the horse was looking at. She could see nothing on the far hill but sagebrush and cacti.

Black Jack snorted and moved restively until he was at the end of the reins, stretching them taut.

"Stand," Libby crooned. She knew she had to get up and get back to the stables. Still feeling dizzy, she urged Black Jack toward her. Reaching up, slipping her hand into the stirrup iron, she pulled herself to a standing position. The vertigo increased and she leaned heavily against the gelding, gripping his mane.

Had she suffered a concussion? Of all the days not to wear her hard hat—something she normally wore without thinking, especially on an A trail, where the going was difficult, anyway. Now, as Libby drew the reins across Black Jack's head and neck, she chastised herself for her carelessness.

Mounting was difficult. They were in a small steep-sided ravine and Black Jack was jumpy. Each time Libby tried to place her boot in the stirrup iron, he'd sidestep away from her. Curbing her impatience and trying to steady herself, Libby pulled the reins tightly against the pommel to force the nervous horse to stand still—at least until she could mount.

If it had been Shiloh, he'd have stood like a statue. But Black Jack was a trail horse without years of dressage training behind him. Libby swore she'd never ride any horse but Shiloh from here on in. Finally, she was able to get into the saddle. Just the quick, upward motion cost her, and she had to rest her head against the horse's neck for a long minute, afraid the dizziness would make her fall off.

The landscape blurred before her eyes as she lifted her head to determine the direction of the stables. Just as quickly, the view sharpened, and she could see fine. Frustrated, and realizing that she must have suffered a mild concussion, Libby eased the reins and squeezed the gelding's sides.

"Get us home," she croaked to the horse. Libby gripped the pommel with one hand, the mane and reins with the other. She was quite unsteady and not at all sure she could stay on the tall horse. If nothing else, trail horses knew the way home—a fact she counted on as never before. As Black Jack slowly moved around the rocks and cacti, Libby clung to him. The stifling heat of the day made her feel sick to her stomach, and she was more sure than ever that she had a concussion.

Her wandering thoughts turned to Dan, who was to meet her down at the stables for his lesson. Libby knew that at this snail's pace she'd never get there in time. Suddenly, she ached for Dan's closeness, for his help. But he wasn't here with her. As she rode, clinging to the horse and saddle, Libby realized just how independent she'd become in the last three years—unwilling to lean on anyone for any reason, too afraid of the consequences to her freedom.

Blood continued to trickle slowly down her temple, along her cheek and jawline. Libby realized she probably looked a sight, with blood dripping down onto her white blouse and yellow breeches. She hoped there would be few people at the stables to witness her mishap—it would be embarrassing, to say the least. Worst of all, she realized, with a concussion, she wouldn't be able to teach riding for at least a week, perhaps more. She began to worry about who would take over her classes. And who would ride Shiloh and keep him in peak condition? Angry over her stupidity in riding the trail horse, Libby had no one to blame but herself. But just the knowledge that Dan would be waiting when she finally made it to the stable kept her going—otherwise, the desire to just fall off and lie still was far too tempting.

Agitated, Dan stood at the gate to the arena, hands on hips, wondering where Libby was. Garwood had told him only that she was out on a trail. Glancing at his watch, he saw that she was half an hour late. That wasn't like her, Dan fumed. Or was it? Maybe Libby was backing away from him, from their agreement to be friends. Had something happened since he'd seen her? He knew all too well

PLAY

BIG BUCKS

AND YOU COULD WIN THE

$1,000,000.00

PLUS JACKPOT!

ONE MILLION $

YOUR PERSONAL GAME CARD INSIDE...

SILHOUETTE

IT'S FUN!

IT'S FREE!

BIG BUCK$

HOW TO PLAY

It's so easy...grab a lucky coin, and go right to your BIG BUCKS game card. Scratch off silver squares in a STRAIGHT LINE (across, down, or diagonal) until 5 dollar signs are revealed. BINGO!...Doing this makes you eligible for a chance to win $1,000,000.00 in lifetime income ($33,333.33 each year for 30 years)! Also scratch all 4 corners to reveal the dollar signs. This entitles you to a chance to win the $50,000.00 Extra Bonus Prize! Void if more than 9 squares scratched off.

Your EXCLUSIVE PRIZE NUMBER is in the upper right corner of your game card. Return your game card and we'll activate your unique Sweepstakes Number, so it's important that your name and address is completed correctly. This will permit us to identify you and match you with any cash prize rightfully yours! (SEE BACK OF BOOK FOR DETAILS.)

FREE BOOKS PLUS FREE GIFTS!

At the same time you play your BIG BUCKS game card for BIG CASH PRIZES...scratch the Lucky Charm to receive FOUR FREE

Silhouette Special Edition® novels, and a FREE GIFT, TOO! They're totally free, absolutely free with no obligation to buy anything!

These books have a cover price of $3.50 each. But THEY ARE TOTALLY FREE; even the shipping will be at our expense! The Silhouette Reader Service™ is not like some book clubs. You don't have to make any minimum number of purchases—not even one!

The fact is, thousands of readers look forward to receiving six of the best new romance novels each month and they love our discount prices!

Of course you may play BIG BUCKS for cash prizes alone by not scratching off your Lucky Charm, but why not get everything that we are offering and that you are entitled to! You'll be glad you did.

Offer limited to one per household and not valid to current Silhouette Special Edition® subscribers. All orders subject to approval.

EXCLUSIVE PRIZE # 4M 663421

BIG BUCKS

$

HURRY!

This lot not be claimed!

Scratch here →

LUCKY CHARM GAME!

Claim 4 FREE books AND a FREE Mystery Gift!

YES! I have played my BIG BUCKS game card as instructed. Enter my Big Bucks Prize number in the MILLION DOLLAR Sweepstakes III and also enter me for the Extra Bonus Prize. When winners are selected, tell me if I've won. If the Lucky Charm is scratched off, I will also receive everything revealed, as explained on the back of this page.

335 CIS ANTT
(C-SIL-SE-05/94)

NAME _____

ADDRESS _____ APT. _____

CITY _____ PROV. _____ POSTAL CODE _____

NO PURCHASE OR OBLIGATION NECESSARY TO ENTER SWEEPSTAKES.

© 1993 HARLEQUIN ENTERPRISES LTD.

PRINTED IN U.S.A.

TWO WAYS TO WIN BIG BUCKS!

1. Uncover 5 $ signs in a row . . . BINGO! You're eligible to win the $1,000,000.00 SWEEPSTAKES!

2. Uncover 5 $ signs in a row AND uncover $ signs in all 4 corners . . . BINGO! You're also eligible for the $50,000.00 EXTRA BONUS PRIZE!

THE SILHOUETTE READER SERVICE™: HERE'S HOW IT WORKS

Accepting free books places you under no obligation to buy anything. You may keep the books and gift and return the shipping statement marked "cancel". If you do not cancel, about a month later we will send you 6 additional novels and bill you just $2.96 each plus 25¢ delivery and GST*. That's the complete price, and – compared to cover prices of $3.50 each – quite a bargain! You may cancel at any time, but if you choose to continue, every month we'll send you 6 more books, which you may either purchase at the discount price...or return at our expense and cancel your subscription.

*Terms and prices subject to change without notice. Canadian residents add applicable provincial taxes and GST.

0195619199-L2A5X3-BR01

"BIG BUCKS"
MILLION DOLLAR SWEEPSTAKES III
P.O. BOX 609
FORT ERIE, ONTARIO
L2A 9Z9

MAIL▷POSTE
Canada Post Corporation / Société canadienne des postes
Postage paid   Port payé
if mailed in Canada   si posté au Canada

Business   Réponse
Reply   d'affaires

0195619199   01

the agony he'd gone through this week—every day a special kind of lonely hell.

Walking past the arena toward the small creek where all the trails converged, Dan tried to tame his own needs and desires for Libby. Last week's hour-long class had been dreamlike. Had it really happened? How many times had he managed to make Libby smile, or heard that wonderful bell-like laughter bubble up from her throat? He'd fallen off Fred twice. And when he'd laughed, Libby had, too—not laughing at him, but with him. He'd taken the falls with good-natured grace—or as much as he could muster. Luckily, the only thing he'd hurt was his pride.

Maybe Libby had enjoyed herself with him too much and it had scared her off, Dan surmised as he made his way to the stream and carefully crossed it. Walking up the steep hill beyond, he thought he might see Libby coming. Maybe she was late on purpose—a subtle warning for him to respect their fragile truce. Rubbing his jaw, Dan dipped his head in thought. Not that he wasn't a gentleman around her, but God help him, he couldn't keep his hunger for her out of his eyes, and he was sure she'd seen it.

As he topped the hill, which flattened out to reveal the surrounding desert of the marine base, Dan hoped he hadn't overstepped his bounds with Libby. She had every right to be wary of him. Lifting his head, he frowned. There, not more than two hundred feet away, was Libby on a black horse. Was that blood on the side of her face, or was he imagining things? Squinting against the sunlight, he lifted his hand to his eyes to shade them. Libby was leaning forward in the saddle, her head hanging. Something was wrong. Very wrong.

Dan broke into a jog and met her and the horse. Automatically, he slowed and gripped the reins to make the animal stop.

"Libby? What's wrong?" Blood had stained her face, blouse and breeches. As she made what seemed like a supreme effort to sit up and look at him, Dan became alarmed. Her flesh was translucent and pasty, her eyes dark and vacant looking. Grimly, he reached for her as she swayed unsteadily in the saddle.

"Hang on," he whispered tautly, "and I'll lead the horse to the stables."

"I—I fell off, Dan...."

"That's all right. Can you stay on? It's just a little farther."

"I—I think so. I'm so dizzy...."

His mind spun with questions about how she'd fallen. Hurrying the horse through the stream at a fast walk and up the other side, he headed for the main office. From there, they could call for a base ambulance. Libby looked shocked and badly shaken.

He looked over his shoulder and at her. Her hair, once bound, had come undone and hung in sable sheets around her pale features. Her lips were parted, and he saw that her eyes were closed.

"What happened, Libby?"

"Someone... was shooting. I—I think two bullets hit close to us and Black Jack reared. I lost my seat and fell off. I feel so stupid, Dan...."

"It's okay, Lib. Just hang on, we're almost to the office."

Now his heart was pounding with real fear and his head was spinning with shock over her answer. Libby had said bullets. But who the hell was firing live ammo out there? That was a restricted area! The only live fire was allowed on Pershing Range, miles away—certainly not here, around the stables area. Quickly tying the horse to the hitching rail,

Dan moved to Libby's side. He placed his hands around her waist and lifted her off.

With a moan, Libby sank against Dan as he allowed her feet to touch the ground. She released a ragged little sigh and clung to him.

"I—I don't think I can stand on my own..."

Grimly, Dan led Libby up the steps toward Garwood's office. "That's okay, just hold on to me. I won't let you fall, Lib."

And he didn't. Just the strength of his arm around her waist made Libby feel better. The dizziness intensified as she walked, and she had no recourse but to lean her head against his shoulder as he guided her into Garwood's office.

"Libby!" Garwood sprang to his feet and came around his desk.

"Call the ambulance," Dan ordered. He guided Libby to the couch. She was semiconscious, barely responding to him.

"Of course!"

Blocking out Garwood's hurried call, Dan focused solely on Libby. As soon as she lay down, she closed her eyes, her arm hanging listlessly off the couch, fingers slightly curled near the wooden floor. Dan quickly opened the collar of her blouse and made her as comfortable as he could. The gash on the side of her right temple wasn't deep, but it was long, and it would take stitches to close it. That was the least of his worries. Libby's skin was so translucent he could see the delicate blue veins beneath her dark eyes.

With trembling fingers, he moved the dusty strands of her hair away from the oozing injury. Garwood came around the desk.

"I'll get a washcloth and some water," he offered.

"Do that." Dan sat tensely on the edge of the couch, facing Libby. She seemed unconscious, her breathing shallow, causing only the barest rise and fall of her breasts beneath the bloodstained blouse. When Garwood came back, Dan took the washcloth from him.

"Thanks." Gently, he placed it across Libby's forehead. Her eyebrows moved slightly and she lifted her hand. Good, she wasn't unconscious.

"What happened?" Garwood demanded, standing next to him.

"Libby said she fell off her horse."

"I see."

Dan shot a look up at Garwood's grim face.

"I don't think so. She said someone was firing live ammo around her."

"Impossible!"

"That's what I'd say, but Libby isn't the kind of person to make things up, and if anyone would know, she would."

"Surely she's mistaken."

Dan kept his gaze on Garwood. "She was married to a marine. She knows all about rifles and gunfire. I believe her if she said there were shots fired."

Raking a hand through his pepper-and-salt hair, Garwood shifted his weight to his other booted foot. "I think Libby is wrong, Captain Ramsey. Eventers like her don't like to admit that they can fall off a horse occasionally. She may be spinning a story to cover it up."

Anger moved through Dan. He heard the ambulance coming. "I don't think Libby is the type to lie, Mr. Garwood."

Moving out of the way, Garwood went to the door and opened it. "Well," he said briskly, "let's just get Libby to the emergency room. We can find out what really happened later."

* * *

Every time a cool, soothing hand moved across her brow, the pain left, momentarily. Libby felt heavy, and her eyelids seemed like they had weights on them. Gradually, the jumble of voices and sounds began to separate and become coherent. She heard Dan's low, strained voice, felt him very near her. It had to be his hand, his touch on her shoulder or brow, that made the pain recede. There was a woman's voice, too. Wrinkling her brow, she devoted every ounce of strength to opening her eyes.

"She's coming out of it," Dr. Juanita Ramirez said, glancing across the bed at Dan.

Dan reached out and gripped Libby's cool, limp hand. Her thick, brown lashes moved slightly, and he saw her lips part. The urge to kiss her, to reassure her, was very real to him. But he was in a military hospital, and he had to remember protocol—much as he didn't want to. Leaning over, his hand on her shoulder, he whispered, "Lib? It's Dan. Can you hear me, honey?"

Just the slightest movement of her fingers squeezing his told him that she had. He smiled a little and watched her struggle to awaken. "Take it easy," he crooned, touching her brow, which was damp with perspiration. "Everything's all right, Lib. You're okay. Don't fight so hard...."

"She's doing fine," Dr. Ramirez said. "Stay with her, Captain, and I'll be back in a few minutes."

Grateful to be alone at last with Libby, Dan leaned down and pressed a small, welcoming kiss on her hairline. They had cleaned the blood off Libby's face and a dressing lay across the recently stitched gash on her right temple. She probably had a splitting headache, for starters. Dan gently grazed her wan cheek and followed the clean line of her jaw with his fingertips.

"Just take it easy," he whispered over and over.

Heartened when Libby stopped struggling, Dan realized his words had affected her, and it made his heart soar with elation. Just getting to touch Libby, to let her know in another way that she was safe and going to be all right, drained some of the tension from him. The last hour had been hell on him until Dr. Ramirez had finally come back from the X-ray department to tell him the good news: Libby had suffered a mild concussion, but it was nothing life threatening.

His smile deepened when he saw the merest hint of green as Libby forced her eyelids open. The pupils were dilated and huge, her eyes vacant looking. For the longest time, as Dan continued to hold her hand and softly stroke her cheek, she stared up at him. Relief was flowing through him. Libby's hair was mussed and in need of washing and combing. Still, she looked like an angel to him lying on that gurney. Her ordinarily red lips were pale and parted. Wanting to follow his heart and lean over and brush them with a kiss, Dan restrained himself.

"Libby? How are you doing?" He spoke slowly and distinctly, because she seemed so dazed.

Her voice was barely a whisper, like a thread of mist, as she closed her eyes and said, "Awful. I feel sick to my stomach, like I'm going to throw up."

He squeezed her hand reassuringly. "The doc said you have a mild concussion, but you're going to be fine. How's the pain in your head?"

Just the caress of Dan's hand on hers brought the dizziness under control and Libby reopened her eyes. How strong and capable he looked standing there beside her, his smile sending a healing warmth flowing through her. "Bad. Really bad," she admitted.

"I thought so. You had to have eight stitches in your temple, so I'm not surprised."

"Ouch..."

"Other than that," Dan went on more lightly, "Dr. Ramirez is giving you a clean bill of health. She said three or four days in the hospital and you'll be fine."

Libby's eyes flew open. It took every ounce of her returning strength to lift her head, her eyes huge with disbelief. "No!"

Dan tensed at her unexpected cry. "Libby, what's wrong?"

Breathing erratically, she tried to form the words that seemed so hard to pronounce. "I won't stay in a hospital!" she croaked, her voice breaking. She had to get out of there. The antiseptic smell was overwhelming, the memories of her time spent in the hospital after losing her baby—and before that, identifying Brad's remains—slammed through her.

"Easy," Dan whispered. He gripped her shoulders as she tried to rise off the gurney. "Lie down, Libby. You can't walk. You'll fall. Come on, relax...."

Gasping for air, her breasts rising and falling sharply, Libby looked wildly around the room. "I want out of here, Dan! Now! Right now! Oh, God, get me out of here! Please!" Tears formed and splattered down her taut cheeks as she looked to him for help.

Shaken by her sudden reaction, Dan got her to lie back down. "Libby, you can't go home. You can't even walk. Dr. Ramirez said you need at least three or four days of complete bed rest."

"Take me home!" she sobbed, the tears flowing hard and fast. "Just get me out of here!"

Libby's sudden emotional storm tore at him. Just then Dr. Ramirez came back in and frowned as she realized Libby was crying. Quickly, Dan explained the situation to her.

"Well," Ramirez said doubtfully, "she'll end up hurting herself worse if she tries to go home."

Libby thrashed her head from side to side. "I won't stay here!" she cried. "You can't make me stay here! Sign me out! Get me out of here!"

Gripping her shoulder, Dan looked across the gurney at the nonplussed doctor. "It's because of something that happened three years ago here at this hospital," he explained hurriedly. "Doc, what are the chances of Libby coming home with me for the next few days? Can I take care of her well enough to make the difference? I don't have any medical training, but—"

Ramirez placed her hand protectively on Libby's shoulder, trying to get her to calm down. "I'll authorize it, Captain. She's almost hysterical, and I can't give her a tranquilizer because of her head injury." With a shrug, she said, "Okay, take her home. If you need any help, you can call here and get directions from me or my staff."

Libby looked from the doctor to Dan, gulping back her panic, her pain. She was going home with him! She was too disoriented to disagree with the impromptu plan. Anywhere was better than here. Libby had sworn after losing her child that she'd never enter a hospital again no matter what.

"I'll get a wheelchair for her," Ramirez said, giving Libby one last pat on the arm, as if to try to reassure her that she could leave.

"Fine. Thanks." Dan helped Libby sit up. He gripped her shoulders as she leaned forward. Her brow rested against his shoulder. "Everything's going to be okay, Libby. You'll come home with me, and I'll take care of you."

Libby could only sniff and then shudder, trying to hold back a sob. Dan meant safety to her right now. How could she tell him that she wasn't herself? That her emotions were fluctuating wildly and she had little or no control over them? He must think her immature at best. It must be the head injury, she thought sluggishly as she felt Dan help her off the gurney. The wheelchair was placed strategically, and she eased into its confines. Hanging her head, her hands pressed to her face, Libby sobbed, "Just get me out of here...."

Chapter Eight

Dan stood just outside the guest bedroom in his apartment. The door was ajar, Libby safely tucked into bed. She'd gone to sleep almost instantly, a mist of tears lingering in her eyes. Should he leave her alone? Or hold her as he had on the way home, her face pressed to his shoulder and his arm about her? Undecided, he exhaled softly.

Why did life have to be so complex? Dan forced himself to move away from the door, telling himself that it was best to allow Libby to sleep. Dr. Ramirez had warned him to wake her if she didn't waken naturally after she'd napped for a while. There was still some worry about possible internal bleeding, and sleeping too long was one of the indicators.

Dan went to his small kitchen and sat down on one of the bar stools and then dialed his office.

"Rose, this is Dan. Is Joe Donnally around? Good. Let me speak to him."

Waiting impatiently, Dan kept replaying Libby's words about the accident. Someone had been firing a rifle or pistol in a restricted area. Rubbing his face, he realized that Libby could have been killed—even if by accident—and that shook him to his soul as nothing else had.

"Sergeant Donnally speaking."

"Joe, I want you to get out to the northeast section about three miles from the stable area. Libby Tyler was out riding in that area and two shots of live ammo were fired around her. The horse she was riding spooked and she was thrown off."

"Live rounds, sir?"

There was disbelief in Donnally's voice. Grimly, Dan rasped, "Yes, live. Dammit, Joe, I want you to find out who did it. Get out there and search the area. When Libby—I mean, Ms. Tyler—wakes up, if she's feeling a little better from the concussion she's received, I'll ask her for more specifics. And check which marine companies are in the area and who might have designated that particular area for live fire. Understand?"

"Yes, sir. I'll get on it right away, sir."

"Good, and Joe?"

"Yes, sir?"

"Thanks. This means a lot to me. Ms. Tyler could have been killed."

"No problem, sir. You want Rose back?"

"Yes, I do."

"Hang on, sir . . ."

"I'm here, Captain. What's Joe looking so upset about? What's happened?"

In as few words as possible, Dan filled in his secretary on what had occurred.

"That's just terrible. You said Libby's with you?"

Dan hesitated and then said, "Yes. She doesn't like hospitals, and the doctor said she wasn't capable of taking care of herself for the next four days."

"I feel so sorry for her. Is there anything I can do to help?"

How like Rose to volunteer. Dan glanced around his sunny kitchen. "I'm not such a great cook, but I think Libby will be able to subsist on my chow."

Chuckling, Rose said, "Captain, I make a mean pot of chicken soup, and that's just what she needs right now."

"Rose, I won't complain if you show up on my doorstep with it."

"Consider it done! I'll make it up tonight and bring it over tomorrow morning."

"I don't want to leave her alone, Rose, at least not for the next two days. Libby can't even walk by herself, she's so dizzy."

"And Colonel Edwards isn't going to be happy to have you call in sick, either. I've got a plan. How about I bring over the most important cases you're working on tomorrow morning, and you can work out of your apartment for the next couple of days? Then, if Libby is feeling better and can walk, I can 'baby-sit' her so you can show your popular face around here and make the colonel smile again?"

"Good idea, Rose. You're a born strategy-and-tactics lady."

"In the meantime, I'll let Private Shaw be our go-between. Anything I think you need to see, sign or otherwise act on, I'll send over via him. He can be a courier of sorts."

"That will make him feel like he's not in the doghouse," Dan agreed.

"Yes, sir. I think it will help him. He's making progress on learning to read, but it's slow, and the kid is hurting emotionally from being left out of the loop on important things. Working directly with you will make him feel a little special.''

"Rose, you're a born psychologist. What would I do without you?''

"You'd probably flounder around a lot, Captain.''

He grinned, his spirits rising a bit. "You're good tonic, Rose.''

"Oh, one more thing.''

"Yes?''

"Corporal Annie Yellow Horse reported for duty today.''

Groaning, Dan said, "I was supposed to see her at 1300. Damn.''

"I took care of it and her. She's quite a young lady and quite a marine.'' In a lower voice she added, "But I don't think she and Sergeant Donnally got along at all. He's defensive toward her.''

"Threatened?''

"Yes, sir. Annie's talents are somewhat legendary, as you know. She's a sharp gal, Captain, and I think you're going to like having her here.''

"Do me a favor?''

"Yes?''

"Send Yellow Horse out with Donnally to investigate the area. Have her look around for footprints or anything like that where Libby was thrown off.''

Chuckling, Rose said, "A man after my own heart. I was going to suggest the same thing. The best way for Joe to get his nose unbent over her arrival is to work closely with her.''

"Yes, well, that system works in some situations.'' Dan sighed.

"My money's on Donnally. He's a macho marine, but eventually he'll come around.''

"I hope you're right. Yes, send both of them out on this investigation. Have Joe call me if he stumbles onto anything."

"You bet. In the meantime, I'll have any important calls routed to your apartment, okay?"

Dan was grateful for Rose's ability to take charge and manage in an emergency situation. "That's fine, Rose."

"You can look forward to Shaw showing up at your door at 0900 tomorrow morning with a big pot of chicken soup and your work for the day."

Smiling, Dan said goodbye to his able secretary and hung up the phone. Just talking to the indomitable Rose had made him feel less shaken and more hopeful. His heart bid him to get up and go check on Libby, which he did, easing the door open enough to look in on her. When he'd put her to bed, Dan had taken off her boots but left her dressed, covering her with a soft comforter.

Libby's sable hair was a dark halo about her pale features. He worried that she still hadn't gotten any color back in her cheeks. Her lips were wan, and blue shadows remained beneath her eyes. Was she breathing? He tried to see the covers rise and fall, but couldn't. His heart suddenly racing, he stepped quietly into the room, alarm filling him. What if her condition was worse than Dr. Ramirez had suspected? Dan knew that concussions were funny things, and sometimes people went into comas or experienced sudden, unanticipated bleeding and died.

As he neared the queen-size bed, sunlight filtered through the pale green floor-to-ceiling sheers at the window, highlighting Libby's form on the bed, and Dan felt a sudden catch in his throat as he leaned over and gently slid his fingers around her wrist. A faint pulse beat beneath his grip, and relief flowed powerfully through him. Unwillingly, he forced himself to release her limp wrist. Wanting to do something, but knowing there was really nothing he could do, Dan fussed with the covers, nudging the comforter gently around her neck and shoulders. Libby slept deeply, completely unaware of him.

Stepping back, he left the room as quietly as he'd entered it. He glanced at his watch as he did so. In another couple of hours, if Libby hadn't awakened, he'd have to wake her and ask her some general questions to make sure she was coherent.

Soft classical piano music gently stole through Libby's awakening state. It was dark when she groggily opened her eyes, except for light cascading into the room from a partly opened door near the bed she lay upon. Where was she? Her head pounded painfully as she slowly sat up to look at her surroundings. Her fingers brushed the gauze dressing on her temple, and she frowned. What was going on?

"Libby?"

The voice, Dan's voice, cut through her confusion. Lifting her head, she saw his darkened shape in the doorway, outlined by the light flowing into the room.

"Dan?" Her voice cracked, rusty from disuse.

Going over to the dresser, Dan turned on a small lamp, and its glow gently lit the room. Libby sat cross-legged in his large bed, the comforter pooled around her. Her hair was straggly and hung around her pale face. Dan sat down on the edge of the bed and faced her.

"You're here at my apartment," he said, seeing the question in her dark eyes. "Remember this afternoon? You were thrown off a horse and hurt?"

"I was?" Libby touched her brow for a moment. Just Dan's nearness stabilized the chaotic emotions running rampant within her. "I fell?"

He smiled a little and stifled the urge to reach out and hold her. For the next five minutes, he went over the events carefully and thoroughly with her. Dr. Ramirez had warned him that she might not have any memory of the actual accident—at least, not for a day or two.

"Gosh," Libby whispered, slowly moving her head to look up at Dan. His face was deeply shadowed, but she saw the worry burning in his eyes. "How did I get here, then?" She looked around the neat, spare room. There wasn't much to Dan's decorating ability—the bedroom contained a bed, a dresser, and green drapes and sheers at the one window. Libby saw no pictures—no hints of a personal touch—and her feelings went out to him and the heartbreaking past he had endured.

Clearing his throat, Dan told her what had happened at the hospital.

Libby sat for a long minute absorbing the explanation. "I feel really stupid. I've had falls before, but never this bad." She glanced at him. "I'm sorry...."

Reaching out, not caring what Libby might think, Dan took her hand in his and squeezed it gently. "I'm not. You're in need of a little care right now, Lib. I'm glad I can be the one to give it to you." And then he smiled, thrilled as Libby's fingers closed around his. "Rose is bringing over a huge pot of chicken soup for you tomorrow morning. She knows my abilities as a cook are desperate."

The strength, the gentleness of Dan's hand sent a ribbon of warmth through Libby, stabilizing her ragged emotional state. Suddenly she wanted to cry again—for no reason, it seemed. "I've always liked Rose. She's a good person."

"I have to be careful not to kill you with my cooking. You're supposed to be here to heal up, not get food poisoning."

Her wan smile increased slightly, and she stared down at their hands. "We'll survive."

Dan wanted to continue to hold Libby's hand, but he knew it wasn't right. Their relationship, what little there was to it, was still tenuous and fragile, and he didn't want to push her or make her feel as if she was trapped here. Extricating his fingers from hers, he smiled slightly.

"I like your attitude. How are you feeling now?"

"Umm, like a truck hit me. I still don't remember falling off Black Jack. My head hurts when I turn it."

Dan purposely kept his voice low. "Something like a migraine headache?" he guessed.

"Exactly."

"Do you remember me waking you a couple of hours ago? I asked you some questions?"

She gave him a puzzled look. "No..."

Dan smiled a little. "That's okay. I just wanted to make sure you were doing okay. Dr. Ramirez said you could have aspirin. Want some?"

Gratefully, Libby met his gaze. "Please."

"Okay, I'll be right back," he said, rising from the bed.

Libby listened as Dan went to the medicine chest in the bathroom. Contentment washed over her as the familiar sounds brought back fond memories of her marriage. As she ran a hand through her hair, she grimaced. It was dirty and matted.

"Here you go," Dan said, returning with two aspirin and a glass of water.

"Thanks," Libby whispered. She took the pills, then drank the rest of the water, suddenly very thirsty.

Dan sat back down on the edge of the bed and took the glass from her hand. "Feel like getting up and taking a bath? Or do you want to just stay where you are?"

"I just want to sleep some more, Dan. What time is it?"

"Twenty-one-hundred hours." And then he smiled sheepishly and amended himself. "Nine p.m. to you civilian types."

She smiled a little in return as she slowly slid back down beneath the blankets. "Once a marine, always a marine," she told him, her voice slurring with exhaustion.

Dan got up and tucked the comforter back around Libby's shoulders. "Go to sleep, Ms. Tyler, and dream sweet dreams. If you need anything, just call me. I'll be out in the living room working on my cases."

Worriedly, Libby lifted her head briefly. "But—where will you sleep?"

"My bedroom is down the hall." Dan saw the sudden concern in Libby's eyes and leaned down to press a chaste kiss on her hair. "It's time to take care of yourself Libby, and not worry about anyone else. Okay?"

Just the touch of his lips grazing her hair sent a delicious warmth through her. Libby lay down on the pillow and closed her eyes. "You're a good person, Dan Ramsey. You didn't have to take me in like a stray."

Dan went over and switched off the lamp on the dresser, then turned. Libby had fallen into a healing slumber before he could answer her. She wasn't some stray to him. Gazing at her a moment longer, he admitted to himself that she was becoming a very important part of his life, whether she realized it or not.

At exactly 0900, Private Shaw showed up at Dan's apartment with the soup. With him was Sergeant Donnally, carrying an armload of case files. Dan invited them in, and while Shaw put the chicken soup on the stove, Joe sat down opposite him at the table.

"Did you find anything in the area where Ms. Tyler was shot at?" Dan asked.

"No, sir." Joe frowned. "And there were no marine companies or squads operating in the area yesterday, except for a recon team. They were carrying weapons, but no ammo whatsoever."

"Damn." Dan looked up at Shaw. "Thanks, Private."

Glowing, Shaw came to attention. "Yes, sir!"

"Shaw, have a seat in the living room. Sergeant Donnally will be with you shortly."

"Yes, sir!"

Dan waited until the private had left the kitchen before speaking again. "Did Yellow Horse find anything?"

Donnally's scowl deepened. "No, sir, she didn't."

Dan felt his sergeant chafing. "We need to pinpoint the exact position where Libby fell. I'm hoping that this morning after she wakes up she can give me the precise location. If so, I'll call and you two can go back out to check."

"Sir," Joe said unhappily, "I can do this by myself."

Giving him a sharp glance, Dan asked, "Problems, Sergeant?"

Moving uncomfortably, Joe muttered, "No...not really, sir."

"What is it then?"

Joe scratched his jaw and shrugged. "I...uh, guess I'm not used to working with a female brig chaser—sir."

"Stereotypes have no place in my command, Sergeant. Absolutely none."

"I know that, sir." Casting him a woeful glance, Joe said, "It's just that...well, Corporal Yellow Horse is a woman."

Dan pretended to look through one of the case files.

"Anything I say will sound like prejudice, sir. I can't put my finger on it, but I'm just not comfortable working with her."

Dan made his voice hard. "Then you'd better adjust, Sergeant. Yellow Horse happens to be the best tracker we've got in the Marine Corps, and I'm not about to make her feel unwelcome just because you've got a problem with her on a personal level." *Great.* Dan had relied on Donnally, more than anyone, to help smooth the rough waters inherent in his new command, especially among the staff. It was obvious by the look of carefully veiled anguish in Donnally's eyes that he wasn't comfortable with Yellow Horse at all.

"I know her reputation," Joe said a bit defensively. "But she didn't turn up anything out there yesterday."

"Maybe you were in the wrong area," Dan snapped. He wasn't about to let Donnally think that he felt sorry for him under the circumstances. The sergeant was just going to have to adjust.

Tensing, Donnally said, "Yes, sir."

"All right," Dan muttered, closing the file, "go about your regular duties today. If I can get anything more definite on the location from Ms. Tyler, I'll be in touch. In the meantime, take Yellow Horse through the motions of normal office routine, will you?"

Donnally rose. "Yes, sir."

"Dismissed." Dan remained seated for a long moment. When he heard the door to his apartment close, he got up to check on Libby. He stopped at the bedroom door and eased it open a bit. The bed was empty. After a momentary start, Dan moved into the bedroom—but then he heard the tub water running in the bathroom. Relief flooded him. Libby must have awakened and been able to walk by herself. *Good.*

Closing the bedroom door, he went back out to the kitchen. His stomach growled, and he decided to make oatmeal. It was bland enough for the queasiest stomach and easy to fix. Puttering at the counter, he found himself pre-occupied with Libby. How was she this morning? He ached to know, to talk with her and dispense with the problems that managing an office always brought to his doorstep.

When he heard Libby enter the kitchen fifteen minutes later, Dan was completely unprepared. She stood there, her hair in damp waves around her face, barefoot, wearing his dark blue terry cloth robe. The dressing on her temple had been removed to reveal a puffy, bruised area around the stitches.

Dan had turned at the slight sound of her entrance, bowls of oatmeal in hand. He tried not to gawk at her, thinking how pretty she was. A slight color had returned to her cheeks, and her eyes looked clearer. He smiled.

"Come and sit down. I've almost got breakfast ready for us."

Libby moved slowly, with mincing steps, to the chair. "I'm not really hungry, Dan. I'm still a little queasy." She gave him an apologetic glance. "The oatmeal smells good to my nose, but not my stomach."

Dan nodded and placed it on the counter, trying to ignore Libby's natural beauty as he set the creamer and sugar bowl on the table. "How about some toast then? Toast's always good for an upset stomach. Come on, you've got to eat something."

"Okay...maybe some toast," Libby agreed tentatively. How handsome Dan looked in his light blue chino slacks and dark blue polo shirt. Still, the marine in him was very apparent in the way he held himself, with unconscious pride and confidence.

"Did you sleep okay?" Dan asked, opening up the package of bread.

"Yes, I did."

"How's your head? Still pounding like a drum?"

"Not as much. I'm still a little dizzy, but I can get around better."

"You should have called me this morning. I'd have helped you out of bed. Dr. Ramirez said the greatest danger is of you falling and hitting your head again."

Libby smiled slightly and touched her damp hair. "I'm okay, really I am."

Buttering the toast, Dan put it on a plate and set it in front of Libby. "I don't think you're used to being taken care of, Ms. Tyler," he teased, taking the chair opposite her.

Libby felt heat flooding her neck and rushing into her cheeks. Deliberately avoiding Dan's intense gaze she picked delicately at the toast before her. "In a way, you're right," she said softly. "When Brad was alive, the world revolved around him. Not that I minded. He loved what he was doing, and I wanted to support him even though the flying scared me to death."

Dan stirred cream and sugar into his oatmeal, although eating was the last thing on his mind. The fact that Libby was here with him, in his kitchen, reminded him of the early years of his marriage—of another breakfast table and happier times. "What about your needs?" he asked gently, spooning up some oatmeal.

Libby shrugged slightly. "I had my horses and classes— teaching children to ride."

"Have horses been prominent in your life since you were a little girl?"

Libby met his inquiring gaze. "I think I hear you asking if horses replaced my parents and Brad?"

"In a roundabout way, yes."

She munched on the toast and slowly looked around Dan's kitchen. It was spare and impersonal, too. Returning her attention to him, she said, "I think I'm just beginning to realize how perceptive you are, Captain Ramsey."

"I hope it's not disturbing to you."

"No... just uncomfortable sometimes."

"Why?" Dan held his breath, the spoon halfway to his mouth. Libby looked lovely in a disheveled kind of way in his oversize bathrobe. Already more color had returned to her cheeks and to her soft, full lips.

"Brad never had that kind of insight into me, and neither did my folks. Not that they didn't love me—they did."

"I think I honed this ability when I was married to Janna," Dan admitted hollowly as he pushed the spoon around in the oatmeal. "I had to try and ferret out the reasons for her behavior, and over the years I began to apply the skill across the board to the people under my command."

"I think it's a fine skill."

"Good." He ate a few more bites of oatmeal. "We need to get you some clothes to wear. I didn't even think about that until you showed up in my robe."

Amused, her head still hurting enough to make talking an effort, Libby touched the terry robe. "I hope you don't mind. I didn't want to climb back into my dirty clothes."

"Not at all. You give new meaning to that old robe."

Flushing, Libby held his dancing gaze, which sparkled with laughter. Dan had a gentleness that made her feel giddy and well cared for, even when he was paying her a decidedly personal compliment. Ordinarily, Libby would have been scared by such a direct remark, but not now. Maybe the concussion had addled her brain.

"What I need are my toiletry items and jeans and a blouse."

"I'll send someone over to your apartment to get them for you."

"Can't I just go home, Dan?"

Dan was careful to keep his expression neutral so she couldn't read his disappointment over her question. "No...not yet. The doc is worried about your dizziness. What if you fell, Libby? Who would know about it? What if you hit your head again and injured yourself worse?"

With a grimace, Libby said, "I just feel awkward here, Dan. You're such a busy person." She motioned to the thick files piled on the edge of the table. "Earlier I heard you talking with your men. I really am putting you out, and I feel uncomfortable about it."

"You're not putting me out," Dan told her lightly. "I can run my office from here for a couple of days, and then Rose will come to be with you during the day, and I'll be here in the evening. It's only four days, Libby."

Four days. To Libby, it sounded like a lifetime in one sense, because Dan was like forbidden fruit to her lonely heart. "Well, I..." She paused helplessly.

"You're staying," he said more firmly. "Besides, it makes this apartment a hell of a lot less lonely than it was before."

Avoiding his gaze, Libby understood only too well what Dan meant. Just having breakfast with him was a wonderful change in her life. The loneliness that normally ate at her was gone.

"I just don't want to be a pain in the rear, that's all."

Chuckling, Dan looked up. "Lady, you're many things to me, but a pain in the rear isn't one of them, believe me."

By two in the afternoon, Libby felt well enough to come out of the bedroom. It took her a lot more time than usual to climb into her jeans and a pale pink blouse. The dizziness came and went, but when it hit, she had to close her eyes, wait and let it pass. Dan had been a thoughtful, sensitive host, checking hourly with her at the bedroom door but never intruding on her space. All day long she heard the phone ringing out in the living room, followed by the sound of his authoritative voice. He was a problem solver, and more than once Libby eavesdropped on his conversation out of curiosity. Not once did she hear Dan get angry or upset—he always spoke in low, sincere tones with whoever called.

An inexplicable longing for his company finally drove Libby out of the loneliness of the bedroom. When she walked slowly into the carpeted living room, she found Dan seated on the couch deep in thought, with about five open files spread out on the long mahogany coffee table in front of him. He had dragged the phone over by him, and the place looked cluttered with work.

Standing for that moment before Dan became aware of her quiet presence gave Libby her first opportunity to study him and the apartment more closely. Dan's profile was set, and she could see he was intent upon the report he was reading. His lips were pursed into a single line, and she knew that was his warrior side, the marine. Her inner voice nagged at her because she realized Dan loved what he was doing. He liked the Marine Corps. He could have been a civilian attorney anywhere in the country, but he'd chosen the corps as a way of life.

Saddened, Libby looked around the apartment. Besides the overstuffed beige couch and chair, a coffee table and a television set were the extent of the furnishings. In fact, she realized, the apartment resembled a barracks in the worst sense of the word, with no pictures on the walls, no photos of family on the TV or any other personal mementos that might make this apartment a home rather than merely a place to live. In that moment, Libby began to understand the real toll that Dan's marriage had taken on him. She didn't know Janna, but it was obvious just by the way his apartment looked, that in a symbolic way, Dan still lived in a prison. She wanted to show him another kind of life. It was interesting, too, Libby thought suddenly, that Dan worked with prisoners, brigs and justice.

The toll on Dan showed in odd ways, she realized as she advanced toward him—as if the spareness of his outer life reflected what he felt inside. And then Libby looked at herself. For her, hadn't horses and teaching replaced the burden of more intimate relationships? Perhaps in her own way, she, too, was "keeping it simple." Maybe they weren't so different after all. The thought gave her hope.

"Looks like you could use some help," she offered as she halted at the arm of the couch.

Dan looked up. Libby stood before him, dressed, her hair combed and a new bandage over her injured temple. He stood up and gestured for her to sit. "You could say that. Have a seat." Leaning over, he quickly cleared a spot on the other end of the couch for her. Libby walked unsteadily, her hand on the edge of the couch as she moved slowly around it. Biting back his worry, Dan placed the errant files on the coffee table. "You must be feeling a lot better."

Libby sat down carefully—any quick movement made the dizziness assail her once again. She folded her hands in her lap and said, "Bored would be closer to the truth."

"Can I get you something to drink? The doc said no coffee. How about tea?"

His solicitude drove tears into her eyes. Surprised, Libby quickly lowered her lashes. "Uh, no, thank you. I'm fine, really. Go ahead and get back to your work."

Dan sat down again with a grin. "Why work when I have your company?"

"I knew I'd be in the way."

"I don't mind, so why should you?"

Giving him a pained look, Libby said, "I'm terribly emotional right now, Dan. I don't mean to be, but I think this crack in the head did something." Touching her temple, she forced a slight smile she didn't feel. "I'm turning into a crybaby."

Dan wanted to reach out, but the distance between them prevented it. Compromising, he placed his arm on the back of the couch. "The doctor said you might be pretty up-and-down emotionally for a while."

"I guess you're used to emotional women, right?" She was thinking of Janna's bizarre and irrational behavior.

"Just a little," Dan said with a sad smile. He gathered up the file before him and set it on the coffee table. "But I think in your case, you've got a lot of leftover tears and anger from three years ago."

"What do you mean?"

"When you realized you were in a hospital you seemed more angry than hurt."

"I hate hospitals," Libby said tautly.

"You have reasons," Dan agreed gently. "Good ones."

Nervously clasping her hands, Libby whispered, "Maybe you're right."

"Did you have anyone to help you through that time in your life?"

"I—no, not really. My folks wanted me to come home, but that's the last place I wanted to be. My dad thinks work is the answer to all of life's problems, and my mother crowds my space when I need to be left alone to think or feel my way through something." She cast a glance at Dan, whose face was tender with feeling. Just the look in his eyes made her go on. "I've never really told anyone how I felt, how horrible the loss of Brad and our baby was."

"I think that concussion probably jolted loose some of those emotional fragments you'd buried somewhere along the way."

"You're right. Last night..." She sighed and looked away. "Last night, I had horrible nightmares of Brad crashing, of losing my baby.... I woke up crying. The more I cried, the more my head hurt, so I forced myself to quit."

Dan couldn't stop himself and he rose in one fluid motion. Sitting down next to Libby, he gripped her cool, knotted hands in his own. "If that happens tonight, will you come and wake me?"

She gave him a startled look, wildly aware of the warmth and strength of his hands around hers. "But...why?"

His mouth stretched into a tender line. "Because, Libby, you're hurting. You had no one after Brad died to hold you, to help you."

Tears stung Libby's eyes and she looked away. "Well, you didn't, either," she accused, her voice cracking. "You lived for years in a hell that I can only begin to imagine."

He studied her suffering profile. "That's why I know the benefits of being held, Libby. I went through that time with Janna alone, too. I know what it's like to suffer, to cry alone. I told myself I'd never try to get through something like that alone again." He forced himself to release her hands. Two tears slid down her cheeks and he gently framed her face. With his thumbs, he removed them. "Will you promise me that if you wake up crying, you'll come and get me? I can hold you. I might not be able to make it better, but at least you'll have someone to lean on when you're hurting."

Choking back an unexpected sob, Libby looked up at Dan's strong, tender face through her tears. "Y-yes, I will."

"Promise?"

"Promise..."

Chapter Nine

The darkness brought out all of Libby's grief. She moved restlessly in the bed, filmy light from the street filtering in, lending the room a gray cast. Her head was hurting more than ever, so she decided to get up and take more aspirin. As she slid from the bed, her feet meeting the wiry carpet, she heard someone moving in the living room. Dan had gone to bed three hours ago, while she had stayed up to read for a while.

"Libby?" Dan hesitated at the open bedroom door, peering through the darkness. His voice was thick with sleep and concern.

"I'm awake," she whispered as she sat on the edge of the bed. When she lifted her head and looked in his direction, she saw that he wore only pajama bottoms. Her eyes widened slightly as the shadows embraced and accentuated Dan's tall, strong form. And suddenly Libby realized just how beautiful—how tempting—he was as a man on a purely sensuous level. His hair was mussed and his face had lost any sternness. No, Dan looked terribly vulnerable as he made his way toward her, rubbing his eyes.

"I thought I heard you," he mumbled as he came and stood next to her.

"Two rooms away?"

The corner of his mouth lifted slightly. "Yeah, I guess that's kind of crazy, isn't it?" Without thinking, he placed his hand on her slumped shoulder. Libby wore a plain white cotton nightgown, but on her, it looked elegant. Kneeling down, he allowed his hand to slide down her arms to access how she was feeling. He could see that the planes of her face were drawn in pain.

"Maybe you need some aspirin?"

"Maybe I do." Wildly aware of his warm hands on her skin, Libby felt an ache squeeze her heart. Her voice wobbled. "I feel so out of kilter emotionally, Dan. I feel shredded...." She met his dark, shadowed eyes which burned with such tenderness that she automatically lifted her hands and placed them on his warm, strong shoulders.

"...I know," he rasped, and sat down. Suddenly, as if he'd been doing it all his life, Dan put his arms around Libby and drew her against him. He bit back a groan of utter pleasure when the silk of her hair brushed against his shoulder as her cheek rested against his chest, her hand curled up beside it. "Just let go, honey, that's all you really need to do," he whispered, his mouth very close to her ear. "I'll hold you. I'll just hold you." Dan began to gently move his other hand up and down her strong, deeply indented spine, the cotton fabric of her nightgown providing a slight barrier between them.

Shutting her eyes tightly, Libby buried her face against Dan, the springy hair somehow comforting, the tensile strength of his chest creating a storm of longing deep within her dormant body. The touch of his hand on her shoulders and back seemed able to pull out all that black, buried grief that she had lived with so long—had thought was gone. But it wasn't gone, and with each stroke of Dan's hand, she felt the fistlike pressure of the held-back pain racing up and choking her throat. The first sob tore from her, and she felt Dan automatically tighten his hold, his head pressed against her own.

The dark world closed in on Libby, but all she was aware of, all she clung to through her sobs of loss, was Dan. He rocked her slowly in his arms, murmured words of encouragement that were drowned out by the animallike sounds tearing from her. Tears splashed from her tightly shut eyes, bathing both of them. The scent of Dan as a man, the brush of his lips against her hair, the even strokes of his hand, created an unfamiliar security for her to give herself up to.

Ever so slowly, the storm within Libby began to abate, and with it came the knowledge that Dan was there for her. He could have taken advantage of the situation, but he hadn't. Somewhere in her aching head and heart, Libby realized he had meant what he'd said—he would be her friend. Shaken to the core, she eased out of his arms just enough to look up into his face. His eyes were dangerously bright with unshed tears, and she stared, stunned. In that moment, she knew they were tears of empathy for her. Reaching up, she touched his face with trembling fingers, aware of the agony so easy to read on his features.

"You don't have to cry for me," she murmured in a broken voice.

With a sad smile, Dan caught her hand in his own. "We need to be able to cry for each other, Lib. I learned a long time ago that crying alone isn't the answer." He tucked her hand beside the one resting on his chest, all the while fighting a clawing need for her unlike any he'd ever experienced. Right now, Libby was completely vulnerable, her lips awash with the remnants of tears, her eyes darkened with spent grief. "You never had anyone to hold you after Brad died. I know that." And then, with a sad laugh, lifting his head and staring into the darkness, he added, "I can recognize myself in you. I cried alone, too. But sometimes—" he shifted his gaze back to her "—I remember sitting and rocking like a hurt kid, wishing someone's arms were around me, just to hold me."

The pain in his eyes made Libby lean upward. For just a moment out of time, she wanted to erase not only his hurt from the past, but her own. Her lashes sweeping down against her cheeks, she opened her mouth slightly and pressed it against the suffering line of his. Instantly, she felt Dan tense—more out of surprise than anything else. Then Libby heard him groan, the sound a sweet reverberation moving through her body like an old, familiar song that she'd longed to hear over the lonely years. His breath, hot and moist, flowed across her and she surrendered to his tightening embrace, to his hungry, searching mouth as it captured hers and moved strongly against her.

The pain in her head and heart miraculously stopped in those molten seconds as he worshiped her lips, molded them to his mouth, slid them wetly in a joyous meeting as the silence ebbed gently around them. Heat bolted deep through her, awakening her hunger to eagerly return his exploring, powerful kiss. Her breathing erratic, her breasts pressed against his chest, Libby eased her arms up and around Dan's neck, wanting to flow into him, to meld into a oneness that her heart told her meant life, hope, and at last, freedom from the pain of the past.

Dan's hands moved against her, not trapping, but evoking. The gnawing need within her spread like out-of-control flames, and Libby found herself wanting him to touch her intimately. Whatever magic was between them gave her the courage to surrender completely to him. As his hands framed her face and he deepened their kiss, Libby moaned, but it was a moan of hungry pleasure. She could feel the strength of his fingers against her face, the rush of punctuated breathing, the monitored power of his mouth finding, capturing and searching hers. Lost in the scent, feel and touch of him, Libby felt life flowing through her as if she were awakening from some deep sleep that she'd been cocooned within for the past three years.

Slowly, ever so slowly, Dan eased his mouth from Libby's ripe, wet lips. He stared down at her through hooded eyes, breathing unevenly and wildly aware of her body molded hotly against his own. He could feel her breasts, the thin barrier of her cotton gown little more than sweet temptation. The rise and fall of her chest told him that she, too, had been swept away by the force of their unexpected kiss. Gently, he eased his hands from her face and smoothed her hair away from her cheeks. It was deliciously mussed, and he had the urge to find a brush and tame those sable strands back into place. The look in Libby's eyes was no longer one of pain or darkness. No, as he searched her gaze deeply in those heated moments, Dan saw desire. The discovery was as tempting as it was off-limits. Even though Libby had initiated their kiss, he understood her vulnerability. It wasn't time to pursue their heated feelings. At least, not yet.

"You're sweet and hot," he murmured, his voice roughened with desire. Barely grazing her arched brow, he tucked a strand of hair behind her ear.

"You made my pain go away," Libby said, her voice unsteady. She absorbed each of Dan's tentative touches, each stroke of his fingers as he moved the tendrils away from her face. For a moment, she'd been close to losing control, giving herself completely to him. Stunned by that knowledge, she tried to order the chaos within her. She saw the burning glitter in Dan's eyes, felt the longing radiating from him, and she soaked it up like a thirsty sponge.

"I think," he said, allowing his hands to drift to her neck, which he caressed with his thumbs, "we made each other's pain go away."

Lowering her lashes, Libby felt suddenly ashamed of herself. She was the one who had reached up to kiss Dan, not the other way around. "I—I don't know what happened... or why," she began lamely. Just the wiry texture of his chest hair against her palms evoked more need in her. "I never realized..."

Dan caressed her shoulders. "What?" How vulnerable Libby was in that moment! He could see she was wrestling with a lot of unspoken thoughts and needs.

"This... I mean, I kissed you."

"I'm not objecting." He chuckled softly. As Libby raised her head, Dan saw the confusion in her eyes. "Are you sorry it happened?"

"I—no..."

"Maybe it was unexpected on both our parts?"

Libby sat in the circle of his arms, hearing the amusement in his voice and seeing the tenderness in his eyes. Any shame or guilt dissolved beneath his warm acceptance. In that moment, Dan looked like a little boy, his mouth quirked at one corner, his face open for her to explore, to know his most intimate feelings. Thrilled and humbled, Libby reached up and grazed his cheek, her whole arm tingling at the exciting roughness of his beard.

"Yes..." Libby allowed her hand to move back to the lap of her nightgown. "You could have taken advantage of the situation... of me...."

Just the pleasure of touching her clean, dark hair was enough for Dan as he sat with her so close to him. "And what would that have gained us?" he asked in a low, deep voice as he searched her eyes.

"Nothing," she agreed, noticing he'd used the word *us* instead of *me*. Clearing her throat, she went on in an aching whisper, "It's just that Brad was...well, different from you. Everything was done on his terms, his time, his needs."

"I see." Dan's hands stroked the length of her arms to capture her tightly wound fingers. "You came second in his life, Lib. I think that's what you're trying to tell me, isn't it?"

Tears stung her eyes. Unable to speak, she could only nod. Dan's hands covered her own, and she liked the warmth that flowed into her because of his simple gesture. After a moment, she said, "It's been hard for me to admit that. He was first in my life. He always had been...."

"Then he missed the best thing of all—you."

With a little laugh, Libby looked up at him. "I guess this concussion really knocked loose a lot of stuff, mostly emotional things, old memories."

"Well," Dan said, "if that's true, then it's time. You need to heal, Libby, so that you can reach out to life again." *To love again.* Those words were begging to be given voice, but Dan held them back on the tip of his tongue. If he stayed here any longer, he knew that his steel control would disintegrate, and Libby would be at the risk of his own naked, selfish hunger. Above all he didn't want to damage the open trust with which she now regarded him.

"How's the headache?" he asked as he released her hands.

Libby smiled slightly. "It really is gone. Can you believe it?"

As Dan rose, he nodded. "Yes, I can. Do you still want those aspirin?"

Mystified, Libby said, "No. I think I can sleep now." As she looked up at him, bathed in the shadows and darkness, she was keenly aware of the burning intensity of Dan's eyes. She felt his hunger for her, and it left her shaky in a good kind of way she'd never experienced in her life. Pulling the comforter and sheet up around her, she whispered, "Good night, Dan—and thank you, for everything."

Dan was working at the kitchen table at ten the next morning when Libby appeared in the doorway. He smiled a good-morning, noting her flushed cheeks and soft returning smile of greeting. Today, Libby wore jeans that outlined her tall form and a mint green blouse. Her hair had been brushed until it shone with gold-and-red highlights. More than anything, Dan felt a difference between them— something good, something profoundly joyous. As she walked slowly toward him, her mouth curved hesitantly at the corners, and he tasted a hunger he'd never felt before. It had taken raw courage for Libby to reach up and kiss him last night, he knew. As he'd worked this morning on his legal cases—the last thing he wanted to concentrate on—Dan had replayed that kiss and their talk a hundred times.

"Good morning," Libby murmured as she halted, her hands on the back of the chair. Dan was in his marine uniform of summer tans, looking every inch the warrior she knew him to be. But searching his eyes, taking in the returning warmth of his gaze, she felt as if she were special to him, allowed to see beyond the tough marine facade. Well, wasn't she? Libby decided it was time to realize that the past had to be released. Dan's kiss had broken loose a dam of old memories and hurts and had somehow transformed them into something beautiful and hopeful.

"It is," Dan agreed, getting to his feet. "Sit down, and I'll fix you some breakfast."

"No... that's not really necessary, Dan. Go ahead, you go back to work. Please."

It took every ounce of his control not to move around the table and take Libby into his arms. How luscious, how vulnerable she looked this morning. "Work when I have you around?" He laughed deeply and moved to the counter to pour her a cup of hot tea. "No way, lady. Go on, sit down. I made some scrambled eggs and bacon earlier. I'll reheat them in the microwave for you."

Touched beyond words, Libby carefully took a seat. The table was a mess of open file folders—cases, she supposed. Dan's scribbled notes were everywhere. The pleasure of watching him work at the kitchen counter was a new experience for her.

"Brad never went anywhere near the kitchen," she remarked wryly as he brought her over a plate of steaming eggs and bacon. "Thanks."

"My mother made sure I knew how to cook the basics before I left home," Dan said, taking his chair opposite her. He cleared away some of the case files and sipped a cup of freshly brewed coffee.

"Do you do dishes, too?"

His grin widened. "When a dishwasher isn't available."

Drowning in his amused look, Libby ate her breakfast. This morning she was hungry, she discovered—and certain that her appetite was due to the man in the marine uniform who sat across from her. "What is Colonel Edwards going to think of you being gone two days in a row?"

"He knows I'm working out of my apartment, so he's not too unhappy. Plus I'm going in for an hour in the morning before the office opens up to deal with any emergencies." Dan glanced down at the watch on his right wrist.

"Matter of fact, I have Sergeant Donnally coming over any moment now." He leaned down and pulled a map out of his black leather briefcase, which sat next to his chair. "I figured you'd be up by this time, and the three of us could zero in on the exact area where you fell. I've got a new brig chaser in my command—a Navajo woman by the name of Annie Yellow Horse who is the best tracker we've got in the corps. I want to send her out with Donnally this morning to search the immediate area and see if we can't find some footprints or maybe locate those spent shell casings."

Libby lost some of her happiness. "I don't think someone was firing *at* me, Dan."

"We don't know that."

"Well," she protested, "who on earth would want to shoot at me? I'm just a lowly riding instructor here on base. That doesn't make sense."

"Maybe not," Dan agreed, not wanting to upset her, "but from the PM's point of view, we have to look at all the possibilities. That's why I want Donnally and Yellow Horse to comb the area."

"I'm sure it was an accident! My goodness, Dan, there's no other sensible explanation."

Libby had just finished her breakfast when Sergeant Donnally arrived. Dan removed everything from the table and placed the map before her, and she took a red pen and detailed her ride for them, circling the exact area where she'd taken the fall.

Dan glanced up at Donnally. "Is this the area you searched?"

"No, sir. We were a little west of it."

"Okay, you and Yellow Horse get on it, then. Also, try to find out which direction the shots came from, and search the general area for shell casings and the like. You know procedure."

"Yes, sir," Joe said, taking the map and folding it up.

Libby remained silent at the table while Dan gave the orders. How different he was in his officer mode—nothing like the way he was with her. The discovery was sweet as well as interesting. When Sergeant Donnally left, she slowly got to her feet, still wary of the dizziness that would suddenly come and go without reason, and moved to the kitchen counter. Dan had returned to the table and replaced his files on it.

"You really like being an officer, don't you?" She poured herself a second cup of tea.

Dan glanced up from the case he'd just opened. "I like managing people," he said carefully.

"You're very stern with Sergeant Donnally," she said as she sat back down, the cup between her hands. "But you aren't with me."

He smiled a little. "I don't have to manage you, either."

Laughing lightly, Libby said, "That's another difference between you and Brad—he never lost that stern officer's facade, even at home."

Dan became more serious and tentatively tapped the end of his pencil on the file. "Sometimes it's hard to let that go, Libby. There are no courses on things like that for us. But I told you before—when I'm at work and wearing this uniform, I'm all business. When I'm not, I'm myself."

Humbled by his admission, Libby said, "I know you told me, but I guess I didn't really believe you. Now I do."

"So you're beginning to see the man behind the uniform he wears for a living?"

Unable to meet his intense, burning gaze, Libby looked down at her cup of tea. Nervously, she laced her fingers around it. "I—yes. Yes, I am."

Relief fled through Dan, but he didn't pursue the topic. "I learned a long time ago," he began slowly, "to take things a day at a time. I don't look back at the past and I don't live in the future. I live right now, Libby. I find if I do that, my life's a little more sane, a little less chaotic.''

"Good advice," she murmured, and met his gaze, now filled with searching tenderness aimed at her. "I guess I've been living too much in the past."

"You can't put the past to rest until you've worked through it and released it, honey."

Honey. The endearment flowed like a sweet, awakening flame through Libby. Dan had said it effortlessly, as if they spent every morning at this breakfast table and were having their usual chat with each other. A frisson of fear clawed up her throat, catching her off guard. Where was it coming from? Confused, Libby sipped her tea, not tasting it at all.

Dan silently castigated himself for using the endearment. He hadn't meant to; it had simply slipped out. Wasn't she like honey, though? Warm, sweet and tempting? Wrestling with a gamut of unleashed feelings, he said, "When Sergeant Donnally reports back to me, maybe we'll have more answers." Frowning, he muttered, "I hope so...."

The first thing Libby noticed when the two brig chasers returned around five that evening with their report was Sergeant Donnally's unhappy expression. Libby was sitting on the couch, reading a magazine, and Dan was out in the kitchen working on cases when they arrived. Libby was struck by the tall, slender marine, Annie Yellow Horse. Dan had told her earlier about Corporal Yellow Horse's Navajo heritage and her legendary tracking skills, and now she discovered that she liked this woman with the short, thick black hair. Annie didn't seem to have any masculine traits at all. Her hand movements were graceful, her voice soft yet firm as she talked with Dan at length about their investigation. Both marines were in their utilities and had arrived wearing soft regulation caps on their heads, which they'd removed once they were indoors. Libby also noticed their highly polished black boots and web belts complete with shining black pistol holsters that held their guns.

"Let's move to the kitchen," Dan ordered. He held out his hand to Libby. "Come on."

Gathering around the cleared-off table, Dan spread out the map again as the four of them huddled around it. Libby stood to one side, near Dan, as they listened to Sergeant Donnally's report.

"Sir, we identified the area where Ms. Tyler was thrown." He frowned. "Corporal Yellow Horse located some blood on a couple of small rocks, and she was able to identify the horse's tracks."

"Excellent," Dan murmured. "What else?"

"She also found two nearby rocks that were hit by bullets."

Dan nodded and looked over at Annie. "Nice work, Corporal."

She bowed her head gravely. "Thank you, sir."

"Were you able to figure out which direction the bullets were fired from?" Dan demanded.

Donnally nodded. "We did, sir." He pulled out a plastic Ziploc bag that revealed two spent shell casings. "M-16, Captain."

"Footprints?"

"Yes, sir, of one person. Corporal Yellow Horse found them, too, and we made plaster casts. They're back at the lab right now."

Pleased, Dan said, "Show me where the shooter was located, Sergeant."

Donnally traced his finger to a position on the map. "Right here, sir. It's a very isolated area, a lot to cover."

"We also found hoofprints in that area, sir," Yellow Horse said softly.

Dan's brows moved upward. "A horse?" He glanced over at Libby and then back at the Navajo woman. "You're sure?" His heart began to pound raggedly.

"Very sure, sir."

"Are the prints the same age?" Dan knew enough about tracking from his youth on the Navajo Reservation to know that tracks could be estimated as to how old they were, by hours or days. He held his breath, hoping Yellow Horse would tell him there was a difference in the age of the footprints of the person who'd fired the M-16 and the hoofprints.

"Sir, they were the same age."

He drilled Annie with a dark look. "You're positive?"

She stood confidently, her gaze unwavering. "Absolutely."

Sergeant Donnally made a sound of protest, then blurted, "Sir, how can you be positive about the age of a set of tracks?" He glared over at Yellow Horse and then looked back to Dan. "I mean, there are plenty of horse trails all over that area. Who's to say that a horse and rider didn't go through there an hour earlier and have nothing to do with this shooter?"

"I see your point," Dan said grimly, "but what you fail to understand, Sergeant, is that Corporal Yellow Horse can expertly judge the age of a track to within ten minutes."

Gasping, Donnally stepped back, his eyes black with anger. "That's not scientific—sir."

Dan smiled a little to ease the sudden tension filling the kitchen. "I grant you, on the surface it wouldn't seem to be, Sergeant. But trackers know."

"It would never stand up in a courtroom," Donnally growled defensively, casting a dark look at Yellow Horse, who stood without defending herself or her statement.

Libby watched the play going on among the three marines. It was obvious that Sergeant Donnally didn't like Annie Yellow Horse at all. Possibly he was threatened by her unique skills and talents. Libby was interested to see how Dan would manage this uncomfortable situation. Annie's face revealed no emotion, except that her brown eyes flashed with disgust at Donnally's reaction. Smiling to herself, Libby was impressed by the other woman's decorum in the face of an attack from her immediate superior, Sergeant Donnally.

Dan straightened and turned to Donnally. "Sergeant, what you should be aware of is that Corporal Yellow Horse has testified as an expert witness at many brig trials over the years on this very subject. She's in the record, and her opinion on the time and age of tracks is acceptable evidence for any courtroom case."

Grimly, Donnally muttered, "I stand corrected, sir."

Dan returned his attention to the map, then glanced at Yellow Horse. "Again, nice job, Corporal."

"Thank you, sir."

"Did you note anything else?"

"Yes, sir, I did." Stepping forward, Annie pointed to the area where the gunman had been hidden. "We followed the horse tracks leading out of the area, and they went back to the stable."

"Oh?" Dan couldn't keep the surprise out of his voice. He felt Libby move in close, resting her hand on his arm as she leaned over to look at Annie.

Donnally edged up to the table in turn. "Sir, we went toward the stable but lost the track near the creek among all the other hoofprints."

Libby gasped. "Oh, Dan, today's the first day of the new moon! Did anyone check on those five horses?"

Annie smiled at Libby. "Yes, ma'am, we did. Sergeant Donnally gave me the initial investigation report to read, and it mentioned those five horses, so we checked them out."

"And?" Libby held her breath, her fingers tightening on Dan's arm.

Donnally cleared his throat. "We found them, Captain. All five were in the paddock and didn't appear to have been ridden at all."

Libby gasped. "They weren't run down or tired? Their coats weren't wet?"

"No, ma'am. They hadn't been ridden," Donnally assured her. He cast a glance at Yellow Horse. "At least, that's what the corporal said."

Dan held up his hand. "Hold it. These two incidents may not be at all related." He scowled. "You weren't able to set up and watch the stables last night, were you, Sergeant?"

"No, sir, I wasn't, not with this other investigation on Ms. Tyler's behalf. I couldn't."

"Understandable," Dan murmured. Frowning, he straightened and thought for a moment. "You lost the print of that horse, right?"

"Well," Annie hedged, giving Sergeant Donnally an apologetic glance, "we did and we didn't."

"What do you mean?"

"I mean, sir, that we could go back out to that area, make a plaster indentation of those hooves and take it back to the stable and try to match it up with the horses that are kept there."

Donnally snorted violently. "Oh, come on, Corporal! You can't tell me horses' hooves are like human fingerprints! This is ridiculous!"

Dan glared at the sergeant, who quickly fell silent. Then he twisted his head toward the woman marine. "Yellow Horse?"

Annie hesitated as she took in Donnally's anger. "Well, sir, it's possible."

"I grew up on the Navajo Reservation at Fort Wingate," Dan told her.

Her eyes grew large. "You did, sir?"

"Yes. I know enough about horses to be dangerous, so you tell me what you think. We're on your turf. Tell us what you can do with this information."

Blushing, Yellow Horse stammered, "Well, sir, if I was given permission, I could take the plaster cast and go through the entire herd there at the stables to find out which horse it belongs to—if any of them. The one that made this print has a chip out of its right front hoof—too deep for a farrier to file off. In fact, the horse might even be lame because of it. I don't know. The shoe was missing on that same hoof, although the other three shoes were still on. I didn't find the missing shoe in the area, but it's probable that the horse lost it because it was being ridden very fast and hard over that rocky terrain. It might have gotten the chip in its hoof on the way out to the area where whoever was shooting wanted to hide."

"Hide?" Libby asked. She was fascinated by Yellow Horse's knowledge.

Dan's mouth quirked, and he gave the marine corporal a pleading look to say nothing. "Just a term we use," he lied to Libby. "Go on, Corporal."

"Yes, sir. I think we might find something based on that chipped hoof. At the paddock, I checked out the five horses that have been ridden hard before, and it wasn't any of them."

"I suppose," Donnally said sarcastically, "that if you find the horse with the chipped hoof, we'll have our culprit?"

"It's possible," Dan growled in warning to the belligerent sergeant. "At least it would be a start."

Chastened, Donnally remained in the background.

Dan swung his attention back to Annie, who stood at ease, her hands clasped behind her back. "All right, I want you to pursue this end of the investigation." Nailing Donnally with a dark look, Dan said, "And you get to ballistics and see if we can find anything further on those shell casings."

"Yes, sir," Joe muttered unhappily.

After they had left, Libby lingered over the map. She felt the tension and worry around Dan as he picked up the file folders and organized them in his large briefcase.

"I never realized horses had such individual hoof-prints," she said wonderingly.

"I learned that from my Navajo friends on the reservation," Dan said. He sat down and shut the briefcase. "I used to go out with them when they had sheep-herding duties. These kids could tell if coyotes were stalking the herd, and how old the tracks were. It always amazed me, but they were never wrong."

Sitting down, Libby rested her chin in her hands and gazed at Dan's closed features. "You're worried about something, Dan. What is it?"

"Nothing much," he hedged.

"I really like Annie Yellow Horse. She seems very professional and thorough."

"I like her, too. She doesn't miss much, does she?" Dan hoped their conversation would veer to anything but what was on his mind.

"She's so pretty in an unconventional sort of way, don't you think?"

He grinned a little. "I don't normally make those kinds of assessments about the people under my command, Libby."

"I think she's very exotic looking," Libby went on primly. "And I also think Sergeant Donnally has a real problem with her because she's a woman and very good at what she does. Don't you?"

With a shrug, Dan said, "Right on both counts."

"Just another skirmish you have to fix, right?"

He smiled up at her. "Right."

"But you like her."

"I like Yellow Horse's abilities. I fought hard to get her here, Libby. After I realized just how big this base is and the fact that we transport a lot of brig prisoners all over the U.S., I wanted someone with Yellow Horse's abilities in my pocket."

Relaxing, Libby said, "You're a very good manager of people, Dan Ramsey. I watched you play Sergeant Donnally. He was getting out of line, but you gave him one look and he settled down."

With a chuckle, Dan stood and hefted the briefcase to the chair. "And I think you're quite perceptive, Ms. Tyler."

"Well, you're a good teacher."

The urge to go over and kiss her was almost Dan's undoing. He stood uncertainly for a moment, bathed in Libby's glowing gaze, which was filled with pride in him. Absorbing her compliment, he smiled slightly. "You must be feeling better."

"Much," Libby agreed. "But I think it's the company I'm keeping."

Dan couldn't disagree. Still, worry chafed at him as he took the briefcase and set it by the entrance to the apartment. Tomorrow morning he had to go to work and leave Libby here with Rose. Nettled by what his brig chasers had found, he said nothing. Libby's life could be in very real danger.

Chapter Ten

On the last day of her stay at Dan's apartment, Libby tried to hide her excitement. Feeling much better, almost her old self, she'd shooed Rose home early and had worked the better part of the afternoon on making Dan a home-cooked meal. Last night he'd brought in pizza for dinner—for the second time in as many days, and she'd realized that he ate poorly living by himself.

When Dan came home, he inhaled deeply. Libby was standing in the kitchen doorway, smiling a welcome. How fresh and wholesome she looked in her jeans and a red tank top. Her hair was swinging about her shoulders and a devilish look shone in her eyes. Ever since their late-night kiss, their relationship had subtly changed and deepened. Setting his briefcase aside, Dan took off his garrison cap and hung it on the brass hat stand behind the door.

"Smells great. What is it?" Shutting the door, he sauntered toward Libby. Her cheeks were flushed and her eyes were sparkling—a sign that she was nearly recovered from the concussion.

"Good old Yankee pot roast, baked potatoes and carrots." Libby had to stop herself from leaning up on tiptoe to kiss Dan's well-shaped mouth which was drawn into a smile of welcome. The day had dragged by without his strong, quiet presence in her life, she'd discovered.

"Mmm, that sounds awfully good." He halted in front of her, achingly aware of the need to touch her. Dan had dreamed about their molten, unexpected kiss three nights ago—about Libby, and how much he wanted to take her not only into his arms, but to his bed. "You're looking awfully pretty this evening, too, Ms. Tyler."

"Thank you, Captain Ramsey. Come on in and we'll start with salad."

"Let me get out of this uniform first."

Libby nodded. "Sure." As she moved into the kitchen to take the salad out of the refrigerator, she marveled at the difference between Brad and Dan. Brad had practically lived in his uniform, not taking it all off until he got ready for bed. But the past two days she'd noticed that Dan shrugged out of the summer tans as soon as he arrived home. He lived in a pair of jogging shoes, old gray sweatpants and a red T-shirt that outlined his deep, powerful chest to perfection. If he was aware of her glances of appreciation, Dan never showed it. And in a way Libby was glad, because so many new and unexpected feelings bubbled up through her in his presence that she didn't know exactly what to do or how to cope with all of them.

At the dinner table, she passed Dan the platter bearing thickly cut slices of roast. "How was your day?"

"Interesting, to say the least." Dan took the platter and set it beside him. "Annie Yellow Horse is proving to be an indispensable asset, I'll tell you."

Libby spooned gravy over her potatoes and beef. "Oh?"

"She's a real bulldog when it comes to following through on an investigation. Not only did she find the horse with the chipped hoof, she found out that it's Stuart Garwood's personal mount there at the stable." Dan cast a glance at Libby, who had a shocked look on her face.

"Stuart's?"

"Yes."

Frowning, Libby chewed slowly, studying the careful, closed look on Dan's features. "What are you saying? That Stuart fired a rifle in a restricted area?"

"I don't know, Libby. Nothing is adding up or making sense yet," he murmured. "I'm running a background check on Garwood right now."

"But he doesn't own an M-16 rifle!"

"I don't know that. At least, I'm not assuming that."

"Dan, I've known Stuart for three years and he's a very nice person. Not only that, but he's been wonderful about expanding the riding programs for the base. He's put in at least ten new trails!"

"I know...."

She put her knife and fork aside and stared at him. "What does that mean?"

With a shrug, Dan murmured, "Libby, I didn't intend to upset you. Sergeant Donnally found out that Garwood wasn't in his office during the time you were fired upon. His secretary, Becky, said he'd come back about half an hour before I brought you to the office."

Her mouth dropped open. "Fired upon?" She blanched.

Dan saw her face go pale with the realization of what he was saying. Reaching across the table, he gripped her hand. "Listen, Libby, something's definitely going down out there at the stables. I don't know what yet, but I suspect Garwood is mixed up in it, somehow."

Moving her napkin aside, Libby pulled out of his grip. "You're implicating Stuart."

"There's a strong possibility he's involved," he replied. "Look, I didn't meant to bring this up now, Libby. It's a great dinner and I've ruined it for you—for us..."

Getting up, Libby moved to the counter and crossed her arms over her breasts. She studied Dan darkly. "Did you have someone at the stables last night to watch those five horses?"

"Yes, and nothing happened. There will continue to be a stakeout for the next three days," he said. Getting up, Dan moved to the counter and placed his hands on her tense shoulders. "I'm sorry I said anything, Libby. I should have timed it better so we could enjoy this meal you worked so hard to fix for us. I didn't mean to upset you like this."

His hands felt stabilizing after the shock she'd received. Allowing her arms to drop to her sides, she muttered, "I just find it so hard to believe you suspect Stuart. Of all people, Dan. He's a respected citizen. He cares about the kids and the dependents."

Giving her a small shake and a slight smile, Dan whispered, "I don't think you ever want to think ill of anyone, Libby. You're an idealist."

With a grimace, she gazed up into his concerned face. "And you're a realist."

"In my line of work, I have to be." His fingers tightened on her shoulders. "Look, until this case is solved, I don't want you riding alone anymore, Libby. There's no guarantee that you won't be shot at again. Next time, you might not be so lucky." He saw the fear in her eyes. "I'm not saying this to scare you, Libby. It's just that I—oh hell, I care a lot for you, and I don't want to see anything happen to you. Okay?"

His admission brought fresh panic on the heels of Libby's fear. She pulled away from him and moved into the living room, her arms wrapped about herself. Feeling him nearby, she cast a glance over her shoulder. Dan's brow was furrowed and his eyes were dark and unreadable. "The last four days have been like heaven and hell for me," she admitted, her voice husky with feeling. "Heaven because of you."

Dan moved to within a foot of her. "And the hell?"

"The past, old fears, old patterns raising their heads."

"I think I understand what you're saying, Libby."

With a sigh, she shook her head. "Then you're further ahead than I am. Being here with you makes me see so much, Dan." It made her want him, but she didn't dare say that. Anyway, Libby wasn't into disposable relationships. She never had been and never would be.

Standing behind her, he placed his hands on her shoulders. "What we have," he told her quietly, "is more heaven than hell. It's about separating the past from the present, Libby."

Closing her eyes, she leaned back against his stalwart, seemingly inexhaustible body. "You've worked through a lot of your past already, and I haven't. I need time, Dan."

"You have all the time you want," Dan assured her, forcing himself not to lean down and kiss her lower lip, barely quivering with the admission. Libby was afraid, and he, better than anyone, understood those feelings. Turning her around so that she faced him, he smiled tentatively. "Tomorrow morning when I take you home, I want you to promise that you'll continue to rest. I'm sure Dr. Ramirez isn't going to let you go riding right away."

"You don't want me at the stables?"

Dan shook his head. "Not right now. And I know how much you love to ride and teach your kids."

Libby wrestled with his request and understood it—from his perspective. In her heart, she didn't feel Stuart Garwood could be a killer, much less the one who had fired that rifle. But the reassuring warmth and strength of Dan's hands on her shoulders made her capitulate—for his sake. "Okay, I'll do whatever Dr. Ramirez orders."

"Good," Dan whispered, relieved.

Looking up at his face, at the lines created by the pain of life, Libby had the absurd thought of what it might be like to carry Dan's child deep within her body. The idea was so startling, yet so right, that she couldn't say anything. Instead, she digested the sensation. Unlike Brad, Dan would be a devoted father to his children, she was sure. Dan would look forward to nights off rather than heading back on base to be with the "boys."

"I'll try to be a good patient," Libby said wryly.

Two days later, Libby was back at the stables. Dr. Ramirez had given her a clean bill of health and told her not to do too much riding—whatever that meant. Libby arrived at noon—a time when Stuart Garwood always went to lunch over at the Officers' Club on base. The stable was relatively quiet in the heat of the day, with most of the trail rides over until late in the afternoon. In her riding clothes, Libby went into Garwood's office. No one was there. His secretary, Becky, had gone to lunch, too.

Libby walked into the back room, where Stuart had a large wall map of the riding trails all over the base and began to study it. Planting her hands on her hips, she craned her neck to take in the routes. The light was poor, so she turned on the overhead fluorescent fixtures. The eight-foot-high map displayed a marvel of trails highlighted in red, blue, yellow and green, spreading like tentacles in all directions from the stables. Frowning, Libby moved closer to the map. Someone had used a pencil to trace a new trail west to where the base met the Pacific Ocean and the interstate highway. The trail began at the stables.

"That's odd," she muttered, moving her finger across the faint line. Whoever had drawn it in had then erased it—or tried to. Libby didn't recognize the trail, the only one that stretched twenty miles across the base to reach the highway and the beach. Perhaps Stuart was planning a new eventing trail, which had been one of his longtime dreams. But why erase it, then?

Stymied, Libby decided to go check out the area herself. She left the stables and climbed into her car. It would take about an hour to reach the outlet point of that trail—if in fact there was one to be seen. She settled her sunglasses into place. The day was bright and hot, and she left the windows down in the car, the warm heat flowing through and lifting strands of her hair as she drove off the base.

Pulling to the shoulder of I-5, the huge interstate that ran the length of California, north to south, Libby pulled the hand brake and climbed out. She walked toward the fence marked Government Property No Trespassing. The six strands of barbed wire looked dangerous, and the white sand sucked at her boots as she drew abreast of the barrier. Across the busy eight-lane interstate lay small, white sand dunes that marched in formation to the blue Pacific Ocean. Many times, Libby knew, marines trained on these beaches, particularly when practicing amphibious landing or night patrols.

Approaching the barbed wire, she frowned. Taking off her sunglasses, she saw that the wire had been cut and repaired—not once, but too many times to count. Running her fingers across the wire, she walked another hundred feet. There were many breaks marring the fence—all carefully repaired to make it look as if the fence had never been cut at all.

Looking around, Libby saw no sign of footprints. Or did she? It was impossible to climb under or over the dangerous barbed-wire fence, but tufts of thin salt grass sprinkled the white sands and dunes on the other side. Was she seeing things, or were there hoofprints in the sand? Perhaps the wind had merely arranged the sand to make it look like prints of some kind? Libby wasn't sure at all.

A shiver moved up her spine, and she snapped her head up, feeling as if someone was watching her. Looking around, she saw only the nonstop traffic that moved between San Diego and Los Angeles speeding along the interstate. The dunes were empty except for some low-flying seagulls looking for food along the beach. Rubbing her arms, she decided to get back to the car. More than anything, she wanted to tell Dan of her discovery.

Dan didn't hide his surprise when Libby called on him at his office.

"Hi..." she said tentatively, sticking her head around the partly open door. "Do you have a few minutes?"

"For you, sure. Come on in and shut the door." Dan set aside a file and came around the desk. Libby looked windblown and breathless, her cheeks flushed a bright red. When he realized she was in her riding gear, he frowned.

"I know what you're going to say," Libby said, closing the door and standing with her back against it, "but I wasn't out riding."

"That's a relief." He grinned a little and gestured to the chair in front of his desk. "Come on in."

"I'll stay only a moment. I know you're busy." His desk was cluttered with more files than Libby could count. When the phone rang, he picked it up.

"Rose, hold my calls, will you? Thanks." He gestured toward a coffee dispenser in the corner. "Did Dr. Ramirez say you could drink coffee yet?"

"She did, and I'll have a cup," Libby said, sitting down. It had been nearly two days since she'd seen Dan, and she hungrily drank in the sight of him, feeling her accelerated heartbeat at his nearness. The heated look he gave her as he handed her the white ceramic mug made her suddenly nervous.

"How are you feeling?" Dan asked, dropping into his creaky chair behind the desk.

"Good as new," Libby said, sipping the coffee.

"You're up to something," he murmured. "I can see it in your eyes, Lib."

Smiling a little, she set the cup on the desk. "I don't know if I like a man who can read me so well."

Chuckling, Dan said, "In your case, it's probably a distinct advantage, Ms. Tyler. You get into trouble very easily."

Laughing, Libby stood up and borrowed a pen from his desk. She took a piece of paper and came around to where Dan was sitting. "I can't dispute your wisdom on that point, Mr. Prosecutor." Quickly, she told him about the map in Garwood's rear office and about checking out the fence line where the trail ended. Drawing a careful picture, Libby showed Dan what the repaired wire looked like.

"It's almost as if someone doesn't want anyone to know the fence has been cut, Dan."

With a scowl, he glanced up at her. "You say all six wires were cut, not just one or two?"

"All of them. Isn't that unusual?"

"Sure is." Dan studied her drawing. "I think we need to go out and take a look at it." Giving her an appraising glance, he said, "Nice piece of investigation."

"Thanks."

Dan put his hand over hers. "Next time, come to me with any ideas first, Libby. Please?"

His hand was warm and inviting. "I wasn't in any danger."

"I'm not willing to take that chance."

Her skin tingling, Libby withdrew her hand. The look in Dan's eyes left her needing him, the ache spreading through her like a hungry fire. There was no doubt in her heart or mind that Dan liked her and wanted her. All of her. "I guess I'm not used to being protected," she muttered, and took a step away from the desk.

Rising slowly, Dan said, "Libby, you have more ways to court trouble than anyone I've ever run into, with the possible exception of Annie Yellow Horse. Wherever she goes, trouble follows." He smiled a little when he saw her open her mouth to protest. "Maybe this is Annie's fault and not yours." Picking up the phone, Dan called his secretary.

"Rose, have Sergeant Donnally and Corporal Yellow Horse meet me down at motor pool in fifteen minutes. Thank you."

Hanging up the phone, he cast Libby a worried look. "I guess you need to come along and show us exactly where the fence is cut."

"I guess I do."

The cross-country ride in the official, olive green Humvee, a new generation spin-off of the Jeep, to reach the site from within the base caused Libby a lot of bruises. The three marines seemed impervious to the jolting ride. The Humvee whined as it crawled up and around the desert terrain, reminding Libby of a slow-moving plow horse. There was no road near where the wire had been cut, so the last mile was tortuous for Libby, who sat in the back with

Annie Yellow Horse. Dan sat in the passenger seat, a map spread across his lap, giving directions to Sergeant Donnally, who drove.

A little apprehensive because the two brig chasers were fully armed with pistols and M-16 rifles, Libby said little during the trip. She was amazed at Annie Yellow Horse's stoic features, which gave nothing away. The Navajo woman, who must have been in her late twenties, had an exquisitely carved face, high cheekbones and a beautiful copper complexion that emphasized her black hair. Her cinnamon eyes constantly scanned their surroundings, almost as if Annie had some kind of invisible rotating radar inside her head, Libby thought. Had Dan given his brig chasers orders to stay tense and alert?

"That's it!" Libby said, leaning forward, straining against the confining seat belt. She pointed her finger between Dan and Joe. "Right there in front of you."

Dan nodded and squinted against the bright sun that had dropped low on the western horizon. "I see it. Sergeant, let's stop here. If there are any tracks or footprints around, I don't want any treads chewing up the evidence."

"Yes, sir." Donnally brought the vehicle to a halt and shut off the engine.

Dan twisted in the seat, his gaze on Libby. "I want you to stay inside the Humvee."

Her mouth fell open. "But—"

Grimly, Dan looked out the window and then back at her. "This could be dangerous."

She shut her mouth and nodded. It hadn't been dangerous before, but then she remembered the cold, shivery feeling of someone watching her. "I'll stay here," she murmured.

"Good. All right," Dan told his chasers, "let's go and keep a sharp eye out."

Once outside the vehicle, Dan watched as Annie stood beside the Humvee, quickly appraising the surrounding white sand. He saw a lot of prints, but most of them had been nearly erased by the shifting sand and constant wind off the ocean, less than a quarter-mile away. Donnally watched his step and moved toward the fence to check it out, the M-16 on his hip, locked and loaded. Looking around, Dan saw what he thought were remnants of a trail leading inland.

"Give me a shout if you find anything, Yellow Horse."

"Yes, sir."

The farther inland Dan walked, the more visible the little-used trail became protected from the wind by the surrounding sand dunes. Hoofprints were clear here and there, deep and obvious. Cupping his hands to his mouth, Dan called for Annie who came quickly, jogging easily despite the gear she carried. Dan pointed to the prints.

"What do you make of this, Corporal?" He followed her as she knelt over the first set of prints.

Touching the surrounding sand, Annie said, "These are old, Captain."

"How old?"

"Hard to tell. Sand's different than soil."

"Your best guess?"

"Maybe three weeks?"

Dan straightened, keeping watch. "That would have been the last new moon."

"Sir?"

"Good work, Corporal. Can you tell me how many animals were here?"

Moving slowly down the trail carved into the sand, Dan watched her work with quiet precision. Yellow Horse was a godsend, he decided. No one else on the base had this kind of experience or savvy with tracking. She got to her feet and walked back to him.

"Four, maybe five horses."

"Probably five."

"Sir, they were very heavily loaded down."

"Oh?"

Annie pointed to one of the prints, almost six inches deep in the sand. "Yes, sir. Look here. The horse had to be carrying close to a hundred to a hundred and fifty pounds beyond a normal rider's weight to make a print that deep."

"Get Sergeant Donnally to take photos of whatever you deem worthy. And hunt around for anything else that might give us a shred of evidence."

"Yes, sir."

Dan made his way back to the Humvee. In full daylight, the place seemed safe enough. He opened the vehicle's door and sat down in the driver's seat.

"Something's going on here," he told Libby, and he filled her in on what they'd seen. She looked very still and pale in the back seat. And very much out of place in the military vehicle in her civilian clothes. Dan could see from the tension around her eyes that she wasn't relaxed.

"It doesn't make sense, Dan," she said finally. "I mean, if they were human footprints, then I'd say illegal aliens from Mexico were stealing across the base at night, trying to make their escape into the U.S."

"I know, I thought of that, too. The interstate is one of the main routes north for illegals. We're always catching them trying to cut across base property, too. But horses? Could it be that illegal aliens are being transported across the base at the darkest time of the month on stable horses?"

Shrugging, Libby said, "I don't know. I guess that's a possibility."

"Well, I'm going to check out that fence." He reached between the seats and gripped her hand. "You okay?"

"Yes, just a little jumpy, that's all."

His smile deepened. "And yet you were the one who was out here today all by yourself."

"That was different." Libby looked around the Humvee. "I don't like military things, Dan. I never have. Sitting in this thing is like sitting in a prison to me."

Squeezing her hand, he whispered, "I know. I'll make this investigation as quick as possible and we'll get back to the office."

"Okay..."

"You doing anything tonight for dinner?"

She saw the gleam in his eyes and went warm all over. "No."

"How about if I take you out?"

"For pizza?"

His laugh tore at her senses and made her ache to kiss him. "No, I promise, I won't take you out for pizza tonight, honey."

"Then I'll come." *Honey.* That one, wonderful word filled Libby with such powerful longing that she didn't want to look too closely at the feeling. Suddenly she felt euphoric—joyous and free. Free? Yes, she realized, Dan gave her a sense of freedom she hadn't known was hers to grasp. Sitting there, whispering his name in her heart, Libby watched him move toward the fence line. When he was in uniform, he was all business, and it was obvious the people under his command respected him. Dan was a good leader, Libby observed, but then he was good with her, too. She smiled softly and leaned back, not feeling as claustrophobic in the Humvee as before. Tonight, she thought, was going to be special. So very special...

* * *

Nervously, Libby turned in front of her bedroom mirror to look at the dress she'd chosen for dinner with Dan tonight. Castigating herself silently over such a trifle, she laughed out loud, the sound light and happy. The pale pink, side-draped jacquard dress had a V-neck and was softly shaped with a crossover surplice bodice that was caught into a very feminine bow on her hip. Because she was tall and, with her curvy figure, not the "ideal" of a thin model, she wondered if she was quite right for the dress.

"Well, it's too late to change your mind, Libby," she muttered, pushing her fingers through her sleek, burnished sable hair which shone with highlights in the light overhead. She'd chosen her mother's single strand of pearls and small pearl earrings as accents. Hurrying to the dresser, she touched dabs of spicy perfume to her pulse points and set the cut-glass container aside. There. Slipping into white heels and picking up her white purse, she was as ready as she'd ever be. The indelible memory of her kiss with Dan sizzled provocatively as she walked into the living room of her apartment. Her heart began to pound at the sound of the doorbell. It was Dan coming to pick her up.

Wetting her lips, Libby answered the door. The man who stood before her wasn't a marine anymore; her eyes widened as she took in the sight of Dan Ramsey. A teal blue, double-breasted sport coat emphasized the breadth of his shoulders and chest. The white silk shirt showed off a contemporary tie in shades of brown, yellow and teal, perfectly matching his tan slacks and dark brown loafers. His smile was very male as he met her gaze.

"I'd say this is one of the few times I'll ever catch you speechless."

With a laugh, Libby moved out onto the doorstep, locked the door behind her and stepped to his side. "I'd say you're right. I just never saw you dressed up. I mean—"

Dan laughed pleasantly. "You've never seen me in anything formal except a marine uniform."

Blushing, Libby murmured, "Precisely. You can put words in my mouth anytime, Counselor."

He'd like to kiss those ripe, red lips, not place words in them, Dan thought, but he kept the comment to himself. He was having trouble not staring like a love-starved sixteen year old at Libby. The silky material of the dress outlined her figure to stunning perfection, with a quiet elegance that set his blood pounding and an ache building deep within him. Taking her by the elbow, he guided her down the sidewalk toward his Corvette.

Sunset tinted the sky a pale pink, with the cover of darkness hovering not far behind. Dan drove to a quaint seaside restaurant in Carlsbad, a small town on the Pacific, south of Oceanside. The Stonegate Inn was a five-star restaurant that served the finest nouvelle cuisine in California, as far as Dan was concerned. Although the atmosphere was somewhat haughty, Dan liked the highly private booths, the low lighting and waiters who knew how to leave a couple alone to talk intimately.

He felt good about his choice when Libby recognized the restaurant. Her hands flew to her mouth, and those wonderfully liquid eyes widened with appreciation.

"Oh, Dan! This is such an expensive place!"

With a chuckle, he drove up to the front, where a valet waited to park the car. "An expensive place for a lady of quality. I hope you're hungry."

She turned and placed her hand on the arm of his jacket. "You constantly surprise me."

Glancing at her as he pulled the car to a stop beside the valet, he said, "Disappointed I didn't take you to a pizza place?"

Laughing, Libby slid out of the car when a second valet opened the door for her. Suddenly, all the trauma and confusion of the past few months lifted. When Dan offered her his arm, she took it shyly, moving with him into the elegant restaurant, her feet barely touching the ground.

"Tell me about your growing-up years," Dan said as he finished his soup.

Touching her lips with the fine linen napkin, Libby shrugged. "I was an only child. Mom and Dad married late, and she was thirty-eight when she had me. To say the least, I was a surprise to them.

"Actually, they both had been divorced before they met each other. Mom thought she was infertile." Chuckling, Libby said, "And here I am. Mom told me later that because she thought she couldn't have children, they didn't take any precautions. I was born nine months to the day after they were married. Pretty good, huh?"

"It sounds like even if you were a surprise, you were wanted." Dan smiled a little and enjoyed the low light touching Libby's face. She looked fully recovered from her accident except for the stitches that she'd carefully covered with her soft, curving hairstyle.

The waiter came and discreetly removed the soup dishes, placing small palate-cleansing dishes of sherbet in front of them.

"Wanted? Are you kidding? Mom had been dying to have a zillion kids."

"A zillion?" Dan baited her with a grin, spooning the orange sherbet into his mouth.

"Maybe that's a bit of an exaggeration."

Laughing, Dan enjoyed her impish expression. "Obviously loved."

"Very much so." Libby moved the sherbet aside and simply absorbed Dan's shadowed features. "I think we both were, and maybe that's what has given us the strength we've needed later on in life."

Reaching out, he captured her hands in his. "No doubt."

"Do you have any brothers or sisters?" Libby asked, feeling the warm strength of his hands on hers.

"Two younger brothers. Gil still lives in Fort Wingate and runs my folks' grocery store for them now that they've retired. In his spare time he's a volunteer firefighter and works a lot with the Navajo people."

"And your other brother?"

"Craig works for a company known as Perseus."

"Perseus?"

"Yes. It's a highly secretive company that has ties with the U.S. government."

"Sounds awfully exciting."

"Dangerous." Dan frowned. "Craig was in the Marine Corps as an aviator until he had a bad crash that killed his best friend. After he got out of the hospital, he walked away from the corps and joined this organization."

Moistening her lips, Libby said softly, "It sounds like he's had a rough life."

"Well," Dan said unhappily, "if he thought he was in hot water in the Marine Corps, Perseus is worse. It's sort of an undercover arm of the government, for when they need someone to pinch-hit who isn't in the FBI, CIA or national security."

"Like a mercenary?"

"Exactly."

"You worry for him, don't you, Dan?"

Gently turning her hands to admire their graceful length, Dan nodded. "Yes. Craig's the youngest. He's always been a rebel. I don't know, maybe Perseus is exactly what he needs. I hardly ever hear from him except on the rare occasion when he's returned to the U.S. from some assignment somewhere in the world."

"Makes being a prosecutor in the Marine Corps seem kind of tame in comparison?" Libby baited, seeing Dan wrestle with a gamut of emotions.

"The life of a mercenary isn't for me. I like working within the law and making it work for all of us."

Detecting some bitter feelings between Dan and his brother, Libby decided to change the topic back to herself. She found she wanted to open up to Dan and share her earlier years with him. "I know I always wished for a little sister. I never got one, but I think you're lucky to have two brothers. When I was growing up, I was horse crazy. My parents gave up trying to get me to ski. I didn't like the snow, either." She smiled fondly. "I guess that's why I moved to Florida, where I met Brad. I was happy when he got transferred to sunny southern California."

"Don't your parents want you to come and run the family business at some point?"

Libby shrugged lightly. "Dad would love nothing better, but I'm not the hard-nosed business type. I like the freedom of riding, taking off when I want to. Believe me, I know the responsibilities and hard work behind running a ski resort town, and I wouldn't like it."

"How do your folks feel about that?"

"Mom understands, but Dad is kind of sad about it. After Brad died, they tried to get me to move back to Vail, but I said no. Dad even offered to start up an eventing stable, hire a qualified trainer and all the horses I wanted as a carrot to get me back to Colorado."

He held her warm, lustrous eyes. "You're a tough lady to take on."

"You can't take me on unless I want you to."

"I'm finding that out." He grinned.

The waiter returned with their salads. After he left, Libby said between bites, "I've been thinking about what you said before—how I've used horses in my life as a replacement for the rest."

Dan knew "the rest" meant her marriage to Brad. "And?"

"I've just never met someone who had your insight, Dan." She nibbled at a piece of carrot. "Sometimes that scares me."

"In a good kind of way?" he suggested hopefully.

"Yes. How did you know?"

He smiled despite her ire. "Being the oldest of three brothers, I learned real fast to pay attention to small details—or get blamed for them."

"You should have been a psychologist," she accused sourly.

"I like being an attorney, thank you."

The main course came—*tournedos aux champignons.* The tiny tender steaks were served in a cream-and-red-wine sauce. Libby saw the pleasure in Dan's face as he slowly ate each succulent bite.

"There's no secret about how a woman can get to you— through your stomach."

"Guilty as charged."

A sudden joyousness swept through Libby as she met and held his smiling gaze. His fork was midway to his mouth, and he looked so very happy. Inwardly, Libby knew it was more than just the deliciously prepared food and the intimate atmosphere of the restaurant infecting her. She was savoring him as a man, a confidant and finally, as a friend.

The waiter came to offer dessert, and Libby wasn't sure she could eat one more bite.

"Tell you what," Dan said, "let's split a dessert. Your choice."

"Just like an attorney, right? You've learned the art of compromise."

"That way, I get at least half a dessert."

Laughing, Libby chose *charlotte de pommes*—cooked apples, peaches and pears enclosed in a crust shell and served with hot apricot sauce.

Lingering over freshly roasted Brazilian coffee, she held Dan's hooded gaze. The table had been cleared, a vase of fresh red and pink rosebuds lightly scented the air, and she couldn't question that he was the best company in the world.

"This sure beats pizza." She sighed, sipping her fragrant coffee.

"No argument from me."

Returning the fragile cup to its saucer, Libby set it aside. "The last couple of weeks," she began softly, "have been some of the happiest I've ever had, Dan."

"Good." He tried to still his suddenly pounding heart. Libby looked as if she were wrestling to say something important.

"Some of the best and some of the scariest."

"You scared me to death when you showed up on that trail with that injury," he murmured.

"I know...." She tilted her head and held his dark gaze. "There are moments when I feel like a bird freed from her cage, Dan. And other times I want the safety, the continuity of that cage."

"Living takes courage, Libby. It always has and it always will. I saw Craig fall back into the same repetitive lifestyle after his crash. He didn't have whatever it took to face the grief. Instead, he just walked from one dangerous occupation into another without missing a beat.''

"I guess I was an ostrich, too, after Brad and the baby died.''

"Libby, we all go through a grieving period, so don't be too hard on yourself.''

"Yes.'' She sighed again. "But you've been showing me that grief does come to an end, and it's time to pick up and start living again.''

Setting his cup down, Dan reached across the table and held her proffered hand. "I know you're making my life happier,'' he ventured huskily. "And my bet is on you to have the courage to live again, Libby—like you want to....''

Chapter Eleven

At the door to her apartment, Dan drew Libby into his arms. He wanted to say so much to her—how she'd made his life suddenly seem hopeful again, that he was falling in love with her.... But it was too soon. His fingers curving around her upper arms, he smiled down into her shadowed features.

"There's so much I want to tell you, Libby."

"I know," she whispered as she raised her hands against his chest. The evening and dinner had been wonderful, a special world where only laughter and joy existed. She saw the intensity in Dan's eyes and felt that incredible sense of power radiating from him and washing across her. It was a good feeling, one that broadcast his care, his love. Love? As Libby studied his serious features, she realized that somehow, at some time, she had begun to fall in love with this wonderful man.

The thought frightened her badly, and she lifted her hands from his chest. Seeing his disappointment, she forced herself to relax as they remained standing mere inches apart. How desperately she wanted him to kiss her this time. The errant thought had remained a heated, teasing possibility all evening long. Libby agonized over the fear that clashed with her desire. Would the past ever leave her alone enough so she could concentrate on the present? To focus on Dan as a man and not necessarily as a marine?

"A penny for your thoughts?" Dan asked as he slowly ran his hands up and down her arms. He saw the turmoil, the desire in her eyes, and he wasn't about to overstep their unspoken boundaries. Too much was at stake. There was no question in Dan's mind or heart that he loved Libby and that the feeling would only grow over time. She was the one who had to realize that she might love him, too—if only a little bit. Libby was unlike any other woman he'd met, and she was worth risking his heart and feelings for.

With a startled little laugh, Libby bowed her head. She felt the heat of a blush sweeping across her face. "I can't say it."

Dan's mouth curved slightly, and he lifted his hand and placed it beneath her chin. "Look at me," he whispered hoarsely.

Just that one, tender action broke through the turmoil in Libby's questioning mind and caused her to open her heart. His eyes were hooded and dark with desire, and it was as if all the chains from the past slipped free of her as he brought her against him and lowered his head to kiss her. Nothing had ever seemed so right to Libby as his mouth meeting hers, easing her lips apart to taste her. Drinking in his scent, she slid her arms around his neck, melting against him until her whole world was focused only on him. His mouth was strong without being overbearing, eliciting bolts of jagged heat that trembled through her until she sagged against him, her knees weakened by his molten onslaught.

Slowly, ever so slowly, Dan broke the kiss that bound them. They were both breathing hard, his body on fire and demanding. Libby's surrender to him had been unexpected. He'd feared she'd resist his need to kiss her, but she hadn't. As he eased her away just enough to look into her lustrous eyes and see the soft tremble of her lower lip, he began to realize the extent of her feelings toward him.

"Lady," he whispered hoarsely, "you could make a grown man cry for a chance to kiss you again like that."

Dazed, wrapped in the euphoria of longing, Libby gave him a confused look. All her senses were focused on Dan—his well-shaped mouth; his hands, which felt like little brands of fire on her back; the hunger burning in his eyes. Lifting her hand, she grazed his cheek.

"I never knew it could be like this," she whispered faintly, and saw his very male smile appear.

"I didn't either, honey." Dan knew if he didn't let her go then and there, he'd sweep her into his arms, carry her into her apartment and make torrid, nonstop love with her. Capturing the hand that cupped his cheek, he kissed her fingers gently. "Come on, it's past your bedtime."

Belatedly realizing that Dan was right, Libby acquiesced. As she opened the door with trembling fingers, other concerns disturbed her pleasure. "Dan, please be careful tomorrow." He'd told her that he was driving up to Treasure Island with two of his brig chasers to pick up a highly dangerous prisoner, Dutch Gorman, a convicted murderer.

"It will be a piece of cake, Lib." The small worried frown didn't disappear from her brow, so Dan leaned over and kissed it away. "I'll be gone until late tomorrow night, so I'll call you the next day. Okay?"

"Okay." As Libby stood there and watched him walk back to his car beneath the streetlamps, she shivered. It was the same old fear she'd felt every time Brad went out on a night flight. Slowly closing the door, she felt her desire, her longing, being crushed beneath the fear of losing Dan.

Moving through the darkened living room to her bedroom, Libby set her purse on the dresser and slipped out of her heels. She fought the feeling valiantly and tried to tell herself that this time it was different. But was it really? No. Dan worked with highly dangerous navy personnel and marines who had broken the law and were now housed in the military prisons called brigs. She'd tried to hide her worry when Dan had told her that tomorrow he'd be part of the escort bringing Gorman from T.I. down here to the base. Eventually, Dan had told her, he'd be taken to Fort Leavenworth in Kansas as a final destination. But all the paperwork had to be done here at the base, because he was a marine and the crime had been committed at Reed.

Gnawing at her lower lip, Libby undressed and started water running in the tub. Slipping on a housecoat, she stood in the doorway, her mind and emotions swinging erratically. A year ago, Sergeant Dutch Gorman had murdered two fellow marines on the base—in cold blood. He was a dangerous psychopath, not to be trusted. Dan hadn't wanted to tell her, but Libby had dragged the information out of him on the way home from the restaurant. Now she wished she hadn't.

Shutting off the tub, Libby sprinkled lilac-scented bath salts into the water. Putting the robe aside, she lowered herself into the warm, fragrant tub. With a sigh, she lay back and allowed the water to take the edge off her worry for Dan's safety. He'd assured her that Gorman would be at the brig at Reed for only a week during processing. Dan was going to assign Donnally and Yellow Horse to drive

Gorman to NAS Fallon, Nevada. It wasn't uncommon to transport dangerous prisoners by car instead of plane, to protect unsuspecting passengers. Libby was just glad Dan didn't have to go with them.

Tomorrow, since Dan would be gone, she wanted to investigate that trail she'd discovered. Early in the morning, around seven, she would go to the stable, saddle up Shiloh, put a lunch in the saddlebags and try to see if the trail did, indeed, lead from the stable to the exit point along the ocean beach and interstate. She knew Dan wouldn't want her to do it, but her instincts needed to be satisfied. Besides, she didn't believe her life was in danger. The last night of the new moon would be three days from now, and Libby knew Dan carried a paging device on him. If there had been any activity tonight with the five horses at the stable, he'd have been alerted because Donnally had been staked out there earlier.

Closing her eyes, Libby succumbed to the water and relaxed completely. She liked her plan and hoped to have more useful information for Dan when he called two days from now.

"Whew," Libby murmured to Shiloh as she dismounted beneath the hot, overhead sun. It was midafternoon, and she was five miles from the stable area after following the trail to the fence and back to this point. Her gelding was wet with sweat from the constant trotting; they'd covered forty miles since early morning. Discovering that the trail swerved and met a little-used back road, Libby walked around the area, careful not to destroy any tracks.

Shiloh snorted as Libby slowly began her search. The long, hard ride had done her good. She'd missed being in the saddle, missed being outdoors and inhaling deep drafts of fresh air. Today would be a perfect day—except that Dan wasn't with her. She worried about him, and once she got back to the stables and rubbed down Shiloh, she was going to call him on the chance he had returned from Treasure Island.

Spotting a piece of brown fabric clinging to a low brush, Libby went over and gently extricated it from the branches. It was a torn fragment of burlap. Tucking it into her pocket, she continued to search the area for clues, then finding nothing more, decided to get back to the stables.

After rubbing down Shiloh and giving him a well-deserved quart of sweet feed, Libby left the shelter of the box stall. It was after five o'clock, and the wranglers and office workers had left for the day. Climbing the steps to Stuart's office, she found the place empty. Picking up the phone, she dialed the PM's office.

"Hi, Rose?"

"Yes?"

"This is Libby. I'm calling from the stables office. Is Captain Ramsey back from T.I. yet?"

"No, Libby. Why?"

She smiled, liking the secretary immensely. "I was out on that trail that Dan looked at the other day and I found a piece of fabric near it."

"Why don't you drop it off? I can have the lab analyze it for us."

"I think it's just an old piece of burlap, Rose."

"Doesn't matter."

"So you think this burlap might be important?"

"It could be. Until the lab analyzes it, I can't say for sure."

"Okay, I'll be right over."

"See you in a little while."

Libby hung up the phone and exited the office. The sun was hanging low on the horizon, sending long, brilliant shafts across the loaflike hills. Getting into her car, she drove out of the stables area and headed for the PM's office.

Rose smiled in greeting when she entered the facility. "My, you look much improved over the last time I saw you!"

"I feel a hundred percent better," Libby agreed. She pulled the fabric from her pocket and handed it to the secretary. "This is what I found where the trail intersected an old, unused road."

Frowning, Rose gingerly placed the fabric into a small plastic bag and closed it securely. "Do me a favor?"

"Sure."

"Draw me a map of where you found this." Rose handed her a small copy of a base map.

Libby came around the desk and bent over it, pen in hand.

"Does the captain know you were out snooping around?" Rose asked in a low voice.

"No. He'd hit the roof if he found out, too."

Rose shrugged. "I can't hide this information from him, Libby."

"I know," she said, concentrating on the map. "He just worries about me, that's all."

"No kidding." She gave Libby a pointed look. "The guy is head over heels for you, in case you didn't notice."

"Rose!"

"Libby!" Rose wagged her finger in Libby's face. "And don't pretend you don't know it."

Sobering, Libby finished the drawing and handed it to the secretary. She kept her voice low, not wanting the other office people to overhear. "He's wonderful, Rose. A dream come true."

"So what's your problem? Instead of running to him, you're running away."

Rubbing her hands on the thighs of her breeches, Libby held the secretary's blunt stare. "It's just that—well—I'm afraid, Rose."

"Afraid?"

"Yes. Afraid that Dan could get killed just like Brad did."

With a snort, Rose muttered, "Libby, you could get killed just as easily, probably easier, on that horse of yours!"

"I hadn't looked at it that way."

"Yeah? Well, I know Dan does."

"Really? How do you know?"

Rose glanced around and said gruffly, "Because he's said so, that's why! Sometimes when I barge into his office, he's standing at the window in thought. I can tell he's worrying. When I bug him about it, he eventually admits he's worried about you, about riding and all. You falling off the other day didn't exactly help his state of mind. The man was wrestling with a lot of emotions after he found out you were hurt, you know."

Avoiding Rose's gaze, Libby whispered, "I didn't know, Rose."

"Maybe it's morbid, but the truth is both of you could either be hurt or killed at any time. You could die in a car accident, for heaven's sake."

"Or," Libby reminded her sourly, "escorting dangerous brig prisoners."

"That's true. What I'm trying to say is that life is full of dangers and potential injury. So why hold the fact that Dan's a marine over his head? You think only marines die in this world? Just take a look at how many people die from cancer or heart attacks, for instance.'' Rose leaned back, her ample girth making the chair creak in protest. ''I think you need to get real about this, Libby. I like both of you a lot. I think you're perfect for each other. And I hate to see you keeping him at arm's length because you're scared. You'd better examine just exactly what you're really scared of. If you ask me, this is about commitment, not about Dan being a marine.''

Libby stood quietly, absorbing Rose's impassioned words. In turmoil, she said in an off-key voice, ''Have Dan call me tomorrow, Rose. I'll be over at the stables teaching classes.''

''Sure....''

Dan tried to ignore the exhaustion he felt as he entered his office the next morning. They'd gotten back from T.I. at 0200, and it had taken until 0330 to finish up the transfer paperwork on Gorman at the brig. As a dangerous prisoner, he'd been taken to solitary confinement for the coming week until it was time to transport him to Fort Leavenworth.

Dan was in his office, rummaging through the stack of phone messages, when Rose entered with a cup of black, steaming coffee. He looked up.

''How did you know?''

Rose grinned and handed him the coffee. ''You've got rings under your eyes, Boss.''

''I was lucky I didn't cut myself shaving this morning,'' he murmured, taking a sip of the hot liquid. ''Thanks.''

Rose waved several papers under his nose. ''Take a look at these. Libby was busy yesterday and found something mighty interesting out on that trail by the interstate.''

Scowling, Dan set the cup aside and took the papers. "What do you mean? Libby wasn't supposed to be riding yesterday. She's still recuperating."

Rose closed the door and said, "Now, you know better than that, Dan. She's not the kind of woman who likes to stay indoors twiddling her thumbs. Look at the lab report. Go on, read it."

Dan swung his attention to the report and his frown deepened. "They found traces of cocaine on a piece of burlap fabric that Libby found yesterday?"

"Bingo. Boss, I think we've got a cocaine connection going on between somebody in the stables and someone out at the highway."

Shaken that Libby had been on that trail and by the possible danger to her, Dan rapidly scanned the results. Then, dropping the paper on the desk, he placed his hands on his hips. "Rose, get Libby on the phone. Right away."

Rose grimaced slightly. "She's at the stables this morning teaching her kids...."

Biting back a curse, Dan nodded. "Okay, just get her on the line. Does she know about the cocaine?"

"No, she doesn't. She thought it was just an old scrap of burlap she found out on the trail."

"Damn," he whispered, rubbing his recently shaved jaw.

"I'll call Libby right away."

"Please. I want to talk to her." Fuming after Rose left, Dan felt his emotions swing between anger and panic. His heart was pounding hard with fear. Fear for Libby. She could have been hurt on that trail. No one knew who was running cocaine, and Dan was sure whoever it was wouldn't hesitate to kill if someone got in their way—innocent or not. Punching his intercom, he called Sergeant Donnally. When the marine appeared in the doorway, Dan waved him inside.

"Sergeant, I think we've tripped onto a cocaine connection."

"Sir?"

"At ease," Dan muttered. He spread the map out on his desk and jabbed his finger at the interstate area where the fence had been cut. "I think I know what's going down. Someone is using five horses from the stable under the dark of the new moon to transport drugs from the interstate, across our base and out the rear gate. That's why that fence has been cut and repaired so many times. Those same horses are used every month because they're dark colored and can't be easily spotted. Yellow Horse said the animals were carrying excess weight. My hunch is that they're carrying large burlap bags in front and behind their saddles, and the bags are filled with cocaine."

Donnally nodded. "And once they get the drugs to the stable, they can be taken by car out the rear gate where there's rarely any inspection done on the vehicles."

"Exactly." Dan's mind was racing ahead. "We know that inspection of every vehicle is mandatory, but at some of the less-used gates, such as the one near the stables, it doesn't happen."

"Or," Donnally murmured, "people who work on the base and are familiar to the gate guards are never inspected."

"Right," Dan whispered roughly.

"Captain?" Rose stuck her head around the door. "Bad news. I can't raise Libby at the stables."

"What?" he growled, snapping his head in her direction.

Rose, obviously worried, entered the office and shut the door. "She's not there. No one's seen her."

Dan glanced at his watch. "It's 0900."

"I know that," she said, trying to keep the alarm out of her voice. "She might be sick. Call her apartment, Rose."

"I already did." She gulped unsteadily and said, "There's no answer...."

His heart pounding harder, Dan tried to control his reeling emotions. He saw the grim look on the sergeant's face and read the same expression on Rose's features. "All right," he rasped tightly, "who knew Libby had found that burlap?"

"No one, as far as I know," Rose said lamely.

"How did you find out about the fabric?" Dan demanded, his hands resting tensely on his hips. He tried to control the panic rising in him.

"She called me."

"From where?"

"Oh, dear. She called me from the stables office." Rose's eyes grew wide and she looked at Donnally and then at Dan. "Someone could have overheard the call. Oh, dear...."

Cursing softly, Dan came around his desk. "Libby may have been kidnapped." Or worse. Trying to get hold of himself, he jerked a look in Donnally's direction. "Get down to the stables and search for Libby. Take Yellow Horse with you."

"Yes, sir!"

Dan stabbed a finger in the sergeant's direction. "Call the moment you find her. Rose, send Shaw over to her apartment to make damn sure she's not there and just not answering the phone."

Dan stood in the gathering silence after his people had left, his chest tight with pain—and real fear. It wouldn't do him any good to go galloping off in search of her. No, he had to remain here, to coordinate the search. But what if they didn't find her? Oh, God. . . . He shut his eyes tightly and leaned heavily against the desk, his fists clenched.

"Captain, I think we found something." Donnally was calling on the phone from the stables.

His hand tightening on the receiver, Dan tried to steel himself. It had been two hours since the search for Libby had been initiated. Shaw had found her apartment empty and Libby's car gone. "What?"

"We talked to one of the dependents out here and she says she saw Libby around 0600."

Trying to keep his voice steady, he said, "And?"

"That was it. She saw Ms. Tyler in Shiloh's box stall, currycombing him."

"And Libby's nowhere in sight?"

"No, sir."

"What about her car?"

"No sign of it, sir."

"Is Garwood there?"

"Yes, sir, and we've been grilling him. He appears to be as worried as we are."

Exhaling, Dan said, "Is it possible Libby left and might be over at the Exchange or something?"

"Anything's possible," Donnally conceded. "Ms. Tyler has a 1600 class here at the stables. If she doesn't show up for that, maybe we ought to get worried."

"You're right, Sergeant. You get over to the Exchange. I'm ordering Shaw to remain at her apartment in case she shows up. This may all be an exercise that means nothing."

"I understand, sir."

Putting the receiver back in its cradle, Dan rubbed his face angrily. Was he overreacting? Was Libby just making her morning rounds, shopping for groceries or running errands on or off the base? Feeling a bit foolish, he sat down. How could he stand to wait until 1600, half a day away, to see if she showed up? His gut clenched at the feeling of helplessness. A call from Donnally at 1600 would confirm if Libby was really in trouble or not. Until then, he had to wait.

Or did he? Sitting up, he hit the intercom button.

"Yes, sir?" Rose said.

"Call the airport, Rose, and order a helicopter to be standing by in half an hour. I'm going to check out that trail by air."

"Yes, sir."

Dan grabbed his garrison cap, settled it on his head and left his office. Somehow, that trail might be implicated. He went first to the lab in the basement of the PM building and picked up the equipment necessary for taking photos and casts of tracks. In the back of his mind, the unused road Libby had stumbled upon while riding the trail kept gnawing at him. Doing something, anything, would help the time pass more quickly.

The helicopter pilot set the aircraft down a quarter of a mile from the intersection between the old road and the trail. As the whirling blades slowed, Dan left the craft. He jogged in the late-morning sun toward the intersection, gear in hand. The day was turning hot and still, and a film of sweat coated his face. The hills around him were silent.

Finding the road, Dan saw where the trail paralleled it. Libby had been right—there were plenty of tracks, both hoofprints and footprints. Unlike sand, the soil held the prints more clearly for a longer period of time. Leaning down, he quickly took several photos of tire treads, wishing that Yellow Horse were here. He felt a sense of urgency to gather the evidence.

Within fifteen minutes, he had what was necessary. The helicopter would make a quick trip back so he could get the evidence to the lab, and then, by late afternoon, they would have some answers. Maybe.

Four hours later, Dan scanned the information the lab had sent him and called in Yellow Horse. When she arrived, she came to attention in front of his desk.

"At ease, Corporal."

She nodded. "Yes, sir."

Dan handed her several photos. "The lab has identified these tracks as belonging to a truck of some sort, probably a heavier model, like a three-quarter-ton size."

Looking over the photo, Annie nodded. "There are several trucks of that size at the stables, sir."

"That was my guess," Dan said, sitting back in his chair. He glanced at his watch. It was 1500, one more hour before Libby was due to show up for her riding class. "Go down there and check it out. You're my tracking expert. See if any of these photos match up with any of the vehicles. If they do, call in the license number. *Don't* try to find out who owns it. I don't want to stir up suspicion. At least, not yet."

"May I make a suggestion, sir?"

"Yes."

Annie looked at her uniform. "Let me go in civilian clothes, so I'll be less obvious. I can check the treads out without attracting attention."

"Good idea," Dan said swiftly. "Sergeant Donnally will go down there on official business with one of our vehicles at 1600."

"Yes, sir, to see if Ms. Tyler shows up. I understand, sir."

As Annie moved toward the door, Dan said, "Just be careful...."

Swiveling in his chair, he stared, unseeing, out the window. Libby still hadn't turned up. His fear was mounting to a point where he felt as if he would begin to howl like a wolf who had lost his mate. The last half day had torn away any doubt that he loved her—unequivocally. And just when he'd found the woman he knew he could share a lifetime with, she could be kidnapped or hurt. Or dead. A bitter taste filled Dan's mouth as he slowly got out of his chair and began to pace. One hour to go, and he didn't know if he could stand the pain of waiting that long.

The phone rang at 1345. Dan grabbed it.

"Captain Ramsey speaking."

"Sir, it's Corporal Yellow Horse."

Dan tried to steady his voice. "Yes?"

"I found an exact match of tread to your photo, sir. It's a black Jeep Cherokee and it belongs to Mr. Stuart Garwood."

Shock rooted Dan to the spot. "Did he see you out there snooping around?"

"No, sir, he was riding a horse in the lower arena and couldn't see the parking area at all. He's still over there."

His heart throbbing in his throat, Dan rasped, "Are you positive the tread is a match?"

"Positive, sir. The photo shows a slight crack between two of the treads that makes a snakelike pattern. Mr. Garwood's left rear tire has the exact same pattern."

"All right, get back here, Annie. You've done good work."

"Sergeant Donnally just drove in."

"Good. Hightail it over here. If Ms. Tyler doesn't show up, then we've got to develop a plan of action."

"Sir, you realize that tonight is the last night of the new moon?"

"It hasn't escaped me, Corporal."

"Might Garwood or whoever he's in cahoots with try to move that cocaine tonight under cover of darkness?"

"Anything's possible. We'll talk about it as soon as we find out if Ms. Tyler is missing."

Every face around the command room table was grim. It was 1700, and Dan had to put his worry for Libby on hold—or at least now show it. All available brig staff had gathered in the large room in the basement of the complex. Libby had not shown up for her class, even though her ten students had. He knew that if she was okay, she'd be there no matter what, so it indicated the worst: she was being held against her will, or... He didn't want to look at the other alternative. Not yet.

"Our plan," Dan said in a low voice to his personnel as he held a pointer to a wall map of the base, "is to let Mr. Garwood and his cronies, whoever they are, think that tonight is a good night to move cocaine via horseback across the base. Recon patrols are already setting up under cover of darkness within half a mile of the trail and will follow any horse and rider's progress via infrared detecting equipment. They will then radio back to me. Half of the brig force will remain at the stables area, out of sight. The other half will be in vehicles, covering the other end of the trail along the interstate.

"I've alerted a navy SEAL contingent, just in case our cocaine connection is coming in by boat off the ocean and not by vehicle. As soon as darkness falls, they will set their people up and the Coast Guard will have a cutter monitoring all boat traffic in the area."

Dan swallowed and continued to look stern. Inwardly, he was dying a little at a time with worry over Libby. "There's a possibility that Ms. Libby Tyler, the base riding instructor, might have been kidnapped. We could end up with a hostage situation. We just don't know. So, be on the lookout for her. Shaw is distributing a photo of her so you can identify her, and be very careful if a firefight breaks out."

Colonel Edwards cleared his throat from his position at the other end of the highly polished oval table. "Just what makes you think Garwood is involved with this, Captain?"

"Corporal Yellow Horse opened up the rear of his vehicle and took dirt scrapings from it. The lab has confirmed small traces of cocaine in the dirt."

Surprised, Edwards nodded. "Good work. Now, what makes you think Garwood and his gang will ride tonight?"

"There's no assurance, Colonel. But it's the last night of the new moon."

"Did Garwood know you were checking him out today?"

"He knew we were waiting for Ms. Tyler to show up, that was all. My people gave no indication that he's a suspect."

"Excellent."

"At 2100, Teams A and B will be in place," Dan ordered. "The recon captain in charge along the trail will call me if they see anything. From that point, I'll orchestrate the capture of whoever we can get at the fence area along the interstate."

"You've no doubt called in the California Highway Patrol and alerted DEA agents?"

Dan nodded. Since they would be operating off government land, the local police and federal officials would have to be in on the bust, should one occur. On the other hand, the recon patrol would be the capturing force should the suspects ride back onto the base. His only unanswered question was where was Libby?

Chapter Twelve

Garwood leaned down and hauled Libby Tyler out of a small cubbyhole between two huge stacks of bailed hay. "Sit up!" he snarled.

Libby moaned as the large, powerful man jerked her upward. It was dark now, and she'd lost track of time since being attacked from behind in Shiloh's box stall this morning. Her hands were bound, a gag covered her mouth and her knees were like jelly, buckling beneath her.

"Dammit!" Garwood growled. He stepped aside and allowed Libby to fall to the straw-covered floor of the hay mow. "Martin! Get her into the trunk. Now!" He straightened, satisfied. They'd gotten rid of her car by parking it off the base so it couldn't be discovered. No one knew her whereabouts.

Sobbing, Libby tried to dodge Martin's hand, but it was no use. Circulation to her legs had long ago been cut off because her captors had literally stuffed her into a tiny room she'd never known existed in the barn at the end of the box-stall area. Tears squeezed from her eyes and soaked into the filthy gag tied across her mouth. She was dizzy, almost incoherent, barely able to control the movements of her body. Once Garwood had pinned her to the floor of Shiloh's box stall, a second man had come in and jabbed a needle into her thigh, and she'd quickly lost consciousness. Martin gave up trying to make her stand and simply threw her over his shoulder.

With a groan, Libby felt her world turn upside down. Where were they taking her? She lifted her head, groggy and disoriented, and tried to see, but the darkness was complete except for the stab of an occasional flashlight. Fear came vomiting up through her as Libby was carried to an awaiting Jeep Cherokee backed up to the barn entrance. She recognized it as Stuart Garwood's.

As her head cleared momentarily, Libby realized she'd been drugged earlier and had collapsed into the straw seconds later. The last thing she remembered was Shiloh jumping to one side and nickering nervously. Whatever drug she'd been given was still potent within her, and with the realization came the fear that her life was in very real jeopardy.

Martin grunted and set her on the end of the opened tailgate of the Jeep. Unceremoniously, he shoved Libby inside, slammed the door and locked it.

"She's in, boss."

"Good. Let's get going."

From the darkness of the rear, behind the seats, Libby felt the Jeep fill up with men. Their voices were low and tense. Frantically, she worked at the gag in her mouth with her bound hands. It was off! Lying there, gasping for breath, Libby felt completely exhausted by her efforts. Her mouth hurt badly and her teeth ached. She had no memory of the tight gag being placed in her mouth or of her hands being bound and knotted with a leather strap.

The Cherokee lurched forward, and Libby was bumping around in the rear. She tried to steady herself with weak legs that refused to respond, and she knocked her head several times before she managed to position herself tightly against the rear seat. Soon the bumping stopped and she realized they were on smooth asphalt highway. Where were they taking her? Her mind was spongy and kept shorting out. She couldn't see distinct shapes, only blurs. And the men's voices sometimes faded, then came back sharply so that she could hear them talking.

"Is Chico goin' to have that Peruvian tuna boat offloadin' the stuff on schedule?" Martin demanded.

"Of course!" Stuart grunted. "This time, we'll pick it up in vehicles. I'm too nervous with those brig chasers snooping around here lately to use the horses."

"Smart move," Martin commented sarcastically. "Why the hell did you drug Tyler."

"She was getting too close," Garwood said.

"That's why the brig chasers were around today, dammit!"

"What was I supposed to do?" Garwood's voice rose with authority as he turned and glared at the man in the back seat. "I heard her making that phone call to the PM's office. I'm sure if they analyze that scrap of burlap she found, they'll be on to us. Hell, I'm not even sure they don't know now."

Libby heard a distinct click, the locking and loading of a weapon, and it made her freeze with terror.

"Well," Martin drawled, patting his M-16 rifle, "we'll blow 'em away if they're on to us. Besides, they're too stupid to put two and two together that fast. If anything, that new captain will have his brig chasers waiting out at that old road on the base!" He guffawed loudly.

Libby tried to steady her breathing and focus solely on the conversation among what seemed to be four men in the vehicle. She worked on the leather strap that had long ago numbed her wrists and fingers. With her teeth, she tugged and yanked at the knot repeatedly.

"Yeah," another man, the driver, said, "just don't get too cocky, Martin. I hear that Captain Ramsey hates drugs. That's why they brought him here, to set up a drug center and put nice guys like us out of business."

Martin snorted. "This last run will net us a cool five million. We'll blow this base and disappear. Ramsey can have it."

"What about the woman?" the driver said.

Libby froze, waiting.

"We'll give her an overdose at the pick-up point. Martin, you take her across the interstate before she collapses on you. Valesquez, who's doing the drop, will take her aboard his boat."

"She headin' to Peru dead?" Martin snickered.

"Her body will never turn up here. I have no intention of taking a murder rap for the nosy bitch, and this is a safe way to get rid of her and the evidence at the same time."

"That Peruvian tuna skipper will drop her body at sea somewhere way south of us, is that it?" Martin demanded.

"Very far south, probably around Colombia."

Her heart pounding, Libby lay very still. Trying to still her panic, she grappled for some kind of coherency. They were planning to kill her! *Oh, God. Dan!* She shut her eyes tightly, tears stinging the backs of them. Why hadn't she listened to him? Her trusting nature had gotten her into trouble. Blinking away the tears, Libby lay there in anguish. Dan would never know she loved him; she'd never have a chance to tell him. And it was love, she admitted with a heartrending finality. He'd never find her body. There'd be no sign of her ever again.

Trying to work the knot loose despite her lack of strength, Libby felt a panic she'd never known before. As she lay in the dark, frantically trying to free herself, she prayed to be given one last chance to escape. Whatever it took, she would make one last bid for freedom. She loved Dan too much not to try.

"They're coming," Donnally said in a very low tone, from his position behind a small sand dune that straddled the fence between civilian and government property.

"Roger." Dan held the M-16 with the infrared scope steady and saw a black Jeep Cherokee slowing down on the interstate. His heart was pounding hard, and he wondered if Donnally and Yellow Horse could hear it. On the other side of the interstate was a recon team, hidden behind the dunes in the darkness. On base property, another recon team waited under the cover of darkness.

"Tiger One, this is Tiger Two. Over."

Dan held the handset close to his mouth, his gaze riveted on the approaching vehicle in front of them. "Tiger One, over."

"The Peruvian tuna boat is anchored two hundred feet offshore. There's a small boat coming ashore with two men in it. Shall we interdict them once they're on the beach? Over."

Dan was grateful for Tiger Two, call sign for the Navy SEAL team that had waited for hours out in the water of the Pacific ocean while the Coast Guard had tracked the foreign tuna boat up the coast. "Roger."

"Two out."

"It's Garwood," Donnally growled, tensing.

Placing the handset close to his lips, Dan waited. The headlights of hundreds of cars racing up and down Interstate 5 flashed constantly. It was hard on everyone's night vision. He saw four men slowly exit the vehicle, all of them looking across the lanes of traffic toward the beach.

"They must be waiting for the tuna boat," Donnally whispered tersely, his M-16 locked and loaded.

"Wait!" Yellow Horse pointed to the vehicle. "Look, Captain!"

Dan's mouth thinned. One of them was dragging a fifth person, someone who was weaving like a drunk, around the rear of the car toward the group. His eyes widened. "It's Libby!" His voice cracked, and he had to force himself not to move. His mind spun with options. With questions. Were there any more cars coming, to be involved in this heist? If he sprung the trap too soon, part of Garwood's gang might escape. He had to wait. It was the last thing he wanted to do as his eyes narrowed on the large man who jerked Libby toward him. It was impossible to determine her condition in the darkness and the flash of headlights.

"They've drugged her," Yellow Horse volunteered, her voice tight with anger. "Drugged or injured her. She can hardly stand."

Cold fury wound through Dan as, tense and alert, he lay on his belly in the sand. How badly he wanted to apprehend Garwood, who stood near the fender, hands on hips, watching the beach for some sign.

"Tiger One, we've got the suspects. Out."

Donnally glanced over at Dan.

"On my order, Tiger Three and Four lock and load," Dan whispered into the handset. "Now. Be apprised that Libby Tyler is their prisoner. She's the smallest person in the group. Try not to injure her. Out."

Libby was directly in the line of fire. Dan saw the guns the men carried, and he knew they'd use them. Libby could be hit. Killed. His mouth went dry as he slowly got to his knees, rifle in hand. There would be no way to warn her.

"Come on!" Martin growled, yanking Libby forward by the shoulder and shoving her toward the front of the Cherokee. He glared at Garwood. "I just shot her up and I'm takin' her across right now! Screw waiting. They're late!"

"All right, all right!" Garwood said impatiently with a wave of his hand. "Get rid of her!"

At that moment, Libby, who had still been pretending to be unable to stand, turned on her heel and shoved savagely at Martin. With a surprised yelp, he threw both his hands up and fell backward into the sand. Dizzy and weak, Libby lurched toward the four lanes of heavy oncoming traffic. She'd rather be killed by a car than by a bullet from one of Garwood's men, she thought determinedly. Curses exploded. She dashed drunkenly across two of the four lanes of traffic. An oncoming car slammed on its brakes, its horn shrilling.

A rifle was fired. And then another. And another. Libby sobbed and lurched drunkenly across the third lane. Suddenly, she saw an eighteen-wheel truck bearing down on her in the fastest lane of traffic. The lights pinned her. She froze. The horn bellowed through the chaos. In those last seconds, as she heard the trucker hit the air brakes, the rubber of his tires biting and squealing into the pavement, Libby saw her short life pass before her eyes. She raised her hand to protect herself, unable to move out of the way.

Then she felt a blow that sent her spinning and sprawling off onto the median. Sand flew up, blinding her eyes and getting into her mouth. The shriek of brakes continued. She heard the rending crash of autos ripping the night apart with screeching metal on metal. Dazed, she stopped rolling, the wind knocked out of her.

"Libby!"

She looked up. Disbelief made her cry out. "Dan!"

He scrambled out of his crouched position and dragged her farther into the median. "Stay down," he gasped. "Stay down!" He covered her with his body, his rifle aimed at the ongoing scene across the lanes of traffic.

Sobbing, her head buried in her arms, Libby felt herself sinking more deeply into the drugged state. As suddenly as it had begun, the screech of tires, the blasts from rifles, stopped. She felt Dan breathing raggedly above her, his body a shield to keep her safe. His hand was gripping her shoulder, pressing her into the sand. Just that touch of his hand sent a wave of relief through her, and she didn't struggle. She couldn't. It had taken every last ounce of her reserve strength to push Martin away and make her dash for freedom. Over and over in her head, she kept hearing her heart pounding, *Dan is here. Dan is here.*

Closing her eyes, Libby heard the sounds around her begin to meld together, and she realized the drug was going to kill her. Unable to struggle, she collapsed against the hard, sandy ground. Somehow, she had to tell Dan. Somehow...

Carefully, Dan got to one knee, his hand still on Libby's shoulder. Across the lanes of blocked traffic he could see his people rounding up Garwood and what was left of his gang. The bright, flashing lights of the California Highway Patrol were everywhere. Taking the handset, he contacted Donnally.

"Is the area secured?" Dan asked, his voice rough with emotion.

"All secured, Captain," Donnally assured him.

"Roger. I'm bringing Libby across the highway. Call an ambulance."

"Already done, sir. Two of the four perpetrators are wounded."

"Roger, out."

Placing the handset on his harness, Dan put the rifle aside and devoted his attention to Libby. In the sporadic light he could see she was covered with sand, her clothes dirty and torn. As he gently turned her over, he held his breath.

"Libby?" His voice was shaken and hoarse as he pulled her into his arms. She was very pale, the skin around her mouth chafed and swollen. When she opened her eyes, they looked cloudy and vacant. Gripping her more tightly, he brought her against him, crushing her to his chest, gasping her name.

"Are you hurt?"

With a moan, Libby tried to speak, but nothing came out of her mouth. She clung wildly to Dan, finding the scent of him reassuring. His rough clothing was scratchy against her face, but she didn't care. *I love you. I love you.* Her tongue felt wooden, and it was impossible to speak. Nearly helpless from the effects of the drug overdose, Libby could only sag in Dan's arms while wet tears ran down her cheeks.

"Captain!" Donnally came running over to him, panting hard. "Is she injured?"

"I don't know," he rasped, handing the sergeant his M-16.

"Ambulances are on their way. But I've got a recon paramedic available over there."

"Get him," Dan barked, watching Libby's pale face, her vacant eyes. "Hurry." *Oh, God, hurry!* With trembling fingers, he touched her cheek. Her skin was cool and damp. "Hang on, Libby, just hang on," he begged. It was impossible in this light to know whether she'd been shot or not. Worriedly, Dan began to run his hand across her, trying to find any wet spot that might indicate bleeding.

With a moan, Libby tried to speak, but the words jelled together. Dan was holding her. It was as if the adrenalin charge from her extraordinary effort to escape had suddenly left her, and she felt limp as a rag doll in his arms. The desperation in his eyes as he hunted for injuries made her sob. He cared more than she had ever suspected. Just the way he held her told her that.

More dark shapes danced above her, and she saw two marines come to her side. Her vision blurring, she gasped as the one with the black-and-green-painted face reached out to touch her.

"Lay her down, Captain," the recon ordered, out of breath.

"It's okay, Libby," Dan said, "he's a paramedic. Just lie still, honey, he's going to check you for wounds."

Closing her eyes, Libby capitulated. Her brain and body weren't hers to control now. She felt the swift, sure movement of the paramedic's hands as he rapidly assessed her condition. Through it all, as she lay in the grass of the highway median, Dan's hand never left her shoulder. She honed in on his low, strained voice, struggling to stop her slide toward semiconsciousness.

"I think she's been drugged," the paramedic rasped after examining Libby's eyes and taking her blood pressure. He darted a worried glance across the interstate. "There's the ambulance. I'll put her on an IV and we'll get her to the base hospital—it's the closest. Captain, will you help me carry her?"

"I'll do it," Dan said, and gently scooped Libby into his arms. She was no lightweight, but just holding her made him feel better. Donnally brought along his rifle and the paramedic jogged across the lanes to prepare the IV.

Libby's head had lolled against Dan's shoulder, her one arm swinging free, and she was boneless in his grasp. Panic ate at him. Someone had shot Libby up with a drug. But what kind of drug? Horrible possibilities tore through Dan's mind as he carried her to the ambulance where the recon paramedic waited. She could die from an overdose, if it was deadly enough. What if it was cocaine? It would be like Garwood to do that—kill Libby with an overdose. Time was of the essence. Did they have it?

"Libby?"

Dan's voice, low and broken, cut through the fog of Libby's semiconscious state. Lifting her lashes, she saw him leaning over her, his eyes dark with concern. It was then that she felt his hand resting gently on her hair, his other hand cupping her cheek. Her mouth curved just a little.

"Hi..."

He smiled brokenly. "Welcome back, honey. You gave us a hell of a scare."

Libby became more aware of her surroundings. She realized she was in a hospital room. The drapes were white, the blinds partly drawn, with sunshine slashing through them to make vertical bars of light on the opposite wall. An IV fed her the fluids she'd lost. The room's antiseptic smells were somewhat dulled by Dan's scent. She felt his fingers trace her cheek and jaw in tender exploration. She slowly moved her gaze back to him, back to his worried expression.

"What...happened?"

Straightening, Dan took her hand and held it between his. His eyes smarted with a gritty sensation. He hadn't slept at all since Garwood's apprehension yesterday. "Do you remember anything, Libby, about last night?"

Her mouth was dry, and she slowly shook her head from side to side. "I—I remember going to the stable. And Garwood. Dan, he attacked me."

"I know." Dan's voice vibrated with anger. He tried to hide his fury for her sake and absently patted her hand. "Garwood was running a cocaine operation across the base, Libby. He thought you knew too much. The doctors saved your life, honey. The drug Garwood's men gave you could have killed you. How you managed to push Martin away and run, I'll never know."

Closing her eyes, she sighed. Just the warmth and strength of Dan's hand on hers fed her hope. "I did it... because I love you, Dan." She lapsed back into unconsciousness once again.

The next time Libby awoke, Dan was at her side, sitting in the chair, his expression even more worried, if that was possible. She vaguely recalled him wearing his military uniform before. Now, he was shaved and showered and in civilian clothes. The moment he realized she was conscious, he came out of the chair and gripped her hand.

"Libby?"

"I'm okay...." And she was. More than she could ever tell Dan. As he caressed her cheek, she smiled a little. "I think I'm going to live."

"Thank God," he whispered. "You've been asleep for twenty-four hours. It's Thursday afternoon."

Wrinkling her brow, Libby stared up at him. "But...Tuesday afternoon I was out at the stables...." And then the entire sequence of what had happened struck her. For long minutes, she lay, eyes closed, seeing and feeling the frightening events. Only Dan's touch, his fingers brushing her brow, caressing her hair, gave her any sense of stability, of solace. Taking in a long, ragged breath, she opened her eyes and stared up at him. "I could have died."

With a nod, Dan said, "Yes."

"That truck...I remember a huge semi bearing down on me. The lights blinded me. I froze. I remember I couldn't move."

"That's when I threw myself at you and knocked you out of the way."

Tears burned in Libby's eyes. Dan had placed himself in jeopardy for her safety. "That was a crazy thing to do."

"I happen to love the lady. What was I going to do?" he whispered in a choked voice as he leaned down and covered her dry, cracked lips with his.

Just the tender touch of his mouth against hers fed her strength. Whispering his name against his lips, Libby molded her mouth to his and drank his moist breath, his heat, into her very cold body. His mouth moved tenderly, tears flowed unchecked from her eyes and they shared the salty taste between them. Dan loved her. He loved her. And he'd proven it by nearly giving his life for her when the truck had been about to run her down.

Easing back, Dan looked deeply into her lustrous, half-closed eyes. "I love you, Libby Tyler. This time, you heard me. I know you did."

"When did you say it before?" she whispered brokenly, lifting her hand and touching his cheek.

"Out there on the median. It was so damned dark. I didn't know what was wrong with you. I thought you were shot, bleeding somewhere. I couldn't see. I couldn't be sure." Taking a deep breath, Dan said, "I told you I loved you then. Your eyes were so vacant, Libby. I don't think anything I was saying registered with you."

"Yes, it did," she insisted in a choked voice. "I felt so helpless out there. I couldn't speak, couldn't even lift my hand. It felt like someone else was in control of me."

"It was the drug they shot you up with," he said grimly, holding her hand tightly in his own. "They gave you an overdose, Libby. We almost lost you." He shut his eyes tightly, her hand pressed to his thinned mouth.

Libby absorbed his statement. She'd nearly died from a drug overdose. "I—I was lucky," she said in a wobbly voice. "More lucky than I deserve."

Dan shook his head and kissed her fingers several times. "You deserve the world, Libby, and if I have anything to do with it, you'll have it."

Weakly lifting her head just enough to reach the suffering line of his mouth, she quavered, "All I need, all I'll ever need is your love, Dan...."

Their second kiss was heated, filled with promise and life as Dan met and molded her questing lips to his. Placing his arm behind her head and neck to support her, he kissed her deeply for a long, long time. He wanted to lose himself in the sweet taste of her, the softness of her giving lips and the molten heat that told him that she was returning to him— finally. The hell of the last thirty-six hours was over, and they had both survived.

"I love you," Libby whispered against his lips, and she felt his very male smile. Her eyes closed, she absorbed his touch, his small kisses from the tip of her nose to her brow to her eyes and, finally, back to her parted lips. She couldn't get enough of Dan, of his touch—so full of life, not death.

"If Dr. Ramirez catches us like this she'll probably throw me out," Dan said wryly as he eased Libby back onto the pillow. "I've refused to leave your bedside—except for a half-hour shower and change—since you got here two days ago."

Gripping his hand, Libby felt suddenly very tired, but very good. "Can you get me out of here? You know how I hate hospitals."

He kissed her hand. "Not this time, honey." When he saw her disappointment, he added, "But I promise you as soon as they release you, you're coming home with me. And no argument, Libby."

In a low, emotional voice, she answered. "You won't get any."

Dan watched with pleasure as Libby slowly turned and looked around his apartment. Her eyes were huge as she took in the get-well wishes in the form of bouquets, plants and gifts that her friends had brought over for her. In anticipation of her getting out of the hated hospital, Dan had been bringing them here. Now, dressed in navy blue slacks, a pale pink blouse and brown leather shoes, Libby looked hauntingly beautiful in his eyes as she turned and smiled across the room at him.

"I can't believe it," she said with a sigh, walking toward him.

Dan opened his arms so that she could walk into them and lean against him. "I can't believe you're here with me, Lib." As he embraced her and felt her arms go around his waist, Dan smiled and closed his eyes. He rested his head against her thick, soft hair. This was all he'd ever need. Ever want. Even though Libby was still pale and a little weak from the drug overdose, she was almost herself. Almost. Dr. Ramirez had wanted her to stay another three days in the hospital, but Dan had pleaded with her behind the scenes to release Libby early. She wasn't doing well there, and he wanted her in an environment where he knew she would thrive. And judging from her response to all the flowers and plants, she would be happy here—with him.

"I can't, either," Libby whispered, and hugged Dan with all her returning strength. The last three days had changed her forever. She'd had a lot of time to think in that hospital room, alone in the silence. Easing away from Dan just enough to meet his smiling eyes, she said, "I'll never not tell you how I'm feeling ever again."

"Oh?"

"I mean, not tell you I love you. I was so afraid before, Dan. Before all this happened." She gestured lamely around the living room.

"You were afraid to start living again after Brad's death," Dan said, threading his fingers through her loose, shining hair.

"Yes." She gave him a sheepish look. "Even though you were so persuasive."

Taking Libby over to the couch, Dan brought her into his arms so that she lay across him, her head resting on his shoulder, his arms around her. "Brushes with death are a hell of a quick way to cut through defenses and get down to the nitty-gritty," he said gently. The strands of her sable hair glowed with gold highlights as he eased them through his fingers.

"But you knew," Libby accused, looking up and meeting his thoughtful expression.

"Yes, but I'm a patient man, honey. I knew I loved you and I knew if I just hung in there, you'd eventually see me for the person I am behind the marine uniform I wear."

Sobering, Libby slid her arm around his neck. "I'm just glad it's over."

"It's not over," he warned her grimly. "The PM has assigned me to the case, and I'm more than happy to take Garwood on." He studied Libby's pale features. "But it means you'll have to testify, and I worry about the stress of it on you."

"I can do it, Dan—with you there to help me."

Nodding, he closed his eyes and simply savored Libby's nearness. Stuart Garwood and Bill Martin were in the jail in Oceanside. The other two men were dead, from wounds they'd gotten in the firefight between Donnally and the recon teams that had closed in on the Jeep in the darkness. Dan wanted nothing more than to wreak vengeance against Garwood for nearly killing Libby. The man was a sociopath—greedy for money and power at any cost, even another human being's life. Tightening his embrace, Dan pressed a kiss to Libby's temple and inhaled the spicy fragrance of her perfume.

"Tonight, I want you to sleep with me," he whispered.

Libby roused herself from her position on his shoulder, met and held his questioning gaze. She saw the burning tenderness in Dan's eyes. "Yes, I want that, too," she agreed softly.

A hot bath melted Libby's tension away. It was nearly ten o'clock and she suddenly found herself so incredibly exhausted that it took every bit of strength to make it to Dan's queen-size bed and lie down. Sometime later he came in, dressed only in a pair of pajama bottoms. The light from the hall broke the gloom as he padded over to the bed and sat down next to her. Without saying a word, he lifted several stray strands of hair away from her brow.

"You're exhausted."

"I don't know what hit me, Dan."

He smiled and nodded. "Dr. Ramirez said you'd fluctuate up and down like this, so don't worry. Everything will be okay."

"But—"

"Shh, you need to sleep, Lib." And he pulled the covers up over her.

Ashamed of herself, Libby watched Dan leave to turn out the hall light. More than anything, she wanted to make love with him, but her lids felt weighted and it was all she could do to stay awake until he got back to bed to lie down beside her.

"Dan, I'm sorry," she whispered, her words slurred.

Lying on his side, he caressed Libby's cheek. "Don't be, honey. I'm not. All I want you to do right now is concentrate on getting well. Loving you can wait. I just want to hold you tonight, Libby. That's all I need. All I want...."

Whispering his name, Libby turned onto her side and found herself in Dan's arms. He molded his body against hers, the cotton gown a thin barrier between them. As she relaxed with her head in the hollow of his shoulder, one arm draped across his waist, she smiled tiredly.

"It feels so wonderful to be here with you. So wonderful...." And she fell into a deep, healing sleep within his arms.

Chapter Thirteen

Sometime near morning, as dawn was dissolving the grip of darkness, Libby began to awaken. It was a slow, delicious process as a sense of safety and longing filled her like sunlight caressing the land after some terrible, damaging storm. Her first awareness was of Dan's rhythmical breathing, his soft breath flowing across her cheek and hair. Her head was nestled in the crook of his arm, and she felt his other arm hanging heavily across her. Instead of feeling imprisoned, Libby felt such a surge of love that she lifted her hand and moved her fingertips along his darkly haired chest.

How lonely she had been these past years, she realized as her tactile senses sent ribbons of heat flowing down through her. Drawing in a deep breath, she inhaled Dan's decidedly male scent, laced with the clean odor of the soap he'd used to take his shower the night before. Not wanting to awaken him, because she knew he'd been just as traumatized by the events of the past several days as she had, Libby moved her head away just enough to look at him.

Several strands of hair fell across his smooth brow. She marveled at the discovery that, in sleep, his stern marine-officer mask fell away, exposing his true vulnerability. His spiky, dark lashes rested against his cheeks. The darkness of his beard gave him a dangerous look, but the soft parting of his mouth endeared him to her. It was a mouth that she had seen become hard and unrelenting as he hovered over her, protecting her that terrible night when she'd thought she was going to die. It was a mouth she'd seen relax, curve and draw into a tender smile meant only for her.

Without thinking, guided by her heart, Libby leaned up on her elbow and softly placed her lips against his. Lost in the exploration of him as a man, as someone she loved so fiercely that it freed her to kiss him like this, Libby wasn't surprised when his arms moved and tightened briefly around her. Even more delicious was his returning kiss, his lips molding hers strongly and drawing her toward him until she lay on top of him, their bodies fitting smoothly together.

"You're like sunlight," Dan murmured thickly as he sleepily looked up at her and framed her face between his hands. "All things good."

Flushing, wildly aware of her heart beating in counterpoint to his, she whispered, "Even if I wake you up at some ungodly hour?"

His smile increased as he absorbed Libby's mussed hair, her drowsy eyes and parted lips that begged to be tasted again. "You wake me any time you want, honey. Any time." Dan drew her down upon him and captured her mouth in a hot, binding kiss that told her just how much he loved her, cared for her. The last thirty-six hours of his life dissolved in the mutual exploration of those next few moments. All he wanted was to love Libby the best he knew how, to show her his love in this new and wonderful way.

Lost in the splendor of his touch, Libby felt herself being eased down onto the mattress, Dan's hand moving slowly up her thigh and bringing the cotton nightgown with it. Tingling followed as he slid his hand upward, and Libby divested herself of the gown. She allowed the material to sink to the floor and opened her arms as Dan moved closer. The need to explore him as much as he wanted to explore her took over, a sweet ache filling her as his hand ranged from her thigh across her hip, abdomen and up to her breasts, which he cupped and stroked, one at a time.

Her breath escaped as his lips settled over the first, hard peak, and she shuddered with pleasure as he teased her, suckled and then drew her deeply into his mouth. Her hands opened and closed spasmodically on his powerful shoulders and taut skin. Fire danced through her, leaping flames licking along every nerve, sending a ragged ache through her as never before. Closing her eyes, she surrendered to his molten onslaught.

Her mind shorted out, but this time with the pleasure Dan was sharing with her, and with this most wonderful way of giving herself to him. The darkness ceased to exist. Daylight no longer registered, either—just the scent, touch and feel of Dan against her, his hand ranging down across her belly, his fingers sliding across the apex of her thighs. Moaning, Libby opened to him, wild with anticipation, wanting more.

The moment he touched her, she gave a small cry, a spasm of intense sensation exploding deeply within her as he continued his caress. She lay cradled in his arms, his mouth capturing hers, muffling her moans. Guilelessly, Libby drew Dan onto her, wanting only him—all of him. In those moments, she opened her eyes, breathing raggedly, her hands framing his face. His eyes burned with such intensity and desire that it made her arch to receive him. A whispered cry fled from Libby's lips as she felt him slide deeply into her, and her arms went around him. The rocking motion, his hand on her hip, guiding her more surely, brought more jolting explosions of pleasure within her.

Libby felt like sunlight in Dan's hands, her body a melody of rainbow colors being played by him, responding to him in every possible way. The fierce love she felt for him was like a warm, lush opening in her heart as he gripped her to him, held her tightly, his head pressed against hers, and released his life deeply within her. In those moments out of time, Libby held him with all her womanly strength, their breathing mingling. As Dan eased off her and took her into his arms afterward, she smiled tremulously. Words were useless as he brought up the sheet and tucked it around them.

Her hand upon Dan's damp chest, Libby moved her palm gently across the expanse, glorying in his masculinity, his power and strength. At the same time, he gently ran his own hand across her shoulder and down the curve of her spine. Slowly, their breathing steadied and grew softer as they held each other. Closing her eyes, Libby absorbed each of his tender touches, the occasional kisses to her hair, brow and cheek.

The awakening world gradually impinged on her. She heard a robin outside the apartment singing its beautiful melody. Lifting her lashes, she realized Dan was watching her from beneath hooded eyes, a tender expression in them.

"The song," she whispered unsteadily, "it's so beautiful...."

"Like you," Dan said huskily, and traced her slightly arched eyebrows. Leaning over, he captured her lips with his own and kissed her long and deeply. Gradually, he eased away just enough to see the sparkling light of joy in her eyes. This morning, there was no darkness or fear in Libby's eyes, and for that, Dan was grateful. Her sable hair—that thick, tempting cloak—lay mussed around her face. Moving his fingers through the clean strands, Dan marveled at the rich texture and the sweet fragrance of it.

"I love you," he said, holding her lustrous gaze.

His words fell around Libby like a warm, binding promise. "I love you, too. I guess I did from the first, but I just didn't want to admit it."

His mouth curved rakishly. "I'll never forget my first day at work, my first hour at work, when you came crashing into my office. I never expected it. I didn't know why you were dressed that way, but I sure liked the way it outlined that gorgeous body of yours."

"Dan!"

He raised his brows. "Hey, I'm being honest."

With a giggle, Libby settled back in his arms. "Now I suppose I'll hear the real story of what you thought about me."

Satisfaction soared through Dan. He had Libby in his arms. It was a dream he had longed for, but had thought would never happen. "Honey, if you knew all the things I thought about you, you'd be blushing from this day forward until forever."

Surprised, Libby melted beneath his laughter and the light dancing in his eyes. "You men are all alike."

"Well, in some ways," he said wryly, "I hope we are."

"And marines are worse than most."

"That depends on what you mean by 'worse.'"

With a groan, Libby said, "I keep forgetting you're an attorney and I can't just throw out general statements."

"True," Dan agreed, easing her onto her back. "And I'm looking forward to the conversations we'll have. I think they'll be spirited."

"Oh, sure!"

His smile broadened. "No?"

"Spirited is another word for argumentative."

"No, honey. You're spirited like that hot-blooded horse of yours. Just as you respect Shiloh's unique personality, I'll respect you. I like the way you see the world."

"You're always making fun of my idealism, Dan Ramsey."

He nodded and ran his hand lightly across her collarbone, watching desire come back into her eyes. It thrilled him how readily Libby responded to him. "In my line of work," he told her more seriously, "I can use a ray of sunshine. Just because I'm a realist doesn't mean I don't want to see the sunny side sometimes, Lib."

"So I'm your ray of sunshine?" she guessed, enjoying the movement of his fingers as he explored the curve of her breast.

"All that and more." Dan cupped her breast, then allowed his hand to move to her belly. There, he splayed his long fingers across its soft curves and gave her a tender look. "I want to marry you, Lib. And I'd like you to move into my apartment."

She held his burning look. Marriage. The word held such promise for her—for them. "I do need some time, Dan...."

With a nod, he said, "When it's right, you let me know."

She nodded and closed her eyes, savoring the feel of his hand on her abdomen. The thought of being Dan's wife held a sweet promise, and Libby was grateful that he was going to give her the time necessary to adjust, to allow her past fears to be put to a final rest. The ache to have her body grow with Dan's children within her was almost too much to remain silent about. Placing her hand over his, she whispered, "We've got so much to look forward to. So much, Dan."

"No disagreement from me, honey. In the meantime," he said, drawing her up into a sitting position beside him, "let's enjoy what we've got. It's a lot more than most people ever have."

Later, following Dan out of the bedroom, his hand in hers, Libby silently agreed. They took a shower together, then dressed in his bedroom. There was such a naturalness between them that Libby knew it wouldn't take her long to adjust to him, to their love. Even now, the thought of moving into his apartment, sharing this bedroom, him, his life, was more than just tantalizing. In the kitchen, Dan made the coffee while she fried bacon and eggs. Just as they finished their meal, the phone rang.

Frowning, Dan saw it was nearly 0800, and he was due at the office at 0830. His time with Libby was coming to an end—at least for the day.

"Captain Ramsey," he answered in his official tone.

"This is Sergeant Donnally, sir."

Frowning, Dan glanced over at Libby, who sat nibbling on the last of her whole-wheat toast. "Yes, Sergeant?" It was unusual that he'd be calling at this time of morning unless something serious had happened.

"Gorman made an escape attempt."

With a groan, Dan sat up. "What?"

"He overpowered one of the guards, but the other chasers got to him before he broke free of the brig."

"Good," Dan growled. Pushing his fingers through his short hair, he said, "And he's in solitary confinement?"

"Yes, sir, everything is status quo."

"See if you can't hurry the paperwork through on that bastard. I want him out of my brig and in a maximum-security prison, Sergeant."

"Yes, sir!"

"I'll be at the office at 0830, and you can give me an update on Gorman at that time."

"Of course, sir."

Dan hung up the phone. He tried to hide his irritation and worry from Libby. She had stopped eating and was watching his expression closely. Getting up, he went to the kitchen counter and looked out the window. He could feel her unasked question, her intent gaze. Turning, he glanced at her.

"Just a slight problem at the brig." That wasn't a lie, but it wasn't the full truth, either.

"I didn't know there could be 'slight' problems at a brig. You look upset, Dan."

With a shrug, he muttered, "Some prisoners are a pain in the neck."

"Did it have to do with Stuart Garwood?"

"No, he's in the Oceanside jail. I'll have to go over there today, too."

Libby moved out of her chair and went to Dan's side. She slipped her arm around his waist as he stood tensely at the counter. "Why do I get the feeling you're not telling me everything?" she teased lightly, smiling up into his harshly set features.

Just her touch, her care, broke Dan's tension, and he turned and took her into his arms. "You know what? Just having you here in this kitchen and being able to wrap my arms around you makes everything okay in my realist world."

Feeling happy, she rested her head against his shoulder and held him. "It's a big, bad world that you live in out there, Dan Ramsey."

"But not an impossible one," he reminded her, kissing her hair. "Some days are just more challenging than others."

"And this is shaping up to be one of them?"

Dan knew Libby was fishing for more information, so he eased her away from him enough to meet and hold her curious gaze. "A part of me wants to tell you everything, Libby. But another part of me, the one that worries about hurting you, doesn't."

With a sigh, she raised her hand and touched his jaw. "Brad used to hide everything from me. I don't want that to happen again. It contributed to my fears, Dan." Her brows knitted. "I know that your job is usually safe. Except for what happened a couple of days ago." She frowned. "Rose chewed me out for being afraid to love again. She was right, Dan. I was. I remember thinking about her words, what she'd said, when I was trapped in that little room in the barn." Looking up at him, her voice filled with emotion, she said, "Being in love with you means living one day at a time. I think if you can share what happens at work, it will help, not hurt me—though I realize some of the stuff you do is top secret, and you can't talk about it."

Murmuring her name, Dan held her tightly. "Most of my work would seem pretty boring to an outsider, if you want the truth," he said wryly, "but I will tell you what goes on, honey."

"Thanks...."

Kissing her cheek, Dan said, "Gorman tried to escape the brig but didn't make it. That's what the phone call was all about."

Relieved, Libby felt some of her old fear slip away. "I feel better already. I was worried Garwood had gotten out or something."

He stroked her flushed cheek, thinking how beautiful, how untouched and trusting Libby was. "See? You were wrong."

"My overactive imagination."

"We'll make sure it gets short-circuited," Dan promised. "When we see each other in the evening, we'll swap stories about our days and how they went."

"I'd like that," Libby quavered.

Dan sighed and held her close for another long moment. He knew time was slipping away from him, but he didn't care. If he showed up a few minutes late for work, it was worth it. The urge to push Libby into marrying him was very real. But Dan knew she had to have time to grow out of old fears and old patterns. The chains from the past had been broken, and she'd had the courage to reach out and love him. Nothing else mattered. With time, with patience, they would have a new life together—built on trust, communication and love.

"You're going to be late for work, Dan," Libby whispered, giving him one last kiss.

Grudgingly, he allowed her to move away from him. "It's going to be one hell of a day. I have to try to find out more from Garwood and the other guy, Martin."

"Good luck."

He nodded stoically. "When I get home tonight, *after* dinner, we'll discuss it."

The evening meal had been sumptuous, in Dan's opinion. Libby had rested most of the day, but had felt well enough to fix stuffed green peppers, a salad and baked apples for dessert. While they shared coffee in the living room afterward, Dan decided to tell her about his day. Libby was curled up next to him on the couch, and he had his arm around her shoulder as he sipped his coffee.

"Feel up to hearing about Garwood's confession?"

"I'd like to," Libby ventured. She placed the nearly empty cup and saucer on her knee and held it steady with her hand as she devoted all of her attention to Dan. Just as before, he'd come home, shed his uniform and gotten into some jogging clothes.

"Actually, Garwood wasn't saying much of anything except that he wanted an attorney, who then sat in with him while I asked him questions. It was Martin, his partner, who spilled the beans. He asked for a plea bargain, and I said we might think about one providing he told us the whole story."

"What a lucky break."

"It was," Dan said, and sipped the coffee.

"Did Stuart shoot at me that afternoon?"

With a nod, Dan said, "Yes. According to Martin, who is a corporal here on base and works over at the motor pool, he lent Garwood his M-16. Garwood shot at you to scare you off, not to kill you."

"At least, not that time," Libby whispered grimly. She felt Dan's arm come around her and hold her a little tighter.

"Garwood made the cocaine connection last year when he was scouting around to purchase a three-day eventing horse in Lima, Peru. The drug lord involved was the man he bought the horse from. They also made another agreement. The cocaine was transported by Peruvian tuna boats up the coast. Under the new moon for the last four months, about five million dollars' worth of cocaine was moved by Garwood, Martin and three other men he hired. They took it inland on horseback, across the base and out the back gate in Garwood's Jeep Cherokee. The gate guards were familiar with Garwood, so they never stopped to inspect the vehicle. They just waved him through.

"According to Martin, there was a year's worth of cocaine that was to be shipped this way, but thanks to you—" he gave Libby a look of admiration "—the plan was stopped after five shipments. Martin is also giving us the names of the main distributors, and I've turned over that list to DEA agents to pursue. The Drug Enforcement Agency is going to work with Peruvian officials to try to nail this drug lord, too."

"I didn't realize just how big an operation it was," Libby said in awe.

"Neither did I," Dan admitted. He took Libby's cup and saucer and his own and placed them on the table in front of the couch. Taking her into his arms, he held her for a long time. Just the way she slid her arm around his waist, lying across his body, her head resting on his shoulder, gave him a contentment he'd thought he'd never experience again.

"I hope you realize how brave and smart you are," he told her as he caressed her thick, dark hair. "You had the guts to pursue the lead, Libby, even though Colonel Edwards wanted to sweep it under the rug."

She twisted to look up at his somber features and saw the pride burning in his eyes for what she'd done. "I couldn't have done much else if you hadn't followed through on it, Dan."

"I thought your report was a little crazy at first," he admitted with a chuckle. "I knew you were upset, and I figured it was just a bunch of kids carrying on."

"So did I. We all did."

"Thanks to some good work by Joe and Annie—and you and me—we cracked the case together. I'm going to enjoy putting Garwood behind bars for at least twenty-five years without parole."

"What will Martin get?"

"About seven with a chance of parole. He'll probably do four to five at Fort Leavenworth."

"With the damage drugs do to people, they ought to be put in prison forever," Libby said fervently.

"You won't get an argument out of me. I lost a wife and marriage to drugs."

Her heart aching for Dan, Libby caressed his jaw. "The only addiction I ever want to have is to living."

"And I want to be there to see you do just that," Dan whispered.

Leaning upward, Libby met and clung to his mouth. Dan's arms went around her, strong and supportive, and she surrendered to his superior strength. His mouth was caressing and tender, and she absorbed the molten heat he shared with her. Ever so gradually, they eased apart. Libby saw the burning blue intensity in his eyes as he studied her in the silence.

Words weren't necessary, Libby realized, as she snuggled more deeply into Dan's embrace. Throughout the day she'd had time to look back on their meeting, their being drawn to each other so powerfully despite everything. As she felt Dan move his hand in a caressing manner across her shoulder and down her back, Libby smiled softly. Both of them had lost so much. Dan had spent many years locked in a hell not of his making, and yet he'd tried valiantly to get Janna to become healthy and whole again. How many years had she spent in Brad's larger-than-life shadow, worrying herself into near hysteria every time he left to fly a helicopter?

As Libby closed her eyes, content as never before, she realized that her past was now put to rest—permanently. She would always hold a warm spot for her good memories of Brad. But now her heart was reaching out to embrace Dan. Perhaps just as important, Dan didn't want her in his shadow. He wanted her to take life on her own terms. With a sigh, Libby whispered, "I love you, for the rest of my life...."

* * * * *

MILLION DOLLAR SWEEPSTAKES (III)

No purchase necessary. To enter, follow the directions published. Method of entry may vary. For eligibility, entries must be received no later than March 31, 1996. No liability is assumed for printing errors, lost, late or misdirected entries. Odds of winning are determined by the number of eligible entries distributed and received. Prizewinners will be determined no later than June 30, 1996.

Sweepstakes open to residents of the U.S. (except Puerto Rico), Canada, Europe and Taiwan who are 18 years of age or older. All applicable laws and regulations apply. Sweepstakes offer void wherever prohibited by law. Values of all prizes are in U.S. currency. This sweepstakes is presented by Torstar Corp., its subsidiaries and affiliates, in conjunction with book, merchandise and/or product offerings. For a copy of the Official Rules send a self-addressed, stamped envelope (WA residents need not affix return postage) to: MILLION DOLLAR SWEEPSTAKES (III) Rules, P.O. Box 4573, Blair, NE 68009, USA.

EXTRA BONUS PRIZE DRAWING

No purchase necessary. The Extra Bonus Prize will be awarded in a random drawing to be conducted no later than 5/30/96 from among all entries received. To qualify, entries must be received by 3/31/96 and comply with published directions. Drawing open to residents of the U.S. (except Puerto Rico), Canada, Europe and Taiwan who are 18 years of age or older. All applicable laws and regulations apply; offer void wherever prohibited by law. Odds of winning are dependent upon number of eligibile entries received. Prize is valued in U.S. currency. The offer is presented by Torstar Corp., its subsidiaries and affiliates in conjunction with book, merchandise and/or product offering. For a copy of the Official Rules governing this sweepstakes, send a self-addressed, stamped envelope (WA residents need not affix return postage) to: Extra Bonus Prize Drawing Rules, P.O. Box 4590, Blair, NE 68009, USA.

SWP-S594

COUNTDOWN
Lindsay McKenna

Sergeant Joe Donnally knew being a marine
meant putting lives on the line—and after a tragic
loss, he vowed never to love again. Yet here was
Annie Yellow Horse, the passionate, determined
woman who challenged him to feel long-dormant
emotions. But Joe had to conquer past demons before
declaring his love....

MEN OF COURAGE

It's a special breed of men who defy death and fight
for right! Salute their bravery while sharing their lives
and loves!

These are courageous men you'll love and tender
stories you'll cherish...available in June, only from
Silhouette Special Edition!

WILD RIVER

by
Laurie Paige

Maddening men...winsome women...and the untamed land they live in—
all add up to love! Meet them in these books from Silhouette Special Edition
and Silhouette Romance:

WILD IS THE WIND (Silhouette Special Edition #887, May)
Rafe Barrett retreated to his mountain resort to escape his dangerous feelings
for Genny McBride...but when she returned, ready to pick up where they
left off, would Rafe throw caution to the wind?

A ROGUE'S HEART (Silhouette Romance #1013, June)
Returning to his boyhood home brought Gabe Deveraux face-to-face
with ghosts of the past—and directly into the arms of sweet and loving
Whitney Campbell....

A RIVER TO CROSS (Silhouette Special Edition #910, September)
Sheriff Shane Macklin knew there was more to "town outsider"
Tina Henderson than met the eye. He saw a generous and selfless woman
whose true colors held the promise of love....

Don't miss these latest Wild River tales from Silhouette Special Edition
and Silhouette Romance!

SEWR-4

IT'S OUR 1000TH SILHOUETTE ROMANCE, AND WE'RE CELEBRATING!

JOIN US FOR A SPECIAL COLLECTION OF LOVE STORIES BY AUTHORS YOU'VE LOVED FOR YEARS, AND NEW FAVORITES YOU'VE JUST DISCOVERED. JOIN THE CELEBRATION...

April
REGAN'S PRIDE by Diana Palmer
MARRY ME AGAIN by Suzanne Carey

May
THE BEST IS YET TO BE by Tracy Sinclair
CAUTION: BABY AHEAD by Marie Ferrarella

June
THE BACHELOR PRINCE by Debbie Macomber
A ROGUE'S HEART by Laurie Paige

July
IMPROMPTU BRIDE by Annette Broadrick
THE FORGOTTEN HUSBAND by Elizabeth August

SILHOUETTE ROMANCE...VIBRANT, FUN AND EMOTIONALLY RICH! TAKE ANOTHER LOOK AT US! AND AS PART OF THE CELEBRATION, READERS CAN RECEIVE A FREE GIFT!

YOU'LL FALL IN LOVE ALL OVER AGAIN WITH SILHOUETTE ROMANCE!

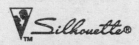

CEL1000

Christine Rimmer

**Three rapscallion brothers. Their main talent: making trouble.
Their only hope: three uncommon women who knew the way to
heal a wounded heart!**

May 1994—MAN OF THE MOUNTAIN (SE #886)

Jared Jones hadn't had it easy with women. But when he retreated to his
isolated mountain cabin, he found Eden Parker, determined to show him a
good woman's love!

July 1994—SWEETBRIAR SUMMIT (SE #896)

Patrick Jones didn't think he was husband material—but Regina Black sure
did. She had heard about the wild side of the Jones boy, but that wouldn't
stop her!

September 1994—A HOME FOR THE HUNTER (SE #908)

Jack Roper came to town looking for the wayward and beautiful
Olivia Larabee. He discovered a long-buried secret.... Could his true identity
be a Jones boy?

**Meet these rascal men—and the women who'll tame them—
only from Silhouette Special Edition!**

JONES1